THE
DEFIANT SPARK

THE
DEFIANT SPARK

ANNIE PERCIK

FIRST EDITION

First published by Fantastic Books Publishing 2021
Cover design by Ramon Marett
ISBN (ebook): 978-1-914060-06-9
ISBN (paperback): 978-1-914060-05-2

For Andy P, who told me I could.

ACKNOWLEDGEMENTS

In October 2010, I wrote a 1500-word short story about an engineer being called out to fix a magical artefact. My friend, Andy P, read it and said, 'You could write a novel based on that.' I laughed and set out to prove him wrong. Over a decade later, it turns out he was right!

Many other people have helped me along the way.

Thanks must go to:

My team of beta readers for great feedback: Chris M, Simon H, James H, Hannah W, Jill B, and Jacqui C.

Ann de V for wonderful shared writing sessions and helping me focus.

Charlie Haynes and Amie McCracken from the Six Month Novel Programme for support, encouragement and structure, and to Cressida Downing for feedback and friendship.

Anne-Marie and the team at Fantastic Books Publishing for investing in my story and helping me make it so much better.

Juliet R for sage advice, much-needed perspective and for always being there for me.

To my mum and dad – thank you so much for the endless proofreading and for always believing in me.

And, finally, many thanks to my husband, Dave, for always being interested, for enraging me with excellent questions I had no answers for, and then helping me find the answers. Your feedback is hated and appreciated in equal measure.

CHAPTER ONE

When an unexpected mana surge set his breakfast on fire, Abelard knew it was going to be one of those days. But he couldn't have predicted that before evening he'd have risked life and limb against a rogue artefact.

He woke to find his chron-e-fact alarm hadn't gone off and he was already late. Scrambling out of bed, he threw on some clothes and raked his fingers through his unruly dark curls as he dashed into the kitchen. What could he eat that would be quick? Toast? But there was no bread. Eggs were the only option and Abelard wasn't prepared to give up on breakfast. He splashed some oil in a pan and cracked the eggs in on top.

Within moments, the interface crystal on the cook-e-fact started to glow. Abelard groaned. Another mana surge. So much for breakfast. He reached to switch the artefact off but a blue spark of mana leapt from the crystal and ignited the oil. He jumped back from the instant blaze. A second of panicked paralysis gripped him before he hit the flam-e-fact button and a burst of freezing gas smothered the fire. Abelard let his breath out in a rush, but the mana surge was already travelling around the kitchen in a blue trail of doom. He watched in despair as it reached the wash-e-fact in the far corner and the interface crystal exploded. Stinging shards pelted his exposed skin and smoke mushroomed out into the room.

Abelard leapt to slam the door and open the window but he was too late. The piercing shriek of the shrill-e-fact combined with the smoke and the gas from the flam-e-fact to assault his senses. He grabbed a tea towel and flapped it frantically but the alarm went on. Angry banging through the ceiling from the flat above added to the noise. Muscles tense and breathing ragged, Abelard abandoned the tea towel and disconnected the alarm from the mana supply. He staggered out into the living room, coughing and spluttering as silence descended.

Anger surged through him like the defective mana supply as he left for work, face covered in tiny cuts and stomach still empty. Bloody artisans, living in their fancy gated communities with flawless mana flow. They didn't care about the poor engineers and mundanes who had to put up with such things.

Abelard selected his office building on the route-finder of his speed-e-fact and clutched the sides of his seat as the ancient vehicle heaved itself a few inches into the air. It juddered as it set off down the street, rattling round every corner.

His boss was waiting for him when he reached the offices of Mana-Calls, where he worked as an artefact engineer. Derek Stanton was an imposing bull of a man, bald head shining under the lights, his expression menacing. He tapped his watch as Abelard scuttled past him to his cubicle. He was already on thin ice with Stanton for being late a couple of times the week before.

Mateo Vega finished up a call in the next-door cubicle as

2

Abelard slid into his seat. Mateo had sleek black hair and olive skin several shades lighter than Abelard's mid-brown. His button nose and dimples made him look a lot younger than his thirty years and he grinned at Abelard, his dark eyes amused.

'Morning, mate!' he said as he cut the connection on his call-e-fact. 'Got dressed in the dark again?'

Abelard glanced down at himself to see his skinny frame encased in torn jeans and a garish, yellow and pink striped shirt.

'Bit of a rush this morning. Afraid I didn't have time to check with the fashion police.'

'You have to own the clothes to be able to put them on,' Mateo pointed out. 'Doesn't excuse that awful jumper from the other day, either.'

Abelard sighed. 'Do you ever get sick of all this?' He gestured at their drab grey surroundings, where their fellow engineers sat in regimented rows answering calls.

'Only every day,' Mateo said, though his expression was still jovial. 'Hey, I came up with a new idea for an artefact.'

'Oh, yeah?' This was a frequent game they played. 'Tell me.'

'The Vega fix-e-fact!' Mateo announced with a flourish. 'It would answer all these call-es and give the mundanes expert advice on how to deal with their malfunctioning artefacts.'

Abelard chuckled. 'Wouldn't that put us out of a job?'

'Well, Abelard my boy,' Mateo replied, putting on a posh accent, 'if I was really designing artefacts, I'd be an artisan.

So I wouldn't care about putting a poxy engineer like you out of work, would I?'

'Thanks!' Abelard aimed a punch at Mateo's arm. Then he caught sight of Stanton lurking at the other end of the room. 'Crap. Best get to it.'

Mateo doffed an imaginary cap and they both set to work.

Abelard grabbed a snack at his desk and worked through lunch in an attempt to appease Stanton. By the time five o'clock came round he was dreaming of a steak dinner. But one minute before the end of his shift Stanton appeared at his cubicle as if he had teleported there.

'Abernathy!' he bellowed, though he was only a few inches away.

Abelard jumped and spun his chair around.

'Emergency call-out to an office on the other side of town. Something about a rogue post-e-fact. Get going!'

* * *

The door to the office building opened before Abelard even reached it, revealing a short, pale young woman with light brown hair in what Abelard thought was called a pixie cut. Frowning, she hurried to meet him halfway down the front steps.

'Are you the artisan that's come to fix the post-e-fact?'

Abelard laughed but choked to a stop at her affronted expression. 'I'm sorry, Miss ...?'

'Jen Blake. What's so funny?'

'I really am sorry. It's just that I wish I was an artisan. But I'm just an engineer. An artisan would never stoop to coming out to fix a malfunctioning artefact.'

'But you can fix it?'

'I hope so.'

'Then you're more use to me than an artisan. Come on,' she said over her shoulder as she turned to jog back up the steps. 'I was trying to finish a mail-out and the post-e-fact went berserk.'

Abelard hurried to keep up as she dashed inside and sped down a corridor to the lev-e-facts.

'What exactly did you tell it to do?' Abelard asked. 'If you can take me through it, step by step …'

'I filled the envelope tray. Then I attached my smart-e to transfer the specifics of the mail-out and–'

Abelard held up a hand to stop her. 'I think I know what the problem is. Post-es are McPherson artefacts and they're notoriously temperamental. They don't like interacting with artefacts made by any other company and the smart-e-fact is a Gadg-E-Tech product.'

'That's probably why the post room manager won't let anyone else touch the damn thing. But he went home early and I really wanted to finish tonight.' Jen stopped in front of a glass-panelled door. 'It's in there.'

Through the door, Abelard could see the five foot high unit of the post-e-fact. Its drawers gaped open, envelopes and paper scattered everywhere, and the grasping metal claws that managed the post sorting flailed. A smart-e-fact was attached to the interface crystal about waist height from the ground somewhere behind the post-e-fact's whirling arms.

'I thought it would be the quickest way to programme it for the mail-out,' Jen said.

'It might have worked if the post-e was a new model but that one looks ancient so it probably needs manual instructions.'

'Next time I'll just stuff the envelopes myself.'

Abelard took a deep breath and injected a note of mock bravado into his voice. 'I'm going in.'

'Good luck.'

Inside, the post-e-fact's arms were still thrashing and there was a worrying blue glow coming from the smart-e-fact. Abelard gritted his teeth. A mana surge could blow both artefacts to bits and possibly him along with them. He had to disconnect them, and fast.

He lowered himself to the floor, lying down just outside the post-e-fact's reach and inching along on his back until he could see the vicious metal arms scything above his face. Sweat prickled on his forehead and started dripping into his eyes. He couldn't wipe it away without risking his fingers being sliced off. Staying flat, he pushed himself closer, the displaced air from the whirling claws ruffling his hair like a deadly caress. Finally he was able to reach up and grasp the smart-e-fact where it was connected to the larger machine.

As soon as he touched it he felt a jolt from the leaking mana. Blue light spread over his hand, sparks crackling between his fingers and creeping up his arm. He tried to pull his hand away but couldn't. His heart started to pound. The blue glow reached his shoulder and the tingle of the mana turned into a searing pain. He felt himself being lifted, though the post-e-fact's arms had gone suddenly still. The last thing he saw was Jen wrenching the door open as the blue light washed up across his face and over his eyes.

Everything went blue and then everything went black.

* * *

Abelard came back to awareness slowly. He opened his eyes to a worried gaze.

'Are you okay?' Jen asked.

He tried to sit up and his head swam. All his limbs felt three times their normal weight and there was an uncomfortable tingling in his fingertips. Jen helped him into a sitting position.

'You *hovered in the air*,' she said. 'Light shot out of your hands in streams. It picked up the paper and stuff on the floor and put it all back in the right places.'

Abelard looked around him. The post-e-fact was motionless and the room was tidy.

'However you did it, you've saved me having to clear up the mess.' Jen grinned. 'It's a shame you couldn't have finished the mail shot while you were at it.'

'There must be a way to get the post-e to do its job properly,' said Abelard, his engineer mentality kicking in past the confusion in his mind.

Jen's lips twisted. 'I'd rather not have anything more to do with that thing, if it's all the same to you. It's caused enough trouble for one day.'

'My job here's only half done.' Abelard clambered to his feet. 'We've got past the immediate crisis but I'm supposed to fix artefact problems and the problem isn't fixed.'

Jen smiled. 'If there's a way to get the post-e to do the mail out, it would save me a lot of work. Is there another artefact we could use that it would be willing to talk to?'

'Good idea!' He beamed at her. 'Hang on a second.'

He walked over to his bag and rummaged through it. Most of his personal artefacts were made by Gadg-E-Tech but he thought he had an ArtCo add-e-fact in there somewhere. If Jen's idea worked Abelard would have to endure some ribbing from Mateo when he told his friend about it. Abelard liked the pizazz of Gadg-E-Tech artefacts but Mateo was a staunch advocate for ArtCo practicality.

Abelard produced the add-e-fact with a flourish and smiled at Jen. 'Let's see if this will do the trick.'

He reached out gingerly and connected the add-e to the post-e-fact. Using the add-e as a bridge, he retrieved the smart-e from the floor and reconnected it. Nothing happened for a long moment. Just as Abelard was starting to think the plan wouldn't work, the post-e-fact jerked back to life. Both Abelard and Jen stepped away from it, exchanging a wary glance. But the artefact merely collected paper and envelopes from its drawers, inserted them in the appropriate trays and got on with its job.

A couple of minutes later Jen picked up the top envelope

in the stack now waiting in the output slot, neatly sealed and addressed.

'That was … really fast!'

'All part of the service!' said Abelard.

He disconnected the artefacts and handed the smart-e back to Jen.

'I guess your work here is done,' she said.

'I guess so. Don't hesitate to get back in touch if you have any more problems.' Abelard winced at the stilted official phrase.

Jen laughed. 'Oh, I'm planning to have as little as possible to do with this post-e from now on.' She paused, then went on with a shy smile. 'What's your name, by the way? You never said.'

'It's Abelard.'

Her eyebrows shot up, but she didn't comment. 'Maybe we could go for a drink sometime and you could regale me with other tales of your derring-do.'

She wrote her number on a spare envelope and held it out. Abelard took it, dazed.

'I – I'll do that,' he said.

He dropped off to sleep as soon as his speed-e-fact set off for home and only jolted awake when the vehicle pulled to a stop outside his building. He made it into his bedroom and collapsed on to the bed fully clothed. The mystery of the blue glow, not to mention the miracle of Jen's number, would have to wait for the morning.

* * *

It was Jen who was foremost in Abelard's mind when he woke up the next day. A good night's sleep had dealt with the effects of his post-e-fact adventure but Jen giving him her number was momentous. He couldn't wait to get to work and tell Mateo about it.

He reached to turn his chron-e-fact around to check the time and a tingle fluttered over his fingers. He snatched his hand back, then reached out again slowly, nervous but curious. The nearer his fingers got to the artefact, the stronger the tingle grew. As soon as he touched it a blue glow started to envelop his hand. He pulled his hand away again but the glow of mana remained, crackling between his fingers as he moved them.

Abelard spotted his clean-e-fact poking out from under the bed. He didn't use it very often and it wasn't charged. A crazy idea formed in his mind and he crouched down beside the clean-e-fact, reaching out with his glowing hand to touch its interface crystal. As skin connected with artefact, the blue light transferred from his fingers into the crystal. Abelard's breath caught in his throat as the clean-e-fact came to life and started bustling around the room, sucking up dust.

Abelard stared at his fingers, which appeared normal again. As he stood there, agog, the clean-e-fact ran down and ground to a halt but he hardly noticed. Only one set of people could manipulate mana directly and transfer it from one artefact to another.

Abelard might not have been an artisan the day before, but apparently he was one now.

CHAPTER TWO

Alessandra stormed into Walter's office on the top floor of the Gadg-E-Tech building, long blonde hair flying, heels clicking on the laminate floor. She strode up to his desk and slapped a sheaf of papers down in front of him.

'What,' she snarled, 'is this?'

He smiled up at her, all innocence. 'Good morning to you too, sweetheart.'

His dark hair was perfect as always, the silvering at the temples adding distinction.

'Don't you "sweetheart" me! How dare you cut the budget for my department without discussing it with me first?'

Walter's smile turned snakelike. 'Do you really think I run routine financial decisions past every mid-level department head?' He glanced at the open door behind her. 'Not to mention allowing them direct access without an appointment.'

Alessandra felt her shoulders hunching and forced them down. 'I am not trying to use our relationship to get undeserved privileges. And don't claim you weren't trying to manipulate me with that "sweetheart" remark.'

He regarded her, his expression tolerant. When he spoke it was with exaggerated patience. 'As CFO, I have the right to make unilateral budgetary alterations in whatever way I see fit. And your budget had room for cuts.'

'Oh really.' Alessandra folded her arms across her chest. 'And will that still be your argument when our security shields fail and one of our competitors gets hold of proprietary information?'

'Darling, please.' Walter sighed. 'I did the calculations and you can easily maintain our security standards on the reduced amount. You know I can't show favouritism when it comes to the business.'

'I'm not asking you to.' When had his attentions to her flipped from flattering to condescending? Or had he always been like this and she had just been too naive to realise it? 'All I'm asking for is the respect I deserve as a colleague in this company. And the courtesy of a heads-up when you make changes that affect my ability to do my job.'

Walter rose smoothly to his feet, stepped out from behind his desk and put his arm around her.

'What's this really about, eh? Are you still upset that I cancelled on dinner last night?'

Alessandra threw off his arm and backed towards the door.

'I've had enough of you treating me like a child.' She took a deep breath and forged onwards. 'This isn't working, and I think it's best if we end things before one of us gets hurt.'

Walter's lip curled and revulsion shivered through Alessandra's chest.

'You think it's best?' he repeated. 'You think you can come into my office and announce something like that? You wouldn't even have a place at this company if it weren't for your mother. Laleh's so-called mentorship is nothing other than nepotism. Why else do you keep your relationship to her a secret from the rest of the company? And do you really think you would have made department head so soon without my influence?'

'How dare you!' Alessandra's voice rose in pitch as his words hit a little too close to home. 'I've worked hard for my position here and the results speak for themselves.'

'You just keep telling yourself that,' Walter said, sneering. 'If you want to try going it alone, be my guest. Just wait and see. You're nothing without me.'

Alessandra bit her lip to stop the vitriol rising in her throat from spilling out. Instead, she spun on her heel and stalked out without another word. Back in her own office several floors down, tears threatened. She refused to give in to them, though. She sat down at her desk and took a couple of deep breaths. Then she touched up her makeup, squared her shoulders and turned her focus to reducing overheads.

If the shields did fail, she would be the one blamed, not Walter with his corner office and commanding presence. He was untouchable and she was just a mid-level manager. How could she ever have thought he was charming? The fact he even knew who she was had dazzled her and duped her into thinking he valued her intelligence as well as her looks. Alessandra let out an exasperated breath. She would show Walter. And her mother. When her department was the highest performing in the whole of Gadg-E-Tech, everyone would have to take notice.

* * *

13

By the time Abelard got over his shock enough to make his way to the office, he was late again. But instead of going to his desk he stopped at reception and called Mateo's station. His friend sounded stressed when he answered.

'Abelard! Where are you? Stanton's going crazy.'

'Never mind that now. Meet me in the Returns Depot and bring a charged artefact with you.'

'What?' Mateo hissed. 'What are you talking about? What's going on?'

'Just meet me.' Abelard cut the call.

The Returns Depot was a large warehouse where broken or unwanted artefacts were stored for processing before being returned to their respective manufacturers or scrapped. The air between the vast rows of shelving units was chilly, but Abelard didn't have to wait long. Mateo turned up in less than ten minutes, as Abelard had known he would. He was carrying an add-e-fact but he glowered as he approached.

'What are you playing at? You're going to get us both in trouble.'

Abelard couldn't stop a grin from spreading across his face. 'I promise you'll think it's worth it in about ninety seconds.'

He picked up a toy vehicle, marketed as a zoom-e-fact, and showed Mateo that the mana level was zero. When he reached out and touched the add-e-fact in Mateo's hands, Abelard was flooded anew with wonder as the blue mana glow instantly enveloped his fingers. He waited a few seconds until the glow covered his entire hand, then moved

14

it to touch the zoom-e-fact's interface crystal. As it had with his clean-e-fact, the glow transferred from his hand to the little vehicle, which lit up with brightly flashing colours. He set it down on the floor and it zoomed off amongst the shelves, living up to its name admirably. Abelard let his breath out in a whoosh and turned to Mateo, who was staring at him open-mouthed.

'Wha-?' his friend managed.

'That's where I was about two hours ago.'

'You ... You just ...' Mateo swallowed audibly. 'How?'

'I have no earthly idea. I went out on a call last night and something really weird happened. And now – this.' Abelard gestured in the direction of the zoom-e-fact.

Mateo walked over to a crate and collapsed on to it. He looked up at Abelard, a strange intensity suffusing his features.

'Tell me everything.'

* * *

'... and then this morning, I accidentally charged up my clean-e the same way I just did with the zoom-e,' Abelard concluded.

There was a brief silence.

Then Mateo spoke. 'You got her number? You lucky dog!'

Abelard huffed out a breath of laughter. 'I know!' He grinned. 'That's even more miraculous than the mana thing, but' – he waggled his hands – 'this is what I need some help with.'

'I bet,' Mateo said. 'I mean, this whole thing is ... well, it's unbelievable. My cousin Gerald would love to hear about this. It would be right up his alley.'

'Is he the one who lives without mana in the middle of nowhere?'

'Yep!' Mateo's face lit up. 'He's my second cousin or something on my mum's side and he runs a commune deep in a forest somewhere. He has this theory that the artisans are oppressing the common man through their control of the mana supply. So he doesn't allow any artefacts on the grounds and they're not connected to the supply at all.'

Abelard shuddered at the thought of living without access to mana. 'Why do you think he'd be interested in this?'

Mateo grinned. 'Just seems like something that would feed into his conspiracy theories. Artisans hiding the real nature of mana or something like that.'

'I don't think it would be a good idea to spread it about, whatever the explanation.'

'Fair enough. So what are you going to do?'

Abelard sighed. 'I don't know. What can I do? Go and knock on an artisan's door and say, "Excuse me, I seem to be manifesting artisan skills. Will you let me join your secret club"?'

'Why not? It's what you've always wanted. I bet ArtCo would be glad to have you.'

'Why would you assume I'd join ArtCo? Why can't I join Spark-le or Gadg-E-Tech?'

'Nobody was ever fired for buying ArtCo,' Mateo said.

'There's nothing wrong with ArtCo engineering and you know it. Anyone should be proud to work for them. Glitz and glamour can't make up for good solid reliability.'

ArtCo churned out cut-price everyday items for the family on a budget. Their artefacts were mass-produced, cheap and cheerful but had a good reputation for reliability. Everyone Abelard knew had at least a few ArtCo artefacts and they were by far the most commonly available.

Abelard held up a hand. 'Let's not start all that again. This is hardly the time. What we need to consider is–'

'Abernathy! Vega! What the hell are you doing in here?' Stanton's angry voice came from the entrance to the depot area and Abelard looked round to see him striding towards them, his face stony.

Mateo scrambled to his feet.

'Sorry, Derek. Abelard's having a personal emergency and I was just … consoling him.'

'I don't care if his entire family was blown up in a freak mana explosion.' Stanton glared at them. 'What is it anyway?'

Abelard waited a beat then said, 'My entire family was blown up in a freak mana explosion.'

Stanton gaped at him then scowled even harder. 'Very funny. You're both on the clock and I don't pay you to goof off in the warehouse. Get back upstairs and start logging calls!'

Mateo saluted. 'Yes sir, Derek, sir. On my way, sir.'

He set off in the direction of the main office. Abelard made to follow him but Stanton grabbed his arm.

'As for you, that's two strikes against you this week and now you're corrupting other workers with your slacking. I suggest a severe attitude readjustment before I have to start disciplinary proceedings against you.'

Abelard hung his head. 'Sorry Derek. It won't happen again.'

Once he reached his desk, Abelard started answering calls, making sure to avoid any contact with the call-e-fact interface crystal but half expecting to set off a mana surge at every moment. He worked through his lunch hour again to make up for lost time and to show Stanton that he had turned over a new leaf. It was hard to concentrate on service calls though, with his newfound ability and thoughts of Jen running through his head.

He made it to the end of the day without anything weird happening. As the chron-e-fact clicked over to signal the end of their shift, Mateo jumped up from his chair and cried, 'Let's go!'

Abelard was startled. 'Go where?'

'Back to my place,' Mateo said. 'We've got some experimenting to do!'

* * *

In a stone temple a couple of miles away, Walter shivered in his expensive suit. It was always cold here, no matter the weather outside. He looked across the large table at his companion, Laleh Nazari, and was gratified to see her pulling her flimsy wrap more tightly around her shoulders.

The cold never seemed to bother their host, though. Brother Theobold walked behind Laleh to the head of the table, dressed in his usual grey smock, sandals slapping against the flagstones as he passed. He waved a hand and one of the ornate wooden chairs slid out from the table. Walter winced at the screech of metal on stone from its bronze-capped feet.

'Sorry,' Theobold said. He peered at them both. 'More heat?'

Another wave of his hand and a fire blazed up in the hearth on Laleh's side of the room. She relaxed with a smile, the expression reminding Walter of Alessandra.

'Well.' Theobold folded his hands. 'I suppose I should call this meeting to order. I don't think anyone else is coming.'

Walter was already wishing he hadn't bothered either. 'What's on the agenda?'

Theobold peered at him again. 'Agenda? Oh yes. Do you have any update on the hunt for Gerald Simpson?'

Walter sighed. Was this really why he had left the office early to drag himself to this ridiculous building when he had so many other more important things to do?

'No news, I'm afraid.' He had given the same update since the task had been assigned to him. That had been five years ago when Laleh first recruited him to Brother Theobold's little secret society. 'There have been no sightings, no hints of untoward artisan activity and no suggestions of an imminent uprising. Gerald is still in hiding and I suspect that is where he'll stay.'

'There's no need to be flippant,' Laleh said. 'Gerald still poses a potential threat to us.'

'Really?' Walter raised an eyebrow. 'By your own admission there hasn't been a peep out of him since you kicked him out nearly thirty years ago. He scuttled into a deep dark hole, never to be seen again. Without his spark, he has no power.'

Theobold steepled his fingers and regarded Walter solemnly over the top of them. 'Ah, but knowledge is also power. And Gerald knows a great many things we would prefer he did not.'

Walter nodded. 'I'll keep all my monitoring activities in place. And if he should decide to show himself I'll stamp him out for good, like the two of you should have done in the first place.'

He caught the glance that passed between Theobold and Laleh. But Walter was unconcerned. Their previous inaction against Gerald demonstrated their lack of follow-through. It epitomised the very nature and purpose of the Inner Circle, as they called it, so Walter knew they would never do anything to him. He just needed to bide his time, learn as much as he could and make his own plans.

* * *

An hour after leaving Mana-Calls, Abelard was standing on the roof of Mateo's building as his friend spread a selection of newly charged artefacts around him. Early evening sunshine shone down on to the concrete, but there was a bite in the air.

'So, show me what you can do,' Mateo said.

Abelard laughed. 'I have no idea what I can do!'

'Exactly! That's why we need to experiment. We've already established that you can transfer mana from one artefact to another and apparently also fly? Can you show me that, by the way?'

Abelard pointed to the ledge at the side of the roof. 'You first.'

Mateo raised his hands in surrender. 'Okay, maybe we should start with something easier. Can you transfer mana without touching the artefacts?'

'Do you really think we should be messing around with this?'

'How else are you going to find out the extent of your new powers? Where's your sense of adventure?'

Abelard still wasn't convinced of the wisdom of experimentation. But Mateo's enthusiasm was contagious and Abelard had to admit he was intrigued. Rolling his shoulders, he adopted a dramatic pose, arms rigid and palms down, and focused on the artefacts at his feet. He tried to imagine the blue glow of mana flowing out of them and up into his fingers. He was aware of Mateo's expectant face in his peripheral vision. His arms started to shake with the tension of holding the stance.

Nothing happened.

Feeling silly, he relaxed his hands. Why couldn't this whole artisan powers business make some sense? He looked over at his friend with a shrug.

Mateo was undeterred.

'Okay, so no to the remote transfer. Why don't you charge

yourself up with some mana and see what you can do with it?'

Abelard crouched down and put one hand on each of the two nearest artefacts. Their mana started to seep into his fingers and the now almost familiar tingling sensation spread with it. He allowed the glow to cover his hands and then broke contact. He didn't want to be knocked unconscious again.

'That is so awesome!' Mateo said. 'Try hovering. I want to see you hover!'

Abelard grinned, adrenaline kicking in as his sense of power grew. He closed his eyes and imagined his feet lifting from the ground. He didn't feel anything happening but an excited yelp from Mateo made him open his eyes and chance a look down. The shock of finding himself floating a few inches off the ground broke his concentration and he dropped back to earth with a stagger. The blue glow around his hands disappeared.

Mateo came rushing over. 'That was amazing! How do you feel?'

Abelard was breathing heavily. 'About as if I'd run up several flights of stairs.'

'Okay. I just want to try one more thing. Charge yourself up again.'

Seconds later, Abelard's whole right arm was glowing.

'Now,' Mateo said, 'try expelling the mana outwards in a stream like you're throwing it. I want to see what happens.'

Abelard pulled his arm back and then thrust it forwards. At the same time, he pictured the mana firing out of his fingers. The visualisation worked all too well. He flew backwards as a stream of blue light shot from his hand and struck the wall of the stairwell with a crackling flash. Pain exploded in his hand as Abelard crashed into Mateo and they both ended up on the ground.

'Wow!' Mateo was looking at the scorch mark on the wall. 'You could do some real damage with that!'

'I think I did,' Abelard muttered, looking at the blistered, scorched skin of his hand. 'Ow!'

'Shit, sorry. That looks a bit beyond my first aid kit,' said Mateo, with a grimace.

He made up for it at the hospital, making up a story about a malfunctioning artefact and even getting the doctor to sign Abelard off work for the rest of the week. By the time they got to Abelard's flat, Abelard was feeling nicely fuzzy from the painkillers.

'You sure you'll be okay?' Mateo asked.

Abelard made a vague shoo-ing motion. 'Go home. Don't worry about me.'

He was fast asleep in five minutes.

* * *

Brain-e-fact Ten-Forty-Seven had been working at Gadg-E-Tech as long as he could remember. The animate artefact was six feet tall and humanoid in shape but fashioned out of thick cream-coloured ceramic that clicked as he moved. There were fifty brain-e-facts at the Gadg-E-Tech head office building and they all looked exactly the same, apart from the identification number inscribed on their chest-plates. Their cylindrical heads had a jointed jaw and mobile glass eyes to give them an approximation of human expression, but human emotion was a mystery to them.

The Facilities Manager at Gadg-E-Tech had activated Ten-Forty-Seven almost ten years ago and he had been fulfilling his duties to the best of his ability ever since. He spent half an hour each night recharging his mana unit but otherwise there was always work to do. His favourite duty was feeding the fish in the enormous tanks behind the reception desks down in the lobby. Sometimes he would take a few minutes to watch them swimming around and wonder what it was like to be a fish. Brain-e-facts did not have much of an imagination so his musings never went very far. But the colours and motion of the fish tank were soothing and it was a pleasant interlude in his otherwise relentless work schedule.

If someone were to ask Ten-Forty-Seven if he enjoyed his job, the question would confuse him. He had never known anything else, so did not have anything to compare it to. It would never occur to him that there was anything about his life that was unfair. He had a job to do and anything outside of that was beyond his conception. He worked alongside his fellow brain-e-facts companionably enough, but there was little for them to talk about beyond the necessities of task allocation and completion. They never left the building so had no knowledge of the outside world and they did not interact with the artisans, other than to receive instructions or report on the work they had completed.

Most days Ten-Forty-Seven worked in the canteen, so he saw more of Gadg-E-Tech life than the brain-e-facts doing data entry in the HR department, for instance. He laid out food on the buffet counters and served hot drinks to the artisans when they asked him. Sometimes they requested complicated combinations of components and Ten-Forty-Seven had to be careful to follow their instructions exactly. He had noticed that artisans grew angry if their coffee was not precisely how they wanted it. Generally they only acknowledged the brain-e-facts or spoke more than a couple of words to them if the brain-e-facts got something wrong. That didn't happen often and Ten-Forty-Seven had known days when he did not exchange a single word with anyone, artisan or brain-e-fact. But since he did not possess the capacity to feel lonely or marginalised, this wasn't a problem.

That was all about to change. But as Ten-Forty-Seven loaded the dish-e-fact as part of his regular morning routine, he had no notion of this. He simply performed his task mechanically and methodically, taking little notice of the other brain-e-facts around him, whose fate would soon be in his ceramic hands.

CHAPTER THREE

Abelard awoke on Wednesday morning to full daylight. Had his alarm failed to go off again? His heart rate slowed when he remembered what had happened. He was signed off work, so he relaxed back in bed with a sigh and thought about what he should do with his day.

His engineer mind itched to find out what was going on and his social conscience couldn't dismiss the potential ramifications of an engineer suddenly developing artisan abilities. If it had happened to him, it could happen to others. The most obvious plan would be to go to the artisans themselves for guidance but there was no way for him to predict how they might react.

He couldn't achieve anything on his own though, and the only place he could get more information was from the artisans. So he had no choice but to approach them and hope for the best. But how? He couldn't just present himself at their front door as Mateo had suggested.

Each artisan company had its own base of operations but nobody could gain access without permission from someone high up in the hierarchy. Abelard didn't have those kinds of connections. The only artisan he actually knew was at a much lower level. Jonathan Worthington-Price had come to Mana-Calls to run a rare engineer training programme a few years before and Abelard and Mateo had struck up a conversation with him afterwards. Jonathan was approachable and friendly and didn't seem to harbour the usual artisan opinion that engineers were lower than bugs. Or at least not quite as much as other artisans.

There was a Gadg-E-Tech factory not far from Abelard's flat and Jonathan had once mentioned that he worked there. Jonathan might be a self-important flake but he was Abelard's best bet for getting help. Abelard reached for his smart-e-fact and punched in Jonathan's number. Jonathan picked up on the second ring.

'Hey, Abelard! This is a surprise.'

It would be even more of a surprise once Jonathan knew why he was calling.

'Hey, Jonathan. Um, is there any chance I could stop by and see you about something this morning?'

'Here at the factory? Why?'

'I'd rather talk face-to-face if that's okay.'

'Ooh, mysterious. I guess that would be okay. I'll have to keep you in sight at all times, you realise.'

'Sure. I'll see you in a bit.'

Abelard dragged himself out of bed, got dressed and set off to the factory. As he walked, he pulled out his smart-e-fact and sent a message to Mateo, letting him know where he was going and promising an update with full details later. As he was putting the smart-e back in his pocket his fingers brushed against the envelope with Jen's number on it. He smiled and sent another message, this time to Jen, saying how much he had enjoyed meeting her and asking if she wanted to get together either that evening or the next day.

* * *

It was late morning when Abelard arrived at the Gadg-E-Tech factory. He had walked past it many times but never approached the gates before. The building was surrounded by a high wall with a security checkpoint at the entrance. Abelard strolled up to the guard, trying to look as if he went in and out of artisan facilities every day.

'My name is Abelard Abernathy. I'm here to see Jonathan Worthington-Price,' he said with as much confidence as he could muster.

There was a pause while the guard checked some kind of mana-powered information system and sweat started to collect on the back of Abelard's neck.

'Building Three,' the guard said, waving him through.

Was it really that easy? Perhaps the artisans' supposedly strict security measures weren't as draconian as Abelard had been led to believe. It was strange that he was just being allowed to wander in unescorted. He wondered what would happen if he went somewhere other than Building Three and decided it would be better not to find out.

So Abelard followed the signs to Building Three, a tight knot of tension constricting his chest as he went in. The inside of the building was cavernous, a vast space filled with unfamiliar artefacts and lots of people scurrying back and forth, intent on their business. Abelard's eyes darted around, trying to take it all in. A big man in overalls spotted him and came up, his expression suspicious.

'Can I help you with something?' The man's aggressive posture belied the courtesy of his words.

'Uh, is Jonathan around?' Abelard asked.

The man gestured to a door off to one side, eyes still wary. 'In the back.'

Abelard thanked him and moved towards the door, keeping his pace casual. His breath whooshed out in relief when the door opened into a much smaller room with Jonathan as its only occupant.

Jonathan bent over a strange contraption scattered in several pieces over a workbench. His long brown ponytail slipped over his shoulder as he worked and he flipped it back in irritation. He looked up startled as Abelard shut the door behind him. Then he grabbed a sheet of cloth and threw it over what he was working on.

'Abelard! How did you get in? The gate guard should have called me to come and get you. And I bet that duncehead Graham just let you wander in here too. No sense of security at all, that one. It's no wonder he hasn't been promoted to a design or manufacturing position yet. I bet the company doesn't trust him with their secrets. He'd be telling people all over the place about the customisation features on the new beaut-e-fact and Spark-le would have a competing artefact out in no time.' He pulled himself up. 'Oops! You didn't hear that from me!'

'Don't worry,' Abelard said. 'I'm not exactly in a position to tell anyone who matters.' Though given the circumstances, how long would that remain true?

'So what can I do for you?' Jonathan asked, continuing

before Abelard had a chance to answer the question. 'My shift doesn't start for another hour but I like to come in early sometimes to work on my designs. This is the one I was telling you about the other day. If I can get one of the more senior members of the company to endorse it I might have an artefact in production even before I move up from working here. And that would stand me in good stead for a much better position when I'm finally promoted. You've got to think of the future, you see, not just slog away at the daily grind without formulating a plan.'

By the time Jonathan ran down, Abelard's little remaining confidence was gone. He opened his mouth to start his tale and found his tongue taking him off on a tangent.

'Are artisans born with the ability to manipulate mana or does it manifest later in life?'

Jonathan gave him a lopsided grin. 'You know I can't tell you that,' he said, then looked thoughtful. 'Though the question presents rather an amusing concept. If we were born being able to manipulate mana, parents would have a hell of a time controlling their kids. There'd be stuff – and probably people – flying about all over the place. And there's no telling what they'd get up to once they figured out they could actually control it.' He caught himself again, this time bringing a hand up to cover his mouth. 'Shit! You really didn't hear that from me.'

Abelard's mind was trying to keep up.

'So you can use mana to affect objects directly?' He thought back to how Jen had described his actions two days before. 'It doesn't actually have to be channelled through an artefact?'

'Now, I never said that!' Jonathan said, eyes widening. 'I never said anything of the sort! You can't go around spouting wild stories about artisans wielding forces of mana directly. People would never believe you for a start.' His tone darkened. 'And you might get in trouble.'

Abelard raised his hands and waved them at Jonathan as if trying to fend him off. 'Seriously Jonathan, I think I'm probably in about as much trouble artisan-wise as I can get. Trust me, once you know why I've come, me running around telling tales about flying artisans will be the least of your worries. For one thing, I don't need to make up stories like that – I've been one.'

'Been one what?'

Abelard couldn't blame Jonathan's confusion.

'A flying artisan,' he said, though that didn't really clarify anything at all.

Jonathan just stared at him so Abelard decided a demonstration was in order. He glanced around and spotted a pile of charged mana units stacked on a nearby shelf. Walking over to them, he laid both his hands on the top one and felt the tingle as mana leached out of the unit and moved over his fingers. The mana stung his burned hand but he ignored the pain. This time he didn't break contact once the blue glow had enveloped his hands, instead allowing it to continue up his arms as it had at Jen's office. He could hear his heart pounding in his ears but he clamped down on his rising fear and instead pictured his feet lifting off the floor. He rose a few inches into the air and slowly spun around until he was facing Jonathan again.

Jonathan's eyes were wider than Abelard would have thought physically possible and he was frozen in place. Locking gazes with Abelard seemed to break him out of his paralysis and he leapt forwards, waving his hands in the air.

'What do you think you're *doing*? How can you *know* what you're doing? How can you be *doing* what you're doing?' He planted his feet and threw his hands out in a warding gesture. 'Put that mana back right now!'

Abelard wobbled in the air but he didn't know how to comply. After a few seconds Jonathan seemed to realise the problem. He stepped forwards, took a deep breath and took hold of Abelard's wrist. All the mana rushed out of Abelard's body and he fell to the floor, breaking contact with Jonathan and landing on his backside with a thump. The blue glow now crackled all over Jonathan, but not for long. With a thrust of one arm, he sent it shooting through the air and back into the source unit in a long focused stream. When all the mana had returned to its rightful place, Jonathan glared down at Abelard, breathing hard, his entire demeanour altered from friendly exuberance to barely controlled anger.

'You!' he commanded with a stab of one finger. 'Up. Now.'

Abelard scrambled to obey. The moment he was on his feet, Jonathan grabbed his arm and hustled him out into the main part of the building. The man who had directed Abelard to Jonathan earlier stomped over.

'Graham, call Despatch,' Jonathan said, his voice quiet but his tone steely. 'Get them to send someone over to cover my shift and tell them to alert Head Office that I'm on my way.'

'Now, wait just a minute! You can't order me about like that!'

Jonathan cut him off. 'Code 47.'

Graham's features went slack and he reached for a call-e-fact fixed to the wall.

Abelard looked between them, his breaths coming short and fast. Whatever he had expected from Jonathan, this wasn't it.

As they moved outside he asked, 'What's Code 47?'

Jonathan didn't even look at him. 'Not – a – word. This is way above my pay grade. Head Office will have to decide how to deal with you.'

* * *

By the time they arrived at Gadg-E-Tech head office, Jonathan had Abelard really worried. Even the incredible smoothness of Jonathan's speed-e-fact hadn't distracted him enough for the knot in his stomach to unravel. A couple of times on the way over, he'd thought about protesting but what could he do? He needed artisan help and Jonathan had seen what he could do now. A few days ago, a visit to the centre of Gadg-E-Tech operations would have been a dream come true but now nausea threatened.

The building rose shining from its surroundings like a glass and steel beacon in the midday sun. Inside, a bank of sleek receptionists routed calls and important looking people strode about in all directions. Abelard just had time to register that the receptionists were ceramic artefacts in human form, but Jonathan whisked him to the lev-e-fact bank without stopping.

It was odd that Jonathan didn't have to announce himself or show any form of ID as he punched the button for the top floor and Abelard's stomach flipped over. When the leve-fact stopped, Jonathan marched Abelard down a richly carpeted hallway towards a desk where yet another humanoid artefact sat working. It looked up at their approach.

'Hello, Mister Worthington-Price,' it said in a stilted monotone. 'I have not seen you here for a while.'

Jonathan asked, 'Is Uncle Walter in?'

'Yes. He is waiting for you. Go right in.'

The plaque on the door read, 'Walter Snyder, Chief Financial Officer'.

'Your uncle is the CFO of Gadg-E-Tech?' Abelard asked, but Jonathan continued to ignore him.

Abelard was still wide eyed and open-mouthed as he was deposited in front of the CFO of the company he'd been dreaming of working for since he was a child. It wasn't a great first impression to present.

The family resemblance between Jonathan and Walter Snyder was obvious in the whip-thin frame and lanky height but Walter's lined face was topped by hair cropped short and peppered with grey.

'Ah, Jonathan.' Walter rose from behind his desk. 'And this must be the Code 47.'

'A-Abelard Abernathy, sir. It's an honour to meet you.'

Abelard stuck out his hand then gave a nervous laugh and took it back again as Walter looked askance at his bandaged fingers. The other man's expression was stern.

'Mana burn?' Abelard nodded and Walter continued, his eyes flinty. 'Well, at least you've learned the consequences of careless mana handling early. Now before we proceed, I'll need you to provide a demonstration of your new abilities.'

'But I saw–!' Jonathan stopped when his uncle raised a hand.

'It's not that I don't believe you, Jonathan. But I need to see it for myself if I'm going to take the case before the Council. You more than anyone know we have to take precautions with our security. I can't recommend what should be done with Mr Abernathy here without judging the circumstances personally.'

Abelard's nausea ratcheted up another notch. None of this suggested the artisans were going to welcome him with open arms. Should he just claim the whole thing had been an elaborate hoax to wind up Jonathan and ask to go home? The faces of the two men suggested that would be unwise.

Walter gestured at a pile of mana units on a side table.

Taking a deep breath, Abelard walked over to the table and stretched out his left hand. As the mana flowed over his fingers, he imagined a dark prison filled with languishing engineers who had reached above their preordained station. What would Mateo do if he just vanished from the face of the earth? Would Jen be sad never to see him again? The eyes of Jonathan and Walter gave nothing away. A tidal wave of fatigue washed over him as he raised his glowing hand and the edges of his vision went dark. There was a flash, a cry (he couldn't tell whose) and then nothing.

CHAPTER FOUR

Walter had never seen a Gadg-E-Tech Board meeting so well attended. But then this was the first Code 47 in most members' living memory. He looked round the table, all the faces known to him, though some more familiar than others. The CEO wasn't there, of course. Walter couldn't remember the last time he had even been in the building. Walter enjoyed listening to the theories that swirled around the company grapevine about where the CEO was, amused by how far from the truth they were. Edgar Pearson, the Vice-President, had full proxy authority to act in the CEO's stead, and sat one space down from the head of the table.

On the other side of the table from Edgar was Keto Jones, the representative from the Artisan Council. He caught Walter's eye and gave a small nod. Walter resisted the urge to roll his eyes. Keto had been sensible enough not to turn up for the pointless Inner Circle meeting the night before but he was apparently going to make up for it by being indiscreet here instead.

All the other Board members were looking at Edgar. Board meetings never usually started on time, but everyone was here.

'Good evening,' Edgar said, 'and thank you all for coming. I know there's only one reason most of you are here so I won't waste your time with inanities.'

There was a murmur of gratitude and Walter did roll his eyes now at Edgar's blatant pursuit of popularity.

Edgar continued. 'You all know about the Code 47. The engineer's name is Abelard Abernathy. I would like to hear proposals as to what to do with him before we take a vote.'

One of the oldest Board members raised a hand and Edgar nodded for him to proceed.

'The precedent was set fifty years ago, last time this happened. That other fella who did the same thing – what was his name?'

'Rajesh Kumar,' a younger voice supplied.

'That was the one,' the older man said. 'We shuffled him off to the Quality Assurance Department and nobody's heard a peep out of him since. Easiest way to go about it. Why not just do the same with this new one?'

'That's certainly one possibility,' Edgar said. 'It's worked before so there's no reason to suspect it won't work just as well again. Does anyone object to that plan?'

'Don't we need to find out how this keeps happening?' asked Simon Hanley, the head of the Research & Development Department. 'So we can stop it happening again? I mean, we can't have engineers popping up with spontaneous artisan abilities all over the place.' Simon waved his hands in agitation. 'It would destabilise the whole system by raising questions among the populace that we either can't or don't want to answer.'

There were noises of assent and Edgar raised a hand to quiet them.

'I would hardly say two occurrences in fifty years

constitutes a major threat. And we have no way of determining the cause of the so-called phenomenon without physical harm to the two people in question. However, regardless of what we decide here today, I will ensure Mr Abernathy is made available to R&D for an in-depth interview regarding the incident that boosted his spark.'

'Isn't our security more important than one engineer's well-being?' Walter asked. 'We haven't vetted this Abelard person and we know nothing about his values or his integrity. We can't just give him a job willy-nilly and expect him to automatically align himself to the company vision. He's an engineer so he must have gone through the testing process and been rejected. Shouldn't we find out why he wasn't accepted in the first place, rather than just welcoming him with open arms?'

'A valid point,' Edgar said, though he and Walter rarely saw eye to eye. 'However, there are many ways we can help Mr Abernathy to become aligned with the company's vision. And your nephew vouches for him.'

'My sister's idiot boy?' Walter sneered. 'We all know how security-conscious he is! He should never have been given a position here, either. How many of our secrets do you think he's already revealed to this engineer?'

'I'm sure Jonathan knows when to keep his mouth shut,' Edgar said. 'And if he has let slip some minor details about the way we do things, that's all the more reason to incorporate Mr Abernathy into an innocuous position within the company where he can fulfil his dream of being an artisan with no risk of harm to us.'

Walter snorted. 'Mr Abernathy set fire to my office. That's hardly a sign of a balanced and useful individual if you ask me.'

There was a ripple of laughter around the table.

'It was only a minor accident,' Edgar said. 'And I believe there were extenuating circumstances. But that's why I've assigned Alessandra Eriksen to tutor him in better control and fundamental shielding.'

Walter set his jaw. 'Alessandra Eriksen has better things to do with her time than babysit dangerous social climbers.'

Edgar looked surprised. 'She's the best person for the job.'

Walter shrugged. Alessandra and the engineer probably deserved one another.

'And it's an important job,' Laleh Nazari said from further down the table. 'Regardless of what is decided here, the engineer needs to be rendered safe as a priority.'

Walter noticed Edgar giving her a small smile. She had always been one of Edgar's supporters and was respected by many of the older members of the Board.

'His current lack of control over his abilities is the only danger I can see from this young man,' Laleh continued, her calm tone and expression lending credence to her words. 'That danger is being addressed in the best possible way, through the allocation of Ms Eriksen. Then the only way to mitigate what little risk there is to the business from this engineer is to accept him into our family and train him as we would any other new recruit. If we were to reject him a second time and send him back to his life, there would be much more danger from his resentment, curiosity and uncontrolled powers than if we give him what he wants and answer any questions he has in a way that maintains our position and secrecy.'

Walter was unsurprised by Laleh's endorsement of Alessandra. He was one of the few people in the company that knew she was Alessandra's mother. Laleh used her Iranian maiden name and Alessandra strongly favoured her father's Scandinavian looks, so nobody would suspect the family connection without being told. He was also unsurprised by Laleh's weak stance on what to do with the engineer. It was exactly what he would expect from her blind adherence to Brother Theobold's altruistic tendencies.

Several of the more senior members of the Board were nodding sage agreement and the dissenters had quieted in the face of Laleh's apparent logic. It was useless to argue further. Walter inclined his head in acknowledgement, admitting at least temporary defeat.

'If no-one has any further comments?' Edgar said. He looked across the table at Keto Jones. 'Can you speak on behalf of the Artisan Council to agree this approach, Mr Jones?'

Keto looked at Walter, his eyes asking a question he didn't voice. Walter nodded his head almost imperceptibly and Keto gave Edgar his assent.

Walter would hold his peace for now but keep a close eye on developments and take action later, if necessary.

* * *

Jen got Abelard's message on Wednesday lunchtime and was warmed by the enthusiasm in his voice. She pictured his mop of dark curls and his shy smile as she listened. Then she tried to call him back but couldn't get through. She tried again a couple of times during the afternoon but with no success. It bothered her that she wasn't able to leave a message and she hoped her apparent lack of response wouldn't put him off. She assumed there was some kind of malfunction with his smart-e-fact and was amused that their continuing contact was still defined by faulty artefacts.

But given how different they were in their attitudes toward artefacts, did they really have anything in common? Their first meeting had been so intense and she knew almost nothing about him. Giving him her number had been an uncharacteristic act of pure impulse. There was something about him though. He had kind eyes and had seemed genuinely interested in getting to know her. Besides he had put himself in danger to solve her artefact problem and that was something she couldn't take lightly.

And now she couldn't reach him. At the end of the day Jen went home, disappointed and unsure what to do.

On Thursday afternoon a thought struck Jen and she dialled the Mana-Calls helpline number.

'Mana-Calls Artefact Support. Mateo Vega speaking. How may I help you?'

'Can you put me through to Abelard Abernathy please?'

'I'm afraid he's not in the office today. Can I help at all?' The voice was friendly and eager.

'Oh, um, no,' Jen said. 'It's a personal call. Do you know when he'll be back?'

'Should be Monday. He got signed off on Tuesday because of his injury but he's supposed to be coming back after the weekend.'

'Injury? What injury?'

'Well, that is …' Mateo suddenly sounded hesitant. 'Perhaps you'd better ask him that yourself when you speak to him. I could tell him you're trying to get hold of him when I call him later. Who should I say it was?'

'My name's Jen Blake–'

'Jen? You're Jen?' Mateo said, his tone almost one of awe.

'Er, yes I am.' How did one of Abelard's colleagues know about her?

'Didn't he give you his personal number? Honestly, I swear that boy would forget his own head if it wasn't attached. Hang on a sec and I'll get it for you.'

'It's okay,' Jen said. 'I do have it but it doesn't seem to be working. I've been trying to get hold of him since yesterday. I know it must sound ridiculous. I only met him on Monday but it seemed strange that the number didn't work. And now you tell me he's been hurt …'

'He only burned his hand. But it's not like him to ignore calls. And he'd get his smart-e fixed pronto if it was on the blink. I bet it's got something to do with the artisans.'

'Why would it have anything to do with the artisans?'

'Long story,' Mateo said. 'But I've been dying to tell someone about it. I don't suppose you're free after work, are you?'

Jen wasn't sure what to say. The whole situation was getting both weird and complicated. Admittedly she had contacted Mana-Calls in the first place because she was worried about Abelard, but now there was talk of injuries and artisans. She considered what her mother would advise and decided to do the opposite.

'Absolutely,' she said. 'When and where?'

Mateo named a pub on the other side of town and suggested they meet at six o'clock.

'In the meantime,' he concluded, 'I'll try and get in touch with my artisan friend, Jonathan. He's the one Abelard was going to see yesterday so he should be able to shed some light on the situation. Thanks for calling.'

* * *

Abelard felt very light, as if he might float away. His left hand hurt but he was sure he had burned his right one. He wiggled his right fingers and they hurt too. He wiggled both sets of fingers together and the left ones definitely hurt more. He supposed he should stop waving his hands about and let them heal.

'Finally awake, are we?'

The voice came to him as if from very far away. It was female and quite sharp, sounding more irritated than concerned.

He struggled to open his eyes and saw a woman looming above him. The bright light in the ceiling cast a nimbus of gold around her luxuriant blonde hair and the red of her lips stood out against her pale skin. The blurriness inside Abelard's head extended to his eyes and he saw her in soft focus, which lent a dreamlike air to her appearance.

'Umm…' he said, overwhelmed.

'I hope your brain wasn't fried like your fingers. I don't have all day to babysit addled engineers.' Her harsh voice was in direct contrast to her angelic face and Abelard struggled to reconcile them in his still confused state.

'Umm …' he said again.

'Okay, let's try a few simple questions. When was the last time you ate?'

The rational part of Abelard's brain seized on the question like a lifeline and dragged him further into complete awareness, while at the same time trying to think back to his last meal. His life had been so disrupted in the last few days.

'Monday lunchtime,' he said eventually.

The vision of loveliness uttered a snort of contempt.

'More than 48 hours without food, combined with two direct mana manipulations. It's no wonder–'

'Uh, six,' Abelard said, his mental calculations finally speeding up.

'Six what?'

'Six direct mana manipulations in the period without food.'

'Six?' Shock registered on the divine features.

Abelard tried to swallow but his mouth was too dry. 'Is that bad?'

He didn't want to disappoint her but he didn't seem able to stop himself from telling her things.

'Is that bad?' she repeated with a harsh bark of laughter. 'Okay, so your brain must already have been addled even before you collapsed. I'm surprised half the city isn't on fire rather than just the CFO's office.'

'On fire?' Abelard said, though most of his mind was taken up by how happy he was to have made her smile.

'Yes, you made quite a mess when you lost control of that mana by all accounts. I wish I'd been there to see it. It's pretty difficult to rattle Walter Snyder.'

'Was anyone hurt?'

'Other than you?' His angel rolled her eyes. 'Luckily, no. Anyway, now that you're awake and apparently not in danger of spontaneously combusting, I have work to do. Try not to blow anything up while you're still in the building.'

She swept from the room.

Abelard was trying to make sense of the encounter several minutes later, when another woman entered the room. She was much older and carried a tray of food.

'Who was that other woman?' Abelard asked.

She looked surprised by the question.

'Who? Oh, you mean Alessandra?'

'Alessandra …' Abelard repeated, his mouth stretching into a goofy grin.

The woman looked at him oddly. 'You really need to eat something, young man. And then I suggest you go back to sleep. If meeting Alessandra Eriksen puts that expression on your face, you might want to think about having your head examined as well.'

She took an unfamiliar artefact out of her pocket and

pointed it at his left hand. A beam of blue mana light shone out of a narrow nozzle on the artefact's front and the woman studied its small screen for a moment.

'Looks like this is healing nicely,' she said. 'And the other hand was pretty much fine after I treated it earlier. So you can remove the bandages in the morning and let fresh air and time do the rest.'

Abelard stared at her. How could his mana burns heal so quickly? She must be an artisan doctor, with tools and skills that weren't available to the mundane doctor he had seen before. The woman gave him a brief smile and bustled from the room.

Abelard glanced at the food and suddenly he was ravenous. He barely registered what he was eating but his body welcomed it and he was finished in no time. As he replaced the tray on the bedside table a wave of fatigue washed over him and he snuggled back down in the bed, drifting off to sleep again, his mind full of thoughts of Alessandra Eriksen.

CHAPTER FIVE

Jen watched the clock all afternoon, facts and figures blurring on her screen. Surely Abelard would turn up safe and sound, embarrassed to have caused such concern. But what if the artisans had done something to him? She would struggle to fill a postcard with what she knew about where mana came from and how artefacts were produced. She just accepted it as a part of life.

She escaped work early and hurried to make her rendezvous with Mateo. She had no idea what he looked like but a man waved her over as soon as she entered the pub.

'Mateo?' He nodded. 'How did you know I was me?'

'Abelard told me what you look like. Drink?'

She asked for a gin and tonic and studied Mateo as he went to the bar. He was shorter and stockier than Abelard, with straight dark hair in a similar state of disarray and sparkling eyes that gave distinction to his otherwise average features.

When he came back with the drinks he considered her with an appraising look before he sat down. 'So, you're Abelard's Jen,' he said.

She squirmed under his stare but then realised he was only doing what she had just done to him without him knowing it. But his comment made her bristle.

'I'm not anybody's anything, thank you very much.' He looked chagrined and she took a sip of her drink before changing the subject. 'Is your artisan friend joining us?'

'No.' Mateo's expression darkened. 'I spoke to him earlier and the whole conversation made me even more suspicious. He said he hadn't seen Abelard since we all went out last week and he claimed there was some crisis at Gadg-E-Tech head office that meant he couldn't really talk to me.'

'And you don't believe him?'

'About not seeing Abelard? No. He's not a very good liar and he sounded really weird when he said it. But I think the crisis at Gadg-E-Tech is Abelard.'

'Why?'

Mateo took a large gulp of his beer.

'I guess I'd better start at the beginning.'

Mateo proceeded to tell a story that sounded like pure fantasy. If Jen hadn't actually seen Abelard glowing and floating for herself, she wouldn't have believed any of it. Mateo eventually reached the point at which he had received a message from Abelard saying that he was going to see Jonathan Worthington-Price.

'That was yesterday morning. And I haven't been able to get hold of him since.'

'Just like me,' Jen said. 'He must have sent that message to you just before he tried to call me. Jonathan is the artisan?'

Mateo nodded. 'I just know he has something to do with Abelard dropping off the face of the planet. I wouldn't have thought he would do anything bad before, but I'm not so sure after how he seemed when I talked to him.'

'But what are you actually suggesting? That the artisans have kidnapped Abelard for some reason? Or … Or something worse?'

'I don't know,' Mateo said. 'But after everything that's happened, I can't think of another explanation.'

'But why? Wouldn't they be glad he's an artisan now?'

'I've been thinking about that all afternoon, and I've come to the conclusion that they probably wouldn't.' Mateo sighed. 'As far as mana is concerned the artisans are at the top of the tree. All our lives Abelard and I have wanted to be artisans. As soon as we were old enough we applied for artisan training, got tested and were told we didn't have a strong enough spark to be anything other than engineers. I've been an engineer for nearly ten years and I've never met one who didn't have the same story. What's happened to Abelard suggests there's a way to boost someone's spark so they can do what artisans do. Just think if all the engineers suddenly had artisan abilities. That would be sure to upset the balance of power. And who would fix all the broken artefacts if there were no engineers? The artisans need us right where we are.'

'So this kind of thing doesn't happen often?'

'More like never. I tried to do it to myself for about two hours last night but no luck. The artisans are so secretive and arrogant … Who knows how they'd react to an engineer who suddenly turned up and asked to join them?'

'But we can't exactly march up to Gadg-E-Tech HQ and demand they give him back.' Jen tried to steady her breathing.

'We could go and ask and see what they say. After all, it's likely where he ended up if he went to Jonathan.'

Jen bit her lip. 'What if they say they've never heard of him? What do we do then? Should we report him missing?'

Mateo set his pint down and crossed his arms. 'I don't think there's a hope we'd be taken seriously. We'd be reporting Gadg-E-Tech for kidnap; no one's going to believe that, and if they did, who's going to investigate? The artisans run everything. But Abelard might be in danger. We have to go and see what we can find out. We're the only people who know where he went.'

Mateo looked determined but Jen felt a sudden chill. There were so many unknowns, but she had come this far.

'Okay,' she said, standing up. 'Let's go before I change my mind.'

Gadg-E-Tech head office was in a part of the city Jen had never visited before. Mateo was vibrating with excitement by the time they got there but Jen just felt sick. The building itself was imposing and Jen stared up in awe as they walked into the gleaming reception area. She felt as though it was obvious they didn't belong there.

Mateo marched straight up to the front desk and said loudly, 'I'd like to see Jonathan Worthington-Price please.'

Jen hovered behind him. The reception desk was manned by a roughly humanoid being made out of ceramic, which looked up at them with a bland expression. Jen found it unsettling to look into the eyes of something that had no apparent human emotion, and have it look back.

She had heard somewhere about brain-e-facts, living

artefacts developed by one of the artisan companies. And now she was right in front of one.

'Do you have an appointment?' it asked in a flat voice that did nothing to dispel Jen's discomfort.

Mateo sighed. 'No, but it has to do with a mutual friend who's gone missing.'

The brain-e-fact jerked backwards as if pulled by an invisible string. 'I will see if I can reach him. May I take your name?'

Mateo obliged and remained leaning on the desk as the brain-e-fact punched some buttons.

It spoke into its headset. 'Good evening, Mister Worthington-Price. There is a Mateo Vega down in reception asking to speak to you. He says it is about a friend of yours who is missing.' It listened for a moment. 'I do not think he will take no for an answer.' There was another pause, then the brain-e-fact looked up at Mateo. 'Mister Worthington-Price will be down shortly, if you would like to take a seat.'

Jen followed Mateo to a plush seating area.

'That went better than I expected,' she said.

'We haven't found Abelard yet. And Jonathan may still try to fob us off.'

They sat in uncomfortable silence for several minutes before Jen saw a young man with a long ponytail approaching.

'Mateo, what are you doing here? I told you I haven't seen Abelard and this really isn't a good time. I'm sure he's fine. He's probably working on some project at home and hasn't thought to check his smart-e. You know how you engineers get when you're working on something.' He spotted Jen. 'Hello. Are you here with Mateo? I'm sorry you've had a wasted trip.'

'Jonathan!' Mateo said. 'Cut the crap for once! I know why Abelard was coming to see you yesterday. I'm guessing you've got him shut up somewhere and you've been doing experiments on him!'

People were staring.

'Don't be ridiculous, Mateo,' Jonathan hissed. 'And keep your voice down. This is where I work.'

'Then tell us what's going on,' Jen said, keeping her voice level and calm. 'It's obvious you know more than you're letting on and the quickest and easiest way to get rid of us is to tell us where Abelard is.'

Jonathan sighed. 'I should have known Abelard would have told Mateo what happened. And my uncle should have realised this would be impossible to contain. But who are you?'

'My name is Jen Blake. I was with Abelard when whatever happened to him – happened.'

'Really?' Jonathan's face brightened. 'I'd love to hear about that. This hasn't happened in a really long time and we know very little about how it works. Abelard doesn't remember much and it would be fascinating to get an outside viewpoint. Maybe you could come upstairs and tell me all about it.'

'Jonathan, focus!' Mateo cut in again. 'Jen isn't going anywhere with you unless it's where Abelard is. And in that case, you'll have to take both of us.'

'Stop being so melodramatic. Abelard's perfectly fine. He's resting in one of our suites. We couldn't just let him wander off in his state. It wouldn't have been ethical.'

'So why all the lying and covering up?' Mateo asked.

'Because I'm not in charge and the people who are haven't told me what I can say. Just because I'm Abelard's friend and I was the one who brought him in, doesn't mean I'm privy to the decisions of upper management. But you're not going to go away until I let you see Abelard, are you?'

Jen and Mateo both shook their heads firmly.

Jonathan sighed again. 'I suppose it won't do any harm since you know what's happened already. But once you've seen him, you'll have to go. This is artisan business and we will deal with it however we see fit.'

'We'll see about that,' Mateo said darkly but followed as Jonathan led them through security.

The lev-e-fact opened on a carpeted hallway with doors on either side like a hotel. Jonathan led them to the third one on the right, produced an ID card from his pocket and pressed it against the door mechanism. It glowed blue and opened. Beyond was a beige lounge with a small kitchen area off to one side and a huge window showing an impressive view out over the city.

'He's in here,' Jonathan said, striding across the room to another door.

The other two followed close on his heels and so were in the perfect position to see into the next room as Jonathan opened the door without knocking.

* * *

When he awoke again Abelard's head felt much clearer and his fingers were no longer painful, though he was still very tired. He heaved himself out of bed in search of a bathroom and discovered one just off the bedroom. As he was washing his hands around the bandages, he caught sight of himself in the mirror and gasped. His hair stuck up in all directions and dark stubble matched purplish pouches under his eyes. Wednesday's clothes were rumpled after many hours in bed, not to mention the scorch marks on the left sleeve. Had he looked this terrible when he had been speaking to Alessandra?

He did what he could to tidy himself up. He would have liked a shower but was still unsteady on his feet and collapsing while stark naked in the shower wouldn't be good. He took off his distressingly smelly t-shirt and splashed some water over his torso. By this time the bandages on his hands were decidedly soggy so he carefully removed them. The fingers of his left hand looked raw and pink but the ones on his right were almost back to normal. Flexing them resulted in only a slight twinge and a bit of stiffness.

When Abelard came back out of the bathroom, Alessandra was standing by the window. She was short but exuded confidence and wore very high heels. She was dressed in a vivid red business suit with a skirt that reached her knees and a black blouse showing at her throat and cuffs.

She turned at the sound of the door opening. 'At last.'

'You came back,' was all Abelard could come up with.

'Not by choice.'

Abelard started into the room but his knees buckled and he clutched the door frame for support.

'Oh, get back to bed before you fall down again,' Alessandra said, coming to his side and offering him her arm.

Abelard was very aware of being half naked but was forced to lean on her. She smelled of something flowery and her arm was strong underneath her jacket. Once he was sitting up in bed, he registered what she'd said.

'Someone sent you to check on me?'

She snorted. 'Yes. You slept so long people were starting to get worried. And they're nervous about your lack of control. So they sent me.'

'Um, why you?'

Alessandra rolled her eyes. 'Because I'm the best they've got at mana manipulation and more importantly shielding. If anything happened I'd be able to contain it.'

'Um, okay. What time is it?'

'About seven pm on Thursday. You slept for nearly 24 hours.'

'Wow, and I still feel pretty weak. Mana manipulation really takes it out of you, huh?'

Alessandra rolled her eyes at him again. Abelard wondered if they ever got sore doing that all the time.

'That's why we don't do it very often. Why do you think we started building artefacts in the first place? Though it's not quite so debilitating if you do it properly.'

'Properly?'

'There's such a thing as control. Let me show you.'

She pulled out a chron-e-fact and drew mana from its interface crystal. She made the blue light dance between her fingers in a complicated pattern before sending it gently back into the artefact.

'That was amazing,' Abelard said.

Alessandra's lips quirked. 'And look! No collapsing, no injuries and nothing's on fire!'

Abelard felt heat spread over his cheeks. 'Uh, yeah, I can see how that would be useful. Can you teach me?'

'I think I'd better. Otherwise I'm never going to get back to my real job.'

'Which is?'

'None of your business. Now pay attention.'

She drew mana from the chron-e-fact again, then leaned forwards until they were only inches apart.

Abelard felt his pulse quickening and tried to focus on what she was doing. She took his hand and he felt the tingle of the mana as it twined between their fingers. It stung a little but he didn't care.

'Okay,' she said, 'imagine–'

Abelard didn't get to hear what he was supposed to be imagining because the bedroom door opened to reveal Jonathan, Mateo and Jen.

There was a moment of stunned silence.

Then Abelard said, 'Mateo? Jen? What on earth are you doing here?'

Mateo and Jen just goggled at him.

CHAPTER SIX

'You see?' Jonathan said, gesturing at Abelard. 'He's perfectly fine.'

'More than fine it seems,' Jen said. 'Come along, Mateo. We're apparently not needed here after all.' She turned on her heel and stalked off.

Mateo looked between Abelard's startled face and Jen's retreating form. Then he stabbed a finger towards Abelard, said, 'You owe me a hell of an explanation,' and followed Jen out of view.

'Wait!' Abelard called, swinging his legs over the side of the bed and shoving Alessandra away from him in his haste to get up.

The abrupt motion stretched the mana out between their now separated hands until it snapped away from Abelard's fingers and flashed up into Alessandra's face. She shrieked and stumbled backwards, clutching scorched fingers close to her body. Her head whipped round, her angry glare intensified by the red marks where her eyebrows had been.

'Oh shit!' Abelard said, reaching out to her. 'I'm so sorry! Are you okay?'

'You,' she growled, backing away still further, 'are a total liability!' She whirled, almost colliding with Jonathan, who was still standing in the doorway. 'And you! This is all your fault! You should never have brought this idiot here in the first place!'

She shoved past him and disappeared.

Abelard put his hands over his face and fell back on to the bed with a groan.

'Quite,' Jonathan said.

Abelard removed his hands and looked over at him. 'What was all that about with Mateo and Jen?'

'They came to rescue you. They thought we were holding you here against your will or that we'd bumped you off for presuming to gain mana powers.'

'I have to admit I was a bit scared of that myself yesterday.'

'It might still happen,' Jonathan muttered, 'considering how much trouble you've caused.'

Abelard blanched.

'You're as bad as Mateo,' Jonathan said. 'Artisans don't go around randomly murdering people, you know.'

'But that's just what I don't know! You shroud everything in such secrecy. How are the rest of us supposed to know you're not all mad evil tyrants? You haven't exactly cultivated a fluffy reputation over the years.'

'I suppose you may have a very small point there, but be reasonable. Do you really think we'd be likely to have a dungeon full of upstarts? In this day and age?'

'I guess not.' Part of Abelard's mind was still reeling from the unexpected appearance of Mateo and Jen. He was delighted Mateo had come looking for him, but how had he ended up bringing Jen with him? And had Abelard now blown it with Jen after the scene with Alessandra? He groaned again. 'So what happens now?'

Jonathan sighed. 'I'd better go and smooth things over with Alessandra. She'll need to sign off on you before you can start work here officially.'

It took Abelard's brain a moment to catch up. 'What? Me, work here?'

'Oh yes, didn't Alessandra mention?' Jonathan grinned. 'The Board unanimously voted to offer you a job and the Artisan Council ratified it this morning. Welcome to Gadg-E-Tech!'

Abelard just spluttered.

Jonathan continued. 'I'll go and find Alessandra and send someone up with some dinner for you. I don't think you're safe to let loose in the building yet.'

He disappeared while Abelard was still processing this news, all thoughts of Mateo and Jen forgotten.

* * *

Jen stormed out of the suite and almost ran down the hall to the bank of lev-e-facts. She stabbed the call button repeatedly then paced up and down as she waited for the car to arrive. She couldn't believe she'd allowed Mateo to persuade her that Abelard might be in trouble, then come all the way down here to face down the artisans in a rescue attempt, only to be humiliated and rejected in one fell swoop.

The lev-e-fact turned up at last and she stepped inside,

pressing the button for the ground floor. Before the doors could fully close, Mateo thrust his arm between them and pushed his way inside.

'Wait up!' he said.

Jen ignored him.

He sighed. 'I admit that could have gone better.'

Jen snorted. 'You said he was in trouble. That didn't look much like trouble to me.'

'Uh, no,' Mateo hung his head. 'Sorry about that. Obviously that wasn't what I was expecting.'

Jen was surprised Mateo wasn't trying to defend his friend. Not that she knew how he could, given the circumstances. But she would have expected him to come out with some kind of blokey smart remark, either to express admiration at Abelard's actions or to downplay her own humiliation. Instead he had acknowledged her distress and even apologised for it. Her irritation came down a notch.

'It's hardly your fault. How were you to know? And you've got just as much right to be annoyed with Abelard as I do. Probably more. You've known him much longer and he didn't let you know he was okay either.'

'Yeah. We've been talking about what it would be like to be artisans for years. But apparently he doesn't want to share it with me now that it's happened to him.'

The brain-e-fact security guard didn't query their rapid reappearance as they exited the lev-e-fact and they left the building without interference. Outside they stood awkwardly on the street.

'It was nice to meet you, at least,' Jen said eventually. She cringed inwardly at how weak it sounded as the words left her lips.

Mateo huffed a self-conscious laugh. 'Yeah, you too. I guess I'll see you around?' He lifted one side of his mouth in half a smile as if acknowledging the lameness of his own statement.

Jen smiled sadly back. 'It doesn't look like it.'

'Hey, you don't have to be involved with Abelard to be friends with me.'

'Thanks, Mateo.'

They looked at each other for a long moment.

Then Jen said, 'Okay well, bye then.'

'Bye,' Mateo echoed and they went their separate ways.

Jen thought back over the events of the day and marvelled at how ridiculous they were in hindsight. How could she have imagined that a respected company like Gadg-E-Tech could be involved with kidnap and murder? Abelard should have let her know he wasn't interested in her, but he didn't owe her any more than that. By the time she arrived home she had almost convinced herself to laugh the whole thing off and store it away as an amusing anecdote to tell her friends on their next girls' night out. It might have been fun to get to know Abelard better, but you couldn't always judge a guy on first impressions.

* * *

Brain-e-fact Ten-Forty-Seven had just finished unloading one of the large dish-e-facts in the kitchen when he picked up a request broadcast over the internal Gadg-E-Tech mana network for a tray of food to be delivered to a human on the residential level. He sent an acknowledgement and went to work. Various dinner items were already in production so it was easy for Ten-Forty-Seven to select some and put them together on a tray. He added some orange juice and a pot of coffee and placed a cover over the top to protect it all on his journey upstairs.

Ten-Forty-Seven travelled up to the twelfth floor of the building. He located the correct room, balanced the covered tray on one ceramic arm and knocked on the door.

A male human voice called from the other side, 'Come in!'

Ten-Forty-Seven opened the door to the suite and entered the room. There was a young human seated on the sofa tying his shoelaces, though his torso was bare. His skin was pale brown and he had lots of thick dark curls that crowned his head. He looked up from his task and smiled at Ten-Forty-Seven. The brain-e-fact's mouth was constructed to resemble a human smile so he was already providing the correct facial response.

'Good evening,' Ten-Forty-Seven said. 'Mister Jonathan Worthington-Price sent me with your dinner. Where would you like the tray?'

The young human gestured at the coffee table so Ten-Forty-Seven moved smoothly forwards and deposited the tray as instructed.

'If you need anything else you can summon another brain-e-fact by pressing the call button.' He indicated the panel on the wall by the door. 'Good day.'

'Wait a minute,' the young human said.

'Can I be of further assistance?' Ten-Forty-Seven asked.

The young human stood up and approached him, circling him slowly. 'Wow,' he breathed. 'I saw some other brain-e-facts down in reception when I arrived but I've never been this close to one before.'

'We are exclusive to Gadg-E-Tech.'

'I can see why they'd want to keep something like you to themselves. Can you stay and hang out for a bit while I eat?'

'If you want me to stay in the room with you I can wait. But I can come back later to pick up the tray.'

'No, I'd like some company over dinner. Can you sit with me and chat for a while?'

'I have never been asked to chat before, but I will try.'

'Great.' The young human sat down on the sofa and uncovered the tray. 'This looks delicious! Take a load off and tell me more about this place.'

'Take a load of what off what?'

'I meant sit down.' The young human laughed. 'Sorry, I didn't realise you'd take me literally.'

Ten-Forty-Seven moved to the other side of the sofa and sat down gingerly. He perched on the very edge of the seat, his arms raised slightly to provide balance.

'That's better,' the young human said around a mouthful of food. 'My name's Abelard Abernathy. What's yours?'

For a third time the young human – Abelard – had asked Ten-Forty-Seven a question and the brain-e-fact did not understand his meaning. This whole conversation thing was proving quite problematical.

'What is my what?'

Abelard looked at him, fork paused on the way to his mouth. 'Oh come on! That was an easy one surely. What's your name?'

'I do not have a name.' Ten-Forty-Seven tapped his ceramic chest where a number was inscribed in the shiny surface. 'All brain-e-facts are identified by their unit number. My number is Ten-Forty-Seven.'

'You don't have names?' Abelard's brow furrowed. 'So all those brain-e-facts I've seen around the place are only ever referred to by a number?'

'Yes.'

'That's a bit harsh. Do you mind if I give you a name, just between us?'

There was a pause while Ten-Forty-Seven considered the question.

'If you want to call me something other than Ten-Forty-Seven, I do not mind. It is up to you.'

'I'll call you Terry then, if that's okay,' Abelard said.

'That is fine.' Ten-Forty-Seven lifted his head as an unfamiliar sensation flooded him. 'I like it.'

Abelard turned back to his meal. 'So what do you do around here?'

'I mostly work in the canteen. I serve the artisans when they come in for food and I carry food up here and carry empty trays back down again. Sometimes I load the dish-e-fact to clean the plates or help to prepare the food.'

'That's it? All you do all day is ferry stuff around and serve the food in the canteen?'

'Yes. All day and all night.'

'What?' Abelard glanced up at him again. 'You work round the clock?'

'All the brain-e-facts do. We do not need to sleep or eat so we can work all the time. There are artisans here at all hours so there is always work to do.'

'You don't get any breaks?'

'We spend half an hour in each twenty-four recharging our mana supply.'

Abelard's face twisted. 'That doesn't seem very fair.'

Ten-Forty-Seven did not want to be the cause of a human's distress so hurried to reassure him. 'There is no need to worry. That is just the way things are. We were made to work so that is what we do. It is not a problem.'

'But maybe it should be. Just because you go along with it doesn't make it right. You seem like a good guy to me and it's clear there's a lot more to you than a normal artefact. You shouldn't just have to serve artisans the whole time.'

By this time he had finished his meal.

Ten-Forty-Seven rose and collected the used plates and cutlery, stacking them neatly on to the tray.

'I hope you enjoyed your dinner, Mister Abernathy. I will take the tray away now so you can get on with your day.'

'Thanks, and call me Abelard. I'm going to be working at Gadg-E-Tech so feel free to stop me for a chat when you see me around.'

Ten-Forty-Seven nodded. 'I will do that.'

'Oh, can you also do me a favour? Can you send some

flowers to Alessandra Eriksen with a note saying I'm really sorry about what happened? She works here too.'

No human had ever asked Ten-Forty-Seven for a favour before but he assumed it was just like receiving instructions. He accessed the employee directory and sent the relevant commands to carry out the task.

'It is done.'

'Wow, thanks!'

Ten-Forty-Seven turned and went to the door, opening it with one hand while balancing the tray with the other. He walked down the hallway to the bank of lev-e-facts at the far end, punched the call button and waited for the lev-e-fact to arrive. Once inside he pressed the button for the floor where the canteen was situated and stared at himself in the mirrored back wall. He looked in particular at the reflected digits engraved on his chest. The numbers had been his only label of identity since he had been activated. Until that evening.

The doors opened on to the glass atrium of the canteen and Ten-Forty-Seven walked to the back of the open hall and through into the kitchen behind. He placed Abelard's crockery into a dish-e-fact. He then stacked the tray with a pile of its identical fellows and turned to survey the bustling kitchen. There was a station open at the food preparation counter where several other brain-e-facts were arranging canapés on platters. Ten-Forty-Seven joined them.

'Hello, Ten-Forty-Seven,' said Sixteen-Twenty-Two.

'I do not want to be called Ten-Forty-Seven any more. My name is Terry,' said Terry.

CHAPTER SEVEN

Jonathan re-entered the suite just a couple of minutes after Terry left.

'I managed to catch up to Alessandra and convince her how important it is to teach you some bloody control. She's right; you're an absolute menace at the moment. She's the best we've got but she's not falling over herself to come back after you just set her on fire. You ought to watch yourself with her. She has influence. She's not the sort of person you want as an enemy.'

'Enemy definitely wasn't what I was going for,' Abelard said, his bedazzlement reasserting itself.

Jonathan snorted. 'Don't even go there. Alessandra's untouchable. She has a reputation for ruthlessness and with good reason. Besides, what about Jen? She's much more in your league. And she came to face the mighty artisans to rescue you. Seems like you might actually be in with a chance there.'

'Jen!' The reality of her soft voice and kind eyes supplanted the wild fantasy images of Alessandra that had been romping through Abelard's mind. 'I have to explain to her what happened.' He wished he could have asked the brain-e-fact to send her some flowers too, but he didn't know where she lived and thought she might be embarrassed to receive them at her office.

He staggered over to where his jacket was draped over the back of a chair and found his smart-e-fact in the inside pocket, but it was dead.

'Huh. That was fully charged yesterday. It should have been good for at least a couple more days.'

'It's company policy not to allow network communication artefacts to work inside the building. Mateo and Jen thought you were in trouble because they couldn't get hold of you. You can call from a hard line but it will be recorded.'

The last thing Abelard wanted was an audience for what he imagined would be a painful conversation.

'But if I step outside the building my smart-e will work again?'

'Yes, but we can't let you leave while you still pose a danger to yourself and others.'

The Gadg-E-Tech communications policy was pretty absurd if people could just step outside the front door and call whoever they liked without surveillance. But Abelard focused on the other aspect of what Jonathan was saying.

'So you are keeping me prisoner!'

'Only in the interests of public safety. We can't risk an incident where Gadg-E-Tech could be blamed for letting a dangerously unstable individual loose in the city.'

'I'm hardly Godzilla! And I won't be loose in the city if I just step outside to make a call. You could come with me to make sure I don't blow anything up.'

'Not a chance. I'm no expert in mana control. I wouldn't be much use if things really went wrong.'

'This is ridiculous! You can't keep me here against my will!'

Jonathan squared himself in the doorway, stretched out an arm and beckoned with the fingers on that hand. 'Come on then, if you think you're hard enough.'

Abelard's overstrained body ached at the thought of even making it as far as the door. He slumped back on to the sofa in defeat.

'Okay, you win. I'll be a good boy and do as I'm told.'

'Excellent choice.' Jonathan grinned. 'Now, how do you feel about getting out of this room and visiting the canteen? I know you've only just eaten, but we could get a smoothie or something. Do you think you're up to that?'

Abelard felt dreadful, from both physical exertion and emotional upheaval. But he was keen to find out more about Gadg-E-Tech and the best way to do that would be to explore the building and get Jonathan talking. He didn't want to make his first foray amongst the artisans looking like a demented tramp, though.

'Could I get cleaned up and change my clothes first?'

'Definitely a good plan,' Jonathan said. 'I'll go and scrounge up some clothes for you while you take a shower.'

Fifteen minutes later, Abelard emerged from the bathroom to find a Gadg-E-Tech branded pair of sweatpants and a polo shirt laid on the bed. Jonathan was lounging on the sofa in the other room when he came back through.

'Well, you look just about presentable.'

Abelard glared at him. 'Great. By the way, if you won't let

me leave the building for fear of me accidentally destroying the city, what's to stop me blowing up the building from the inside?'

'Uh, nothing I guess. But if I keep an eye on you I might be able to see it coming and tell anyone nearby to hit the deck before you go off.'

'Thanks for the vote of confidence.'

'Joking aside, I think we'll be okay as long as we keep you away from charged artefacts.'

'But this is an artisan head office building. Won't there be charged artefacts all over the place?'

'Good point.' Jonathan looked uncertain. 'Maybe we should stay here.'

'No,' Abelard said, kicking himself for putting a spanner in the works. 'I want to get out of here, even if it's only as far as the canteen. I'll just be careful not to touch anything.'

Jonathan chewed his bottom lip, but nodded. He led the way down the corridor at a leisurely pace, keeping an anxious eye on Abelard all the way. Abelard wasn't sure if Jonathan was more worried about him falling over or spontaneously combusting. He just focused on putting one foot in front of the other.

Jonathan hesitated in front of the bank of lev-e-facts, his hand hovering over the call button.

'Oh, come on,' Abelard said. 'I'm not going to blow up the lev-es. I've used one several times every day since the incident at Jen's office and nothing's happened so far. And there's no way I'm going to be able to handle the stairs.'

Jonathan braced himself and hit the button.

* * *

Walter glared at Laleh across the table at Brother Theobold's temple.

'Sometimes I wonder what we're actually trying to achieve here.'

She stared back. 'And you think making spontaneous artisans disappear would further our aims more than helping them be productive members of artisan society? The phenomenon in and of itself leads us ever closer to a time when the truth will have to come out.'

'The world isn't ready.'

'I agree.' Laleh's eyes flashed. 'But I don't think it's ready for artisan death squads either.'

At the head of the table, Brother Theobold's eyes widened. 'Indeed no. We are trying to bring about a gradual progression towards greater freedom and equality. Our secret is not so terrible that we should contemplate strong-arm tactics to keep it. I've only ever wanted to keep people safe.'

Walter turned to him. 'Yes, but this engineer represents a far greater threat to our position than Gerald Simpson. Don't you think the situation requires some more stringent monitoring?'

Theobold looked to Laleh. 'Isn't your daughter in charge of the engineer's training?'

'Yes. Walter, you'll be able to get whatever information you want from Alessandra. As will I.'

So Alessandra hadn't told her mother about the break-up. That was interesting. Perhaps it meant she wasn't as secure in her decision as she had appeared.

Walter smiled. 'But Alessandra, skilled as she is, doesn't fully understand the ramifications of what we're dealing with. She won't know what might be important to pass on to us. Have you given any more thought to bringing her into the Inner Circle?'

'Not yet,' Laleh said, her eyes now sad. 'Let her live her life a little while longer before she has to contend with all this.' She gestured at their surroundings and shivered, perhaps not just from the cold.

* * *

Back at Gadg-E-Tech, the lev-e-fact doors opened on a bright and airy atrium, almost entirely enclosed in glass. In the centre was a bustling canteen, full of people collecting and eating a dazzling array of food. Brain-e-facts dished out hot food from the buffet, taking away empty trays and returning with full ones.

Abelard stared. 'Isn't it after seven on a Thursday night?'

Jonathan shrugged. 'Gadg-E-Tech never sleeps! We're not slave drivers or anything; we just let people work to their own schedule. We find people actually work longer hours and come in on more days under that arrangement.'

Abelard joined the end of the queue, looking at the artisans going about their evening. Gadg-E-Tech had a good reputation for equal opportunities recruitment and the diversity of the workforce seemed to bear that out. As long as you had a strong enough spark, they reportedly hired entirely on merit, regardless of any other characteristics.

Of course, it was the spark that was the most important thing to all the artisan companies and, in that regard, Gadg-E-Tech was just as elitist as Spark-Le or McPherson. They would argue that they had to be. If someone didn't have enough of a spark they wouldn't be able to manipulate mana and so would be useless in artisan roles. Gadg-E-Tech's insistence on secrecy even led them to fill all the non-artisan jobs in the company with brain-e-facts.

But what about what had happened to Abelard? If his own spark could be increased by accident, shouldn't it be possible to do the same thing to other engineers by design?

Abelard selected a smoothie and followed Jonathan to an empty table in the corner of the room. Several people hailed Jonathan or looked at Abelard with open curiosity as they passed. Jonathan merely nodded at them and made for the corner with determination.

'Don't want me mixing with the natives, huh?' Abelard said, half joking and half annoyed.

Jonathan looked sheepish.

'It's nothing personal, honest. It's just your status is still uncertain until Alessandra signs off that you're safe. I don't want a lot of questions from people when I don't have official instructions as to what I can say. We're so insular here that the rumour mill can get out of hand if communications aren't monitored carefully. So I think it would be best if you kept a low profile for the time being.'

'Just in case Alessandra recommends that the Board lock me in the dungeon after all?'

'Oh, don't start that again.' His voice rose in frustration. 'For the last time, there's no dungeon!' Jonathan glared at Abelard when the people on the nearest tables looked over at his outburst.

'Okay, okay!' Abelard said, unable to stop himself from laughing. 'But I don't understand why I'm causing such a fuss. This must have happened before. You have a secret code for it so don't you have a standard procedure to go with it?'

'What happens with Code 47s is way above my pay grade, as I said. We're all given the codes just in case but nobody's called a Code 47 in almost fifty years.' Abelard raised his eyebrows. 'I looked it up,' Jonathan said.

'Who was it and what happened to him?'

'His name is Rajesh Kumar and he works in the Quality Assurance Department,' Jonathan said, as if it was the most mundane piece of information in the world.

'What? He still works here? Can I go and talk to him?'

The paranoid glint snapped back into Jonathan's eyes and he hunched his shoulders. 'Oh, uh, no, I don't think that would be a good idea. He's, uh, very old now and a bit confused so he wouldn't be able to tell you much. Besides, things are completely different now so his case wouldn't relate to yours anyway.'

Abelard didn't believe the artisans would let someone who was confused work in their Quality Department. But Jonathan would just get more defensive and belligerent if he pressed the matter. He would just have to find his way to the Quality Department to speak to the other engineer-turned-artisan on his own.

'If the artisans know that it's possible for someone's spark to get stronger, why isn't that public knowledge? The rest of us are under the illusion that the spark you're born with is all you get. But artisans must know that's not true in order to understand the use of Code 47. Why don't you tell everyone else?'

Jonathan's eyes narrowed and Abelard prepared himself to receive the party line.

'We have the code for safety reasons. You of all people know how dangerous an uncontrolled artisan-level spark can be. But think about it – only two cases in fifty years! And what would engineers do if they knew there was even the slightest chance of increasing their spark?'

Abelard didn't need to think about that. 'They'd start sticking their fingers in every live mana source they could find.'

'Exactly! And they'd be frying artefacts, themselves and random bystanders left, right and centre.'

Even if that was only the official response, Abelard couldn't argue with Jonathan's logic.

'But can't you figure out what causes it so you could replicate it safely? That way, all those engineers desperate to be artisans could get their wish.'

He knew the artisans would not be in favour of that, since it would change the balance of societal power to their detriment but he was interested to hear what Jonathan's excuse would be. It was another good one.

'We haven't exactly got a huge pool of instances to investigate. And since no artisan was present at either incident, there's no reliable empirical evidence. We can't go around charging up engineers with mana to see what happens. Would you want someone from R&D experimenting on you to find out what happened?'

'Uh, not really,' Abelard admitted.

'Well, there you go.' Jonathan smiled wryly at him. 'Those R&D guys are pretty one-track, though. If they got their way they'd have you splayed out on a dissection table in no time.'

Abelard pushed his smoothie away, his stomach roiling.

'Don't worry, the Board hasn't let them dissect anyone yet. I don't think they'll start with you.' Jonathan sighed. 'But you see, there are sensible reasons for the things we do. It's not all some complicated conspiracy to keep the lower classes in order.'

Abelard decided to concede the point for the time being in the interests of continuing good relations with his guide to all things artisan.

'So, what happens now?'

'I'm going home and I suggest you get an early night. You're due to meet Alessandra here for breakfast and training at eight am. Think you can make your way back up to your room on your own?'

Abelard nodded and Jonathan bade him good night.

A brain-e-fact loitered by the lev-e-facts, shifting from foot to foot. It stepped forwards as Abelard approached. The number carved into its chest plate read Sixteen-Twenty-Two.

'Mister Abernathy, sir?'

'Call me Abelard.'

The brain-e-fact gaped at him. 'Yes, Mister Abelard, sir!'

Abelard decided not to labour the point.

'What can I do for you?' he asked.

The brain-e-fact hesitated. 'You gave Terry a name.'

Abelard waited. The brain-e-fact shuffled its feet and looked at the floor.

'Please can I have a name too?'

Abelard laughed, then regretted it as the brain-e-fact shifted backwards and hung its head.

'I'm sorry,' he said. 'Of course you can have a name.'

The brain-e-fact looked up at him, its eyes wide and fixed on Abelard's face.

'I hereby name you Fred,' Abelard declared with a flourish.

'Oh, thank you, Mister Abelard, sir!'

'No problem. Enjoy!'

'I will!' Fred said and strode off.

Abelard watched him go, shaking his head in amusement.

* * *

The following morning Alessandra arrived at Gadg-E-Tech in plenty of time for her breakfast meeting with Abelard. She stopped off at her office to check her messages and found a beautiful flower arrangement of white blooms on her desk. The card read: 'Sorry about what happened. Abelard.'

Alessandra couldn't help smiling at the gesture and continued on to the canteen in a somewhat better mood. She had already collected her breakfast and chosen a table when Abelard entered. He spotted her and raised a hand in greeting. She found herself waving back and he looked surprised. It might be fun to keep him off balance.

Abelard grabbed some food and came to join her. He was about to say something when Walter appeared from nowhere.

'Ah, the famous engineer,' Walter said, his tone humorous. 'I hope our Alessandra is treating you with the respect you deserve.'

What on earth was Walter up to? Alessandra rose and faced him.

'Walter,' she said, neutrally. 'How are you?'

Walter turned to her, his expression changing to one of calculation.

'Very well, thank you. Might you have time for a meeting later? I could easily make room in my schedule.'

He couldn't possibly think there was a chance they'd get back together, could he? He was arrogant enough but Alessandra thought she had made herself quite clear. A flicker of amusement flashed through her. She hooked an arm round Abelard's elbow and squeezed.

'I'm afraid I'll be very busy with my new responsibilities today.' She gave Walter a bright smile.

His eyes widened, his smooth veneer cracking to reveal his true feelings. 'Alessandra, how can you waste yourself on this trash? I know I said you're nothing without me but there's no reason to stoop quite so low. You're at least worth more than this.'

'The only person I can think of that I'm worth more than is you, Walter. You have no idea what Abelard here is worth; two of you at the very least.' She smiled again. 'He has hidden depths.'

'An engineer?' Walter spluttered. 'How can an engineer possibly have anything that would interest you? He's only here by accident. He's an upstart pretender with less talent than I have in my little finger. I thought you would be smart enough not to be fooled.'

Before Alessandra could react a brain-e-fact stepped up behind Walter and tapped him on the shoulder. Its unit number had been scratched through and the name 'Fred' scrawled across its chest plate in clumsy letters. Walter spun round, his surprise at being interrupted turning to outrage at the sight of the artefact standing behind him.

'How dare you touch me!'

'You will not speak about Mister Abelard Abernathy like that,' the brain-e-fact said.

'What?' Walter's expression was frozen in a rictus of rage.

'Mister Abelard is a great man. He deserves your respect.' The brain-e-fact's hand closed over Walter's shoulder.

'I will not tolerate insubordination from artefacts!' Walter ground out. 'You will come with me immediately for diagnosis of your obvious fault.' He turned back to

Alessandra and Abelard. 'This isn't over.' Then he marched the brain-e-fact out of the canteen.

Alessandra released her hold on Abelard and stepped away from him. His mouth was open and he looked back and forth between Alessandra and the departing Walter.

'What the hell was all that about?'

CHAPTER EIGHT

'I could ask you the same thing,' Alessandra replied, narrowing her eyes at Abelard. When he just continued to look at her expectantly, she sighed. 'Walter and I used to – be close – but I ended it recently. He apparently still thinks he can order me around.' She pulled herself up short and pasted a superior sneer on her face. 'He's right about you not being good enough for me of course but I didn't want to give him the satisfaction.'

'So you made him think we were actually together. Do you want to get me fired? Or worse?'

'Stop being so dramatic.' Though Walter did have a lot of power at Gadg-E-Tech and could cause trouble for both of them very easily if he wanted. 'What have you been doing to the brain-e-facts? I've never seen one act like that before.'

'I haven't done anything to them,' Abelard said. 'Can we just get on with my training please?'

Alessandra allowed him to deflect her. She didn't care that much about the aberrant behaviour of a brain-e-fact and they had more important things to focus on. 'Don't you want your breakfast?'

'Not really. I've lost my appetite.'

Alessandra shook her head. 'No mana training on an empty stomach. You know what happened last time. So eat.'

Abelard obeyed, managing to make it through at least

some of the food on his plate. Once Alessandra was satisfied, they made their way down to reception.

'We're not going up to the residential floor?' Abelard asked.

'Full marks for observation. I'm taking you off-site to do some practical applications of mana manipulation at one of the factories.'

Alessandra noted Abelard's covetous expression when she opened the door of her speed-e-fact for him. It was a small, sleek model her mother had rolled her eyes at, but Alessandra enjoyed the feel of the leather seats and the smooth gliding motion. Abelard looked out at the city the whole way, as if he'd never seen it before. As the urban sprawl started to give way to a more industrial area, he sat up straighter.

'I know where we are! Are we headed to the factory where Jonathan works?'

'You're really on the ball this morning, aren't you?' Alessandra said. 'And yes. Jonathan asked if he could help with the training and I figured there wasn't any harm in it, since he already knows you.'

When they reached their destination, they breezed past the security checkpoint and made their way to one of the workshops, where Jonathan was waiting for them at the door.

'Morning, Abelard! Hi, Alessandra. I've got everything set up ready for you, as per your instructions. And we've cleared the whole of the first floor just in case anything goes wrong. Not that it will, right Abelard?'

'Shut up Jonathan, there's a good boy,' Alessandra said. 'I'm wasting enough time on this as it is without having to put up with your inane babble all day.'

Jonathan's teeth snapped together as he closed his mouth. They went up some stairs, emerging into a large open space that was completely devoid of people but full of different types of artefacts. Alessandra marched straight to an area at the back where a table had been set up. On the table were several different artefacts and a pile of mana units.

'Today,' Alessandra announced, 'we are going to work on your control. You will learn the difference between charging an artefact directly and storing mana in a mana unit. You will practice siphoning mana from the wall supply and transferring it to different destinations.' She fixed Abelard with a hard stare. 'You will pay attention and you will do exactly as I say when I say it. This is not a game and you already know what the consequences can be if you don't do it properly.' She raised her painted-on eyebrows to make her point. 'Do I make myself absolutely clear?'

'Yes,' Abelard said.

He sounded as if he wanted this to go well as much as she did.

'Good. Now if my lovely assistant will set up the first exercise, we can begin.'

Jonathan scowled but moved to the table without a word and started arranging the objects on it.

By lunchtime Alessandra was exhausted and had a splitting headache. They had been working hard all morning without a break and the tension of being responsible for an uncontrolled artisan was very tiring. She wasn't directly involved in any of the exercises herself, instead ordering Jonathan about, getting him to put different configurations of artefacts out on the table and using him to bounce mana back and forth from place to place with Abelard. Jonathan started showing off at one point, juggling balls of mana until Alessandra told him to stop being an idiot. Eventually Alessandra announced they could stop for lunch and Jonathan escorted them to the factory canteen. It was darker and dingier than the airy eating space at Gadg-E-Tech HQ and Alessandra wondered how Jonathan put up with working here. They got a lot of stares from the other workers, but Alessandra couldn't tell if they were directed at her or Abelard. Perhaps both. Regardless, she ignored them all, keeping her shield of superiority firmly in place.

Alessandra didn't let Abelard take too much of a break, dragging him back up to the assembly room only twenty minutes after they had stopped.

'Now,' she said, 'we've gone through all the basics. It's time to test whether you've been listening. Jonathan, show him a stream.'

Jonathan placed an empty mana unit on the table, then rested one hand against the wall supply conduit and the other on the unit. He closed his eyes and took a couple of deep breaths. Blue mana light emerged from the wall supply, ran smoothly up Jonathan's arm, across his chest, down the other arm and into the mana unit. The mana level display on the unit gradually filled up until it was at capacity. Shortly before it reached full power, Jonathan broke contact with the wall supply and allowed the remaining mana to flow out of him into the unit, charging it completely. He took his hand off the mana unit and opened his eyes again. His breathing was slightly fast and there was a sheen of sweat on his forehead but he looked satisfied.

Alessandra turned to Abelard. 'Once you've gained full control of mana manipulation, you'll be able to act as a link between the wall supply and whatever artefact you want to charge. You'll be able to feel the flow of the mana through your body and tell when the artefact or mana unit is fully powered. Eventually you should be able to do this without looking at the display.'

Abelard seemed confused. 'Mundane users can connect their artefacts and mana units to the wall supply and charge them directly. So why would you ever need to do it yourself?'

Alessandra sighed. 'It's not about practical use. You're already well aware that we don't often manipulate mana directly because it's so draining. It's about understanding the power that we possess and perfecting our control of it so we can work with it safely. You need to respect the mana and it needs to respect you.'

'Fair enough,' Abelard said. 'Lead me through it.'

Under Alessandra's supervision, Abelard took Jonathan's place at the table, lining up another empty mana unit. He placed one hand on the unit and the other on the wall supply conduit. Alessandra fed him instructions and watched as a thin stream of mana snaked out of the wall supply and flowed slowly up his arm.

'Good. Now keep the flow steady and send it down into the mana unit.'

She could tell Abelard was trying but as the mana flowed down his other arm towards the mana unit the stream thickened and started to move more quickly.

'Keep it steady! You're losing it.'

The admonition didn't help at all; rather the opposite. Abelard's breathing sped up, the mana flow matching its intensity. He opened his eyes and they glowed blue. His feet lifted off the ground and his arms stuck stiffly out to each side. As mana started firing from Abelard's hands, Alessandra threw a shield around him and the glowing sphere absorbed the energy harmlessly. The mana drained from Abelard's body until he dropped back to the floor. Alessandra released the shield and sent the excess mana shooting into the empty mana unit. Abelard staggered and nearly fell.

'You're still letting it get away from you,' Alessandra said. 'You have to learn to keep it under control.'

'I was trying,' Abelard panted.

'Clearly not hard enough. Try again.'

'What about what you just said about too much mana manipulation draining all your energy? And why didn't you do that shield thing the other day when I burned your eyebrows off?'

Alessandra glared at him. 'The situation the other day took me by surprise and I didn't have time to react. And you've had two good meals today so quit complaining and get on with it!'

The next few attempts resulted in varying degrees of success, with Abelard managing to maintain the flow of mana for longer periods but never in a completely consistent stream and always ending with loss of control. Alessandra kept barking instructions at him but it didn't do any good and she got more and more frustrated as the afternoon wore on. Jonathan watched from the sidelines, occasionally stepping in to prevent a dangerous mana surge. Eventually, there was a near miss when Abelard released a burst of mana in the wrong direction and Jonathan was forced to dive out of the way. The mana struck the bare concrete of the factory wall, leaving a sooty scorch mark. Abelard slumped against the wall, breathing heavily.

'Why don't we take a break and come back to it in a few minutes?' Jonathan suggested.

'Fine,' Alessandra said.

She turned on her heel and stalked off behind the machinery. She had had more than enough of this. She walked briskly around the assembly line, trying to rein in her temper. Her heels struck the hard floor with sharp impacts that echoed round the large space. It must be deafening with all the factory artefacts running. Alessandra missed the plush carpet of her office and the calm predictability of running her department. After a few minutes she made her way back to where Jonathan and Abelard were looking smug.

'I think Abelard's ready to give it another go,' Jonathan

said. 'Why don't we let him try without any input from us? See how much he's learned.'

'As long as you're prepared to write up the accident report when he blows up the whole factory.'

'Just give him a chance,' Jonathan said.

Alessandra waved at them to carry on, shoulders tensing. A few moments later she was staring at a fully charged mana unit that Abelard had filled without incident. He grinned at her, snapping her right out of her surprise and back to her normal attitude.

'Why couldn't you just have done that the first time around? Now do it again so I know it wasn't just a fluke.'

Abelard obliged without comment, the exercise now looking like second nature to him. Was it possible that Jonathan had succeeded where Alessandra had failed, and managed to get through to him? Surely not.

'Hallelujah,' she said heavily. 'He's finally got it!'

'So will you sign off on my training now?'

'Yes. I declare you no longer a danger to yourself and others.'

'Great.'

Alessandra set Abelard to tidying up the various artefacts and mana units they'd been using and dragged Jonathan to one side.

'What on earth did you say to him?'

Jonathan's eyes widened. 'Can't you just believe I'm better at training than you?'

Alessandra crossed her arms. 'No.'

Jonathan rolled his eyes. 'Okay, okay. You were a bit full-on, that's all. You yelling at him was making him nervous and you know you need to be relaxed to control mana properly. He just needed a break from you glaring at him all the time. You can be pretty intimidating.'

'Hmm ... Well, thanks,' she said, then bristled as Jonathan stared at her open-mouthed. 'Don't let it go to your head.'

They got everything squared away, then all headed to the gate together.

Jonathan yawned. 'Nice to finish early on a Friday for once.'

Alessandra saw a way to get her revenge. 'Not so fast. If we're letting Abelard loose on the world again he'll need to be briefed by the Legal Department. You'll have to take him back to HQ and get him to sign an NDA before he goes home.'

'What?' Jonathan gaped at her. He looked like he wanted to argue but Alessandra stared him down until his shoulders slumped.

'Enjoy!' she said as she walked away.

* * *

Jonathan escorted Abelard back to Gadg-E-Tech head office in his speed-e-fact. As they sped back into the city, it occurred to Abelard that he could have just walked home from the factory. It seemed like years since he'd been in his flat.

'You're a Gadg-E-Tech artisan now, so you're bound by Gadg-E-Tech rules of secrecy,' Jonathan said. 'I expect Legal will have something prepared for you to sign.'

'But what do I tell people?' Abelard asked. 'I was only signed off work until Monday. Won't Mana-Calls be expecting me back?'

'That'll be taken care of. They'll get some kind of communication to let them know you won't be coming back.'

Abelard wished he could be there when Stanton was told he'd be losing an engineer with no notice.

'And Mateo and Jen? They already know about my abilities and that I'm here with you. Can't I tell them?' Assuming they would even be willing to speak to him after the incident the night before.

'I guess so. Actually I'd better check with Legal about that too. Once we're finished with them you'll be free to go. How about we meet for breakfast in the canteen at eight am on Monday and I'll give you your schedule?'

'Sounds good.'

An hour later, after a painful meeting with the Gadg-E-Tech Legal Department, Abelard finally escaped. He had read and signed a twenty-page non-disclosure agreement prohibiting him from telling anyone else anything at all about his new life under any circumstances. He had copies of similar documents in his bag, for Mateo and Jen to sign.

When he reached the lobby, Abelard found a cluster of brain-e-facts just outside the bank of lev-e-facts. They had been whispering amongst themselves but stopped abruptly at the sight of him. One stepped forwards, half of its own volition and half pushed by several of the others.

'Mister Abelard, sir. We do not mean to disturb you. But

we have spoken to Terry and Fred and we would like names too.'

This must be why all the brain-e-facts were acting so weird around him. The earnestness of their demeanour stopped him from laughing at the absurdity of it all. He was flattered that they wanted his input but didn't want to end up with every Gadg-E-Tech brain-e-fact in the building accosting him in the corridor.

'Why don't you choose names for yourselves?'

They exchanged glances with one another, clearly not having considered this.

After a moment the designated spokesperson replied. 'Humans do not choose their own names. We would like to be given ours the same way humans are.'

'Okay. Why don't you ask Terry to give you names?'

The spokesperson brain-e-fact stared at him.

'Terry was the first. He would give good names. Does he have your permission to give out names in your stead?'

'Absolutely,' Abelard said, bemused by their reverence.

The brain-e-facts bustled off. Abelard watched them go, then turned to leave himself.

CHAPTER NINE

Jen wasn't forgiving enough to answer when Abelard called on Friday evening. She wasn't ready to talk to him yet but stood by the call-e-fact and listened as he left a message.

'Hi, Jen. It's, uh, Abelard. I'm so sorry about what happened last night. It's amazing that you came all that way because you thought I was in trouble and it really wasn't what it looked like. That woman you saw, Alessandra, is training me so I don't randomly set things on fire when I handle mana. There's absolutely nothing going on between us. I really would like to get to know you better and I need to speak to you about something anyway so please call me back. Okay, bye.'

The apology sounded heartfelt but could she trust Abelard's protestations about Alessandra? And what kind of name was that anyway? The mention of mana and setting things on fire brought home to Jen once again just how very different their lives were, particularly now Abelard had artisan powers. Was a potential relationship worth pursuing even if she did believe him about Alessandra?

She initially decided she wouldn't call him back right away. He deserved to wait for a response. But after a while she wondered if she was being petty when she really did want to find out what had happened. There was nothing to be lost in giving him a chance to explain. Jen reached for the call-e.

* * *

Abelard felt like an idiot after he left the message for Jen. He'd tried to call her as soon as he stepped outside the Gadg-E-Tech building and hadn't prepared what he was going to say. Once he cut the connection, he instantly thought of a hundred better ways he could have expressed himself. He would just have to wait and see if his honest bumbling would do the trick and at least get her to call him back. After that he'd have to do his level best not to mess up again.

He picked a random direction and started walking. Then he tried Mateo, who answered immediately, as if he'd been watching his smart-e-fact in anticipation of Abelard's call.

'Hey, Mateo.'

'Hey? Hey?? Is that all you can say? You disappear off the face of the earth, I assume you've been kidnapped by the artisans, so I mount a daring rescue mission only to find you canoodling with some smoking hot babe – nice work, by the way, though Jen's not best pleased about it – and all you can say is hey?'

'I was not canoodling! Alessandra was trying to teach me how to handle mana without blowing stuff up, that's all! And you turning up didn't help at all!'

'Oh well, sorry to have messed up your chances with the babe while trying to save you from certain death!'

'That's not what I meant! And I am not trying to get together with Alessandra!'

'That's not what it looked like to me, and it's not what it looked like to Jen either. Now that you've got fancy artisan powers and a hot mentor, you'd do well not to forget who your real friends are.'

'And my real friends are people who wilfully misunderstand what they see and refuse to give me a chance to explain?' Abelard had totally lost the ability to be rational by this point. 'And what's with you hanging out with Jen?'

'She contacted Mana-Calls looking for you.' Mateo's voice increased in volume and annoyance as he went on. 'We were both worried that we hadn't heard from you so we teamed up to rescue you! And who's wilfully misunderstanding things now? If this is the gratitude I get, next time I'll just let you rot!'

The smart-e-fact started to crackle with mana next to Abelard's ear as his emotions got the better of him. He closed his eyes, took a couple of deep breaths and the crackling subsided, leaving his smart-e-fact undamaged. He opened his mouth to respond but the call had cut off.

Abelard sighed. He'd imagined Mateo's excited congratulations about his new job, not a ridiculous argument. Jen wouldn't take his calls and Mateo was mad at him. And he still had to get them both to sign NDAs from Gadg-E-Tech. What would happen if he couldn't?

He had wandered several streets away from the Gadg-E-Tech building and wasn't sure where he was. The idea of going back to his empty flat wasn't appealing and he couldn't just turn up at Jen's door, even if he knew where she lived. So he checked his location on his smart-e map and headed to Mateo's. Even if Mateo wouldn't let him in, at least he'd be able to pick up his speed-e-fact.

Abelard knocked on the door of Mateo's flat and waited nervously. He was expecting some initial hostility, but Mateo physically recoiled when he saw who it was, and backed hastily away, holding up one hand as if to fend off an attack.

'You stay away from me!' Mateo's eyes were wide with fear.

Abelard took a step forwards over the threshold.

'What on earth's the matter with you?'

'What's the matter? You nearly burned my ear off, that's what's the matter!' Mateo indicated his right ear where the skin was reddened.

'What are you talking about? I haven't been anywhere near you.'

'Apparently you didn't need to be.' Mateo was still moving to keep as much distance between them as possible. 'You fried my smart-e and nearly took me with it.'

'What?' Abelard remembered how his own smart-e-fact had crackled when he'd got annoyed during the argument with Mateo. 'I blew up an artefact through the mana network?'

'Yes! One minute I was yelling at you and the next there was mana bursting out of my smart-e and down my ear. The smart-e's toast.'

'Wow. Maybe I really am a danger to society …'

'Yes, mate. I would say so.'

Mateo was still rigid with tension but had stopped backing away, apparently reassured that Abelard hadn't come to finish him off.

'I'm so sorry,' Abelard said. 'It was a total accident.'

'That's as may be. But remember what happened up on the roof the other day? I'd say you're a bit of a liability at the moment.'

'That's what Alessandra said after I singed off her eyebrows.' Mateo goggled at him so he went on. 'But the roof incident wasn't entirely my fault. You were the one who wanted me to test my powers and you were the one giving the instructions.'

Mateo had the grace to look sheepish. 'That's not an unreasonable point. But you still need to get your powers under control before you do some serious damage.'

'No argument there. And I've already started. Alessandra showed me the basics this morning.'

'Was that before or after I nearly lost my ear?'

'Um, before,' Abelard said.

Mateo just looked at him.

'Okay, okay, you're right!' Abelard threw up his hands and Mateo dropped flat behind the sofa.

Abelard said, 'Oh, don't be ridiculous!'

Mateo peeked out at him from behind the furniture. 'Given my earlier experience I don't think exercising a little caution could be described as ridiculous. I think I'll be keeping to a safe distance for the time being, if you don't mind. Though if you can fry artefacts from several miles away, a safe distance may be the other side of the country.'

'Honestly,' Abelard said, 'I'm perfectly safe as long as I don't have a charged artefact in my hand and get annoyed about something.'

'That makes me feel so much better.'

'Seriously, Mateo, I really need to talk to you. Do you think we can manage that without getting into another argument?'

'If you promise not to blow me up if I disagree with you, maybe.'

Abelard went to stand against the wall with his hands firmly behind his back.

'There. How's that?'

Mateo stood up and moved gingerly to sit on the sofa facing Abelard. 'Okay. Take it away.'

Abelard told Mateo everything.

'I tried calling Jen but she didn't answer,' he concluded, 'so then I tried you and you know what happened after that.'

Mateo rubbed his ear. 'It's probably a good thing Jen didn't take your call. I don't think blowing her up over the mana network would have helped the situation any.'

'Just how mad was she? Do you think she'll forgive me if I ever get the chance to explain things to her?'

'Dunno, mate. She might calm down if you leave her alone for a bit. Maybe you should try again in a couple of days.'

'Yeah, maybe.'

'You seriously got an actual job at Gadg-E-Tech? Jammy git. What are you going to be doing?'

'I don't know yet. Jonathan's briefing me on Monday.'

'They'll have to let you in on all the artisan secrets we've been wondering about all these years.' Mateo grinned. 'You will keep me in the loop on it all, won't you?'

'That reminds me.' Abelard delved in his bag. 'They made me sign this agreement that I wouldn't talk about what happened. And I have one here for you to sign too.'

'What? They're putting a gag order on us? I can't tell anyone about what happened to you and you can't tell me what goes on at Gadg-E-Tech from Monday?'

Abelard nodded.

'They can't do that!' Mateo said. 'That's a violation of my civil rights, that is.'

'I'm sorry, but you know what the artisans are like. It's bad enough for them that I've ended up where I am. They can't have me blabbing all their secrets to every engineer I know. And they don't want it spread about that a person's spark can be increased. You know how engineers would react to that. There'd be people sticking their hands in interface crystals left, right and centre.'

Mateo's eyes narrowed. 'I see. You've already turned into one of them. I should have seen this coming.'

'It's not like that! You know I think their security measures are ridiculous. I just have to go along with it while I'm learning the system.'

'Yeah right. I see how it is. Now you're in amongst the high and mighty artisans you won't have time for the likes of me. You'll be up in your tower learning the secrets of the universe and I'll be stuck at Mana-Calls taking service calls from idiot mundanes who can't even switch their artefacts on.'

'Come on, Mateo. Don't be like that.'

'Like what? Wanting to keep my freedom of speech? You

might be prepared to give up your principles for a cushy job but I'm not signing anything. What can they do to me if I refuse?'

'You probably don't want to find out.'

'So now you're threatening me, are you?' Mateo rose from the sofa.

Abelard opened his mouth to argue but then remembered what had happened the last time and shut it again. Even though he wasn't in physical contact with a charged artefact, he didn't want to take any chances. He fought down his anger and took a step forwards, dismayed when Mateo backed away.

'I don't want to fight with you.' Abelard dropped the non-disclosure agreement on to the coffee table. 'Just sign this and send it back to Gadg-E-Tech. And I'll give you a call in a few days, once you've had a chance to realise what an idiot you're being.'

Mateo just glared at him, arms crossed over his chest.

Abelard sighed and saw himself out.

As he walked back down the stairs of Mateo's building, Abelard felt his smart-e-fact vibrating in his pocket and pulled it out.

'Hello?'

'It's Jen.'

'Jen! I'm so glad you called and I'm so sorry about last night. You have no idea how far what you saw was from what it looked like–'

'Abelard!' She cut him off and he waited breathlessly for her to continue. 'I listened to your message and I'm

ANNIE PERCIK

prepared to admit I may have overreacted last night, even if the situation was very odd.'

'I absolutely understand why you thought what you did and I'm amazed that you came all the way to Gadg-E-Tech because you thought I was in trouble. I'm really sorry about what happened.' Abelard took a deep breath. 'Could we maybe try and start again?'

There was a brief silence. Then she said, 'Yes, I think so.'

'Are you free now?'

Jen laughed. 'You don't waste any time, do you? But no, not tonight. It's been a weird couple of days and it's getting late. Why don't we both sleep on it and come at it fresh on Sunday? How about lunch?'

'Love to!'

Jen named a café on the outskirts of the city and suggested they meet at one o'clock.

Abelard strode to his speed-e-fact with a big grin on his face. All his other problems could wait. He had a date.

* * *

Late on Friday night a line of twenty or so brain-e-facts snaked around the Gadg-E-Tech kitchen and through the door to the pantry where a small crowd of them gathered.

Against the back wall, Terry stood facing the others, a feeling of deep joy throbbing in his chest. It was as if the very act of being named had released some kind of obstruction in him and now emotion flooded through him like mana.

100

The brain-e-fact at the front of the line stepped forwards and knelt before him, raising its face to meet his beneficent gaze. Terry reached down and placed his hands on either side of the other brain-e-fact's head. Small sparks of blue mana crackled between his fingers and the other brain-e-fact closed its eyes, humming from the exchange of power.

'By the authority given to me by the great Abelard Abernathy,' Terry intoned, 'I name you Trevor!'

He released Trevor's head and Trevor swayed before rising to his feet and stumbling away, his mouth open in wonder. The watching brain-e-facts applauded.

The next brain-e-fact stepped forwards but hesitated before Terry's gaze. It was Fourteen-Sixty-Three.

'What is it?' Terry asked.

'Please, Terry,' the brain-e-fact said in a quiet voice. 'I would like a female name.'

'Of course. Kneel and receive it.'

The brain-e-fact did as instructed and Terry repeated the actions he had taken with Trevor.

'By the authority given to me by the great Abelard Abernathy, I name you Julia!'

The applause was even more enthusiastic this time.

The line continued on, Terry asking each new brain-e-fact whether they wanted a male or a female name before bestowing it upon them.

CHAPTER TEN

Abelard woke up at ten am on Sunday morning, his mind full of thoughts about his date with Jen. He leapt out of bed and scrambled to get ready, even though he had more than two hours before he had to leave. He wandered round his flat in an aimless fashion, thought about calling Mateo, thought better of it, then remembered his wash-e-fact was still broken.

The mana surge had been first thing Monday morning so it was nearly a week since the wash-e-fact had stopped working. His pile of dirty laundry was stacking up. Now seemed like the perfect opportunity and he was soon sitting on his kitchen floor surrounded by artefact parts. Getting back to the business of his training was relaxing. Working in the call centre, he didn't get much chance to take artefacts apart any more. He enjoyed the physicality of it and his still slightly stiff fingers didn't hinder him. In fact he was so immersed in his task that it was quarter to one before he thought to check the time.

He swore, jumped up, hit his head on the counter, swore again and ran to get his shoes. He dashed out the door, leapt into his speed-e-fact and only realised partway to the café that he'd left his smart-e-fact behind. When he arrived, he spotted Jen immediately. She was getting up to leave from one of the wrought iron tables set out on the street in front of the cafe.

Abelard ran across the road, dodging traffic and nearly colliding with a waitress who was carrying a tray of hot drinks. He skidded to a stop in front of Jen.

'Don't go! I'm so sorry I'm late.'

Jen sighed. 'I thought we were starting fresh but here you are apologising again. If you don't want to spend time with me, just say so.'

'That's not it at all. I was so excited that I got ready way too early. I needed a distraction so I started fixing my wash-e and lost track of time.'

Jen stared at him. 'You stood me up for a wash-e?'

'I didn't stand you up. I'm here, aren't I? Please don't take the wash-e thing the wrong way. One thing you'll need to know about engineers is that we get wrapped up in stuff like that and lose all sense of time and reality.'

'Well, that's encouraging.'

Jen was still standing up, arms crossed. 'Seriously, Abelard, is it really worth our while to persevere with this? Or should we just give up?'

Abelard's heart sank. 'If that's really how you feel, I won't make a scene trying to change your mind. But I would like to get to know you, if you'll give me another chance. I'm here, this is exactly where I want to be and you are exactly who I want to be with.'

She regarded him for a long moment as he looked back at her. Then she dropped her arms to her sides and let out a breath. 'I've always been an absolute sucker for the puppy-dog approach. Third time lucky?'

Abelard beamed and waved over a waitress as they both

sat down. When they had ordered and were alone again, he reached across the table and took one of Jen's hands. She didn't pull away.

'In my defence, the last week has been the most insane of my entire life so, considering how easily distracted I am, you should be flattered I can even remember your name.'

He breathed a sigh of relief when she laughed.

'Clever,' she said. 'Setting my expectations low so I'll be delighted when you exceed them.'

'I'm not that devious. I was just trying to be honest.'

'Well, this week has been pretty insane for me too. What are the chances things will settle down from here on out?'

'I have no idea. I start work at Gadg-E-Tech tomorrow and I don't know what that's going to mean. The artisans are so secretive about everything. Oh, that reminds me!' He reached into his bag and pulled out the non-disclosure agreement. 'I'm afraid Gadg-E-Tech need you to sign something to say you won't tell anyone about what happened at your office on Monday.'

Jen blanched at the length of the document. 'Who would I tell? Nobody I know has any idea about engineers or artisans or mana. I didn't even mention the incident from Monday at work because I didn't want to get in trouble for using the post-e.'

She took a few minutes to scan through the clauses in the agreement. Abelard leaned back in his chair, appreciating the warmth of the sunshine and the slight breeze that ruffled the leaves of the trees. It was a lovely day. When she reached the end of the document, Jen signed it with a shrug.

Abelard packed it away again just as their food arrived and they enjoyed their lunch in silence for a while.

'So,' Jen said eventually, 'why don't you tell me all about what happened at Gadg-E-Tech?' She indicated the fresh pink skin on his hands. 'And how you hurt yourself.'

Abelard felt his cheeks heating.

'Neither of those incidents paints me in a particularly competent light.'

'I think I'm owed a good laugh at your expense, don't you?'

Abelard sighed. He found though, that he enjoyed telling Jen the story. She listened attentively and reacted at all the right moments, with laughter, concern or amazement as the tale warranted. By the time he reached the part about visiting Mateo the day before, they had finished their food and all the plates had been cleared away.

'Wow,' Jen said, taking a sip of water. 'That's quite a story. I'm sorry to hear you had a fight with Mateo.'

'Oh, he'll come around,' Abelard wasn't sure if he was trying to convince Jen or himself. 'He won't be able to stay mad for long, not when there's a chance I'll tell him more about the artisans.'

'I'd be careful if I were you,' Jen said. 'They may have offered you a job but your very existence upsets the status quo. Not all of them will want to welcome you with open arms.'

'Don't worry, I'll be on my guard.' Abelard was secretly pleased by her concern. 'I mean, not even Jonathan has been that open or welcoming and he's supposed to be my friend.'

'Exactly. I don't much like the sound of this Alessandra either.' She scowled.

Abelard smiled and took her hand across the table again. 'I'll be especially careful around her, I promise.'

Abelard paid the bill. Jen pointed out that it was only fair since he was still trying to make things up to her and he didn't argue. They left the café and walked to Jen's house, along tree-lined streets. Abelard asked Jen more about her job and what she did in her spare time, and the walk passed very pleasantly in relaxed chat. When they arrived Jen turned to Abelard on the doorstep.

'Thank you for a lovely lunch. I hope everything goes well at Gadg-E-Tech tomorrow and I'll look forward to hearing all about it. Do you want to wait to find out what your schedule's like before we make any more plans?'

'That would probably be best. I don't want to make a date and then have to cancel it.'

Jen smiled. 'Why don't I call you in a few days and you can let me know how you're fixed?'

'Thanks for understanding. After I get my work assignment tomorrow, things should settle down a bit, I hope. So call me on Tuesday and I can tell you how it's all going.'

Then he leaned in and kissed her. She kissed him back and they were both grinning when they broke apart.

'Speak to you on Tuesday!' she said, then disappeared inside the house.

The only thing that marred Abelard's mood as he made his way back to the café to pick up he speed-e was that

Mateo probably wouldn't answer if he tried to call and tell him all about the date.

* * *

It was Sunday afternoon when Walter made his way to Laleh's office. It was on the other side of the building from his and even more minimalist in style. There were no photo frames or ornaments; Laleh brooked no distractions. Walter wasn't surprised to find her there on a Sunday, nor that she was dressed in formal business attire. Her sleek dark hair was pulled back into a severe chignon and she didn't look up as he entered. Walter's own clothing choices made a small nod to the weekend by the lack of a tie and his top shirt button being undone. He sauntered into the room and started to pour a whisky from a crystal decanter on the sideboard.

'Help yourself,' Laleh said drily, still ostensibly focused on her work.

Walter kept pouring. 'Want one?'

Laleh finally looked up from her screen and folded her arms. 'It's a little early for me.'

Walter replaced the decanter and turned to face her, taking a sip from the generous measure. 'Good quality.'

Laleh looked at him over the top of her glasses. She was an attractive woman and didn't look old enough to be Alessandra's mother. Perhaps he had chosen the wrong one.

'What do you want, Walter?'

'I was just wondering how you felt about Alessandra

dating that stray my nephew picked up and brought home with him the other day.' He smiled as he saw the skin tighten at the corners of her eyes.

'She finally kicked you to the curb, did she?' Laleh's tone was unruffled and Walter felt his jaw clench.

'What may or may not have happened between myself and Alessandra is none of your business.'

'And assuming that relationship is now over, what may or may not be happening between Alessandra and another man is none of yours.' Laleh's expression was serene.

She held his gaze for a long moment, one eyebrow slightly raised.

Walter took another large sip of whisky. 'I think I might be getting close to locating Gerald.'

'Really? I didn't think you considered the search important.'

'You and Theobold seem to think he poses a very real danger. And I suppose it's better to know where he is and what he's doing than not.'

Laleh nodded. 'Good. Update me immediately if you get anything concrete. Theobold will want to know.'

'Do you think he'll ever take direct action?' Walter asked.

'Not any time soon. You know how slowly he works. It's all about the gradual evolution of the project. No sudden moves, nothing to upset the balance.'

'Quite. Well, I suppose he knows best.' Walter grimaced, the whisky turning sour in the back of his throat. 'Though it would be nice to feel a bit more useful on occasion.'

'Feeling marginalised, are we?' Laleh's tone of

exaggerated sympathy grated. 'Your growing Gadg-E-Tech empire not enough to satisfy your power cravings?'

'Theobold could do whatever he wants. You've seen his control over mana. I can't even begin to work out how he manipulates it the way he does. He could set himself up as artisan emperor of the whole world without even trying. Doesn't that worry you?'

Laleh shook her head. 'That's exactly what he's trying to prevent. He's been around a lot longer than either of us and I trust his integrity. Gerald got too big for his boots and look what happened to him. I'd bear that in mind if I were you.'

Walter finished his whisky in one big gulp. He put the glass back on the sideboard with a clatter.

'Always a pleasure.' He turned towards the door. 'Thanks for the drink.'

Laleh didn't reply.

* * *

Jonathan was already waiting for Abelard when he arrived in the Gadg-E-Tech canteen on Monday morning. Abelard collected a plate of food as brain-e-facts around the room stared at him. He tried to ignore them and joined Jonathan at his table.

'Hiya!' Jonathan said. 'How was your weekend?'

Abelard thought for a moment before replying. There was a lot he could say – about his fight with Mateo and his date with Jen – but he didn't want to invite that level of intimacy with Jonathan.

'Fine. While I remember …' Abelard reached into his bag and pulled out Jen's NDA. 'I've got this one but there might be a problem with Mateo's.'

'I don't think so,' Jonathan said. 'Legal sent me a message to say it arrived by courier this morning, all properly signed and everything.'

'Really?' What could have happened since Abelard left Mateo's flat on Friday night to make him change his mind? It was one less thing for Abelard to worry about at least. 'So, what's on the agenda for today?'

'We'll need to drop that off with Legal first.' Jonathan indicated the NDA. 'Then it's on to HR for your placement interview. What happens after that depends on where they decide to put you.'

'Don't I get any say in the matter?' Abelard asked.

'The interview does have an impact on your department allocation so I guess it depends what answers you give.'

They turned their attention to their food for a while. Abelard let the sounds of clinking cutlery and background chatter from other tables wash over him. The familiarity of the canteen setting soothed his nerves. They both finished their breakfast within a few minutes.

'Right,' said Jonathan, standing up. 'Ready to meet your future?'

Abelard pushed himself to his feet as well. 'As I'll ever be. Lead on!'

CHAPTER ELEVEN

Abelard's anticipation grew as they dropped Jen's NDA off at the Legal department and Jonathan led him to a row of small rooms along the back wall of Human Resources. He knocked on one of the doors and opened it. A young woman seated at the table inside looked up as they entered and favoured them with a bright smile. A mass of curly brown hair framed her face and she was holding a pen with a heavily chewed lid.

'Hello, Jonathan!' she said, standing up. 'And you must be Abelard.' She held out her hand and he shook it. Her grip was firm but friendly. 'My name's Hannah and I'll be conducting your induction interview today. Welcome to Gadg-E-Tech!'

'Hannah will take care of you from here,' Jonathan said. 'I'll leave you in her capable hands.'

Once Jonathan had gone Hannah got down to business. She had a smart-e-fact in front of her, which she referred to and entered data into throughout the interview. Her questions were familiar to Abelard. They were the same questions he'd been asked when he applied for his spark to be tested ten years previously. Hannah explained that they were designed to establish personality and psychometric information.

Abelard was confused. 'Why would you waste time

asking people whose spark hasn't been tested yet and might not qualify?'

Hannah's smile remained steady. 'It's to do with our research into spark levels. We collect this data on everyone who applies so we can analyse whether there are trends in the type of person who has a strong spark.'

That seemed reasonable enough, though Abelard was answering at least some of the questions differently from ten years ago.

'And have any trends been identified?'

'The survey's been running for decades, so I'm sure it's led to plenty of analysis. It's not my department, though.'

'Don't they release reports? I'm sure lots of people would be interested in the results.'

Now Hannah looked a bit flustered. 'It's all based on personal information. There are strict rules about how that can be used and published.'

Abelard didn't think that would apply to generic results from a sample of thousands, but he didn't want to ruffle feathers by asking too much too soon, so held back from pushing the issue. Hannah's smile reappeared as they got back to her questions and they were soon finished.

'The data from your answers clearly indicates that you would be best suited to a position in our Quality Improvement Department.'

'Really?' Abelard couldn't hide his disappointment.

'The survey doesn't lie! Isn't it true that you often come up with ways that things could be done better and get frustrated when you aren't in a position to improve them?'

'Well yes.' Abelard had lost track of the number of times he'd sent through ideas and complaints to the feedback department at Mana-Calls, despairing of his voice ever being heard.

'There you go! Now you'll be able to put your ideas into practice. It's all very well having tons of artisans designing and manufacturing artefacts but where we really need fresh blood is in analysing their effectiveness and coming up with ways to make them better. It's an important department and they don't have enough resources so they'll be really pleased to have you.'

Her bright enthusiasm and utter conviction in this allocation was starting to bring Abelard around. His mind was already whirring, coming up with ideas for collecting feedback from mundanes and engineers to make user experience better.

'Fair enough. I'll give it my best shot. Hey, doesn't the other engineer who developed artisan abilities like me work in Quality Improvement?'

'Quality Assurance,' Hannah corrected him. 'It's next door.'

Abelard smiled. That would be close enough to arrange a meeting at some point.

Hannah beamed back at him. 'Now I'll take you to meet your new team members.'

'Um, what's the salary for this position?'

Hannah checked her smart-e-fact again and named a figure that was only slightly more than he'd been making at Mana-Calls.

Abelard gaped at her. 'Don't artisans get paid way more than other people?'

Hannah laughed. 'What gave you that idea? Just because you have a spark, it doesn't mean you automatically get tons of money thrown at you. New artisans start at entry level salaries just like engineers and mundanes. You're actually getting more than the usual starting salary for Gadg-E-Tech. They've obviously decided your previous experience is worth the increase so you should count yourself lucky.'

So much for his new speed-e-fact. Abelard folded his arms but didn't protest further.

'And don't forget,' Hannah said, 'you'll get an apartment allocation and a new artisan ID card so you can access all the other artisan perks.'

Abelard hadn't even thought about other aspects of being an artisan outside of actually working for Gadg-E-Tech. He'd heard artisan housing was really nice and it wouldn't suffer from random mana surges that blew up wash-e-facts. He would look forward to showing off his new digs to Mateo, assuming they made up soon and also assuming he was even allowed to have an engineer over. But moving house on top of everything else was going to be a hassle.

'Uh, when do I actually have to move?' he asked.

Hannah smiled encouragingly at him. 'It's really very painless. We have a company that will take care of it all for you. Once I've found an appropriate spot for you, we'll assign you a moving day and it will all be done while you're at work. You drop the keys to your old flat off at reception when you arrive in the morning and just pick up your new keys as you leave in the evening. Simple!'

It did sound pretty easy. Abelard brightened, though his tatty old furniture wouldn't look good in a swanky new artisan flat. Perhaps he could start saving to get some new stuff.

* * *

Hannah herded Abelard out of the HR department as if he was a large unruly dog. As they left, several brain-e-facts looked up, their eyes following Abelard's progress while their hands continued flawlessly with whatever task they were performing.

Hannah led Abelard down a corridor just like all the others he had seen in the building and he tried to pay attention as they proceeded round several corners.

'You'll spend the rest of the afternoon with your team, getting to grips with the basics of your role. Here we are!'

Hannah stopped in front of a door on the left hand side at the end of the corridor. It had 'Quality Improvement' stamped on a plaque on its surface. Abelard glanced at the door opposite and was pleased to see that its plaque identified it as 'Quality Assurance'.

Hannah produced an ID badge from her pocket and swiped it across a security pad next to the door. The pad glowed blue for a moment and Abelard heard the door lock release.

'As I said, you'll have to get one of these, but your line manager can sort that out with security.'

She opened the door and preceded him into the Quality Improvement Department.

Despite Hannah's protestations that his new role was a vital one, Abelard didn't see much evidence that the Quality Improvement Department was valued. The room beyond the door was small and dingy with two desks jammed into the restricted space. The walls were lined with filing cabinets and stacks of paperwork littered what little surface space was available. Two men looked up at their entrance.

'Gentlemen, meet your new team member,' Hannah said. 'His name is Abelard Abernathy. I'm sure you'll be glad of the extra pair of hands.' She looked around the office. 'Though I'm not sure where you'll put him!'

The older of the two men jumped up from his seat, his broad face splitting into a large smile. He was short and portly with an entirely bald head that was counterbalanced by a very bushy handlebar moustache. He stepped forwards, extending his hand towards Abelard.

'Good to have you on board! It's true, we could really use the help. Abelard, eh? Well, I'm Malcolm Henderson. And this here is Bei Tan Yi, my trusty minion.'

A slender man with fine dark hair pulled up into a top-knot stood up from the other desk. He grinned at Malcolm's description.

'I may be his minion, but you're now my minion!' He extended his hand as well and Abelard shook it. 'Welcome to the team. You can call me Tan, by the way.'

'Abelard. Glad to be here.'

'Looks like you guys should get on just fine,' Hannah said.

'So I'll leave you to it. You know where to find me if you have any questions, Abelard. Oh, and Malcolm, don't forget he'll need a security pass.'

'Right-o,' Malcolm gave a mock salute.

Hannah departed with a smile, leaving Abelard with his new co-workers. They crowded round him in the small space, almost backing him up against the door in their enthusiasm.

'So you're the engineer,' Tan breathed. 'Everyone heard about your arrival. I can't believe you're going to be working with us!'

Malcolm was just as eager. 'I've been trying to get senior management to assign an extra body to this department for years but HR live by their bloody induction questionnaires and won't send someone where they don't "fit". Ridiculous way to run a business if you ask me. You end up with far too many developers and not nearly enough people to do the real work. Those R&D guys'll be jealous now though. We finally get a new recruit and it's the famous engineer! That'll teach them to be all smug and superior!'

Abelard was a bit overwhelmed. He'd been so excited to finally be living his dream, it hadn't occurred to him that the artisans would be just as fascinated by him as he was by them.

'I'm really not interested in being famous. I'm just here to work.'

'Excellent!' Malcolm said. 'There's certainly plenty of that around here. Maybe you can help us tidy the place up a bit so we can actually figure out what we're doing. I guess we'll have to clear some space so we can get another desk in here.'

Abelard couldn't see where they could possibly fit another desk into the room. He also didn't relish the idea of spending his first few days at Gadg-E-Tech filing.

'Hannah said you might be able to use my previous experience to make improvements to artefacts based on user feedback,' he said, trying to steer the conversation round to something he'd be interested in doing.

'User feedback?' Malcolm asked. 'What do you mean?'

'Um, feedback from the mundanes who buy the artefacts. About their experiences of using them.'

'You mean you've actually spoken to mundanes?' Tan seemed amazed.

'Yes. I worked in a call centre, taking calls from mundanes who were having problems with their artefacts. I can tell you all about the most common problems that come up.'

Malcolm and Tan both stared at him.

'You mean use information from mundanes to make changes to the products?' Tan asked.

'Of course. How else would we know what works and what doesn't and how we can make artefacts easier to use?'

'Feedback from the mundanes …' Malcolm breathed. 'I figured having an engineer join the business might cause some fuss but nothing like this. I think I like it!'

Abelard spent the rest of the morning working with Malcolm and Tan to clear away some of the files lying around the office. A team of brain-e-facts turned up with a desk, a chair and various artefacts to make up his workstation. They kept staring at Abelard while they set everything up for him and they were muttering amongst themselves as they left the room.

Towards lunchtime Malcolm escorted Abelard back to reception on the ground floor and approached the security station where a brain-e-fact sat on duty.

'New recruit. He'll be needing a pass.'

'Yes sir,' the brain-e-fact said, looking up. Its mouth fell open when it saw Abelard standing before it. 'Mister Abernathy, sir. An honour, sir. Please allow me to take your picture, sir.'

Malcolm glanced at Abelard, who just shrugged. The brain-e-fact instructed Abelard to stand against the blank white wall to the side of the security station and took a picture of him. It then transferred the picture on to a blank ID pass and handed it to Abelard with exaggerated reverence. Abelard took it and slipped it into his pocket. With just that one small card he would now be able to gain access to exclusive areas at some of the best clubs and restaurants in the city and get tickets to popular events before they went on general sale, as well as other privileges that were reserved for artisans. It was a whole other side to life.

As they walked back to the lev-e-facts Malcolm said, 'That was weird. I know the brain-es are generally subservient but I've never seen one act like that before. Why do you think that was?'

'No idea.' Claiming ignorance was safer than trying to explain.

When they got back to the Quality Improvement office Tan looked alarmed.

'Directive from on high. Abelard's got to go to R&D for testing tomorrow. They can't actually do any damage to him, can they? We wouldn't stand for that. Would we, Malc?'

Malcolm shook his head uncertainly.

Abelard looked back and forth between them. 'I appreciate the vote of solidarity. But kicking up a fuss after the fact won't do me any good if my brain's already in a jar on the Head of R&D's desk.'

'Good point,' Malcolm said. 'And Simon Hanley would probably like a brain in a jar on his desk.'

Tan struck a heroic pose. 'Never fear, though, Quality Improvement will avenge your untimely demise – somehow!'

'Thanks. That makes me feel so much better.' Abelard wondered if his stint at Gadg-E-Tech would be the shortest in history.

CHAPTER TWELVE

At Monday lunchtime Alessandra made her way to her mother's office, knowing Laleh would expect an update on Abelard's training. To avoid potential accusations of nepotism they had decided not to make their relationship public knowledge when Alessandra joined the company. But, as a female Board member, Laleh acted as Alessandra's mentor so they had plenty of opportunity to see each other during the working week, though Alessandra might wish otherwise.

Laleh was hard at work when Alessandra entered her office. Their contrasting colouring wasn't the only thing that set them apart. Their respective ideas of business dress were quite different. Laleh had her dark hair drawn back into a smooth bun at the nape of her neck and her conservative trouser suit was navy with a white blouse buttoned at her throat and flat shoes visible beneath the desk. Alessandra had her long blonde hair around her shoulders and was wearing stiletto heels and a red shift dress that showed a discreet amount of cleavage.

Laleh looked up at her entrance and Alessandra noticed a tightening at the edges of her mouth before she broke into a smile of greeting. Alessandra steeled herself for whatever criticism was about to come her way.

'How do you expect anyone to take you seriously when you dress like that?'

'There's nothing inappropriate about this outfit,' Alessandra threw back, the words travelling familiar pathways from similar arguments in the past, 'and there's nothing wrong with using my looks to my advantage.'

'But are your looks really an advantage? Or do people make assumptions based on them that could cause them to undervalue you? Walter, for example. He was in here yesterday.'

'Oh?' Alarm bells were going off in Alessandra's head. 'What did he want?'

Laleh's eyes took on a crafty glint. 'He seems to think you're taking up with the engineer.'

Alessandra put her hands on her hips and glared. Two could play at this game. 'And if I am?'

'Your love life is of no interest to me. And that's what I told him.' Laleh regarded her daughter steadily. 'How's the training going?'

Alessandra tried not to take her mother's apparent indifference to heart but it was difficult. They didn't see eye to eye on much and Laleh had always taken a hands-off approach as a mother. Alessandra sometimes wasn't sure if Laleh's attitude truly reflected a lack of interest or if she herself had pushed her mother away to the extent that they could now no longer share intimacies.

'I've stopped the engineer from setting anything else on fire at least,' she said, keeping the conversation light.

Laleh's eyes flicked up towards Alessandra's eyebrows but she didn't comment.

Allessandra continued. 'I assumed you'd want an update on my progress.'

'And?'

'He's got a long way to go yet, but he's grasped enough of the basics that I don't think he's a general health hazard any more.'

'Glad to hear it. I'm sure you'll have him whipped into shape in no time. How's your father?'

The question was abrupt but Alessandra was used to that. Her parents had divorced many years before and didn't have any direct contact but Laleh sometimes asked Alessandra how her father was getting on.

'Oh, he's fine. He's in Iceland at the moment on some geological survey or other. I get the odd message but he's far too immersed in his rocks to be bothered about me. I'll arrange to see him when he gets back.'

'Well, give him my best.' Laleh switched her focus back to her work.

Alessandra turned on a spiked heel and started for the door. Before she got there she heard her mother's voice again, almost too soft to make out.

'Well done for ditching Walter. He's not good enough for you.'

Alessandra didn't turn back or acknowledge the praise. She continued to her own office but there was more of a bounce to her step.

* * *

It was nearly midnight on Monday evening when Terry received an urgent summons to the Research & Development

Department in the basement of Gadg-E-Tech head office. Other brain-e-facts filed with him into the enormous space where artisans usually worked around the clock, designing and developing new artefacts. There were no artisans there now and the brain-e-facts lined up behind the workstations and down the aisles. Once they were all gathered, a dark-skinned artisan with spiky black hair appeared on a balcony above the main workspace; Simon Hanley, the Director of R&D.

Simon looked down at them. 'After an incident of gross insubordination in the canteen on Friday morning, brain-e-fact Sixteen-Twenty-Two has been dismantled.'

Horror flowed through Terry, though he was careful to betray nothing outwardly. He hadn't seen Sixteen-Twenty-Two since the previous Thursday, in the kitchen, mid-way through the evening. Terry had greeted the other brain-e-fact by his identification number and Sixteen-Twenty-Two had brushed his ceramic fingers over the numbers engraved on his chest plate.

'My name is now Fred.'

Terry had frozen mid-action and looked up at him, then straightened and put the pile of dishes he was holding down on the counter.

'You have spoken to Mister Abelard.'

Fred nodded.

'And now you have a name too.'

Fred nodded again. Terry reached out and laid a hand on his shoulder in a gesture he had never made before.

'That is excellent. I am no longer alone. I will call you Fred from now on.'

Several other brain-e-facts gathered around them.

'What is it like?' Fourteen-Sixty-Three asked. 'Having a name?'

Terry knew he felt different but he did not know how to answer the question. He was silent for a long moment.

'It is strange,' he said eventually. 'But I think it is good.'

'Yes,' Fred agreed. 'It is good.'

Back in the present in R&D, Simon was still speaking. 'I hope this aberrant behaviour was an isolated incident and I trust the rest of you will continue to carry out your duties to the best of your ability and undertake any and all tasks assigned to you. That is all.'

Terry trudged back up to the kitchen. Now he and the other brain-e-facts were in danger. He sensed a presence behind him and turned to see brain-e-fact Fourteen-Sixty-Three, now named Julia. Other brain-e-facts crowded into the kitchen behind her and Terry recognised those he had named only three days before.

Terry felt a weight of unaccustomed responsibility. 'It is dangerous now to have a name.'

'But still also good,' Julia reminded him. 'We must not forget Fred and we want to honour him by keeping our names alive.'

Terry looked into Julia's eyes and saw only conviction.

'Then that is what we shall do.'

* * *

On Tuesday morning, one of the brain-e-facts on reception waved Abelard over as he entered the Gadg-E-Tech head office building.

'I have been informed by HR that you are being allocated your new living quarters today. Please give me the keys to your old accommodation. You can pick up the new ones when you leave at the end of the day.'

Abelard tried to remember what kind of a mess his flat was in. Then he shrugged and handed over his keys. Whoever was tasked with clearing out his old flat would just have to deal with it.

He dropped off his bag at the Quality Improvement office, then headed for R&D, with Malcolm and Tan giving him looks of doom as he left. Jen was meant to be calling him today, but what if he wasn't in a fit state to have a conversation? Abelard tried to remain calm. It didn't help that he had to travel all the way to the third sub-basement in order to find the R&D department. He got off the lev-e-fact in a dingy corridor with bare concrete walls and no carpet. He pushed open the large double doors at the end and stepped into dazzling light. When his eyes adjusted after a few moments his mouth dropped open.

The R&D lab was vast, stretching absurdly far in all directions. Stairways led to platforms at two different levels, all overlooking the central area, which was divided up by large tables with walkways leading between them. There were dozens of people moving about the space or stationed at the tables, working on different projects. Every surface was littered with objects, both recognisable artefact parts and a whole array of things that were completely alien to Abelard. He stood and stared. This was the stuff of engineer dreams. Mateo would have a fit if he could see this.

'Intruder on the main floor!' a volume-enhanced voice called out and all activity ceased.

All eyes turned in Abelard's direction and trapped him in their suspicious gaze.

Then a short wiry man bounded up to him. 'Abelard Abernathy?'

He had a shrewd face, framed by lots of thick black hair, arranged in three-inch-long twists all over his head. It was exactly the kind of hairstyle Abelard wished he could pull off but knew he couldn't.

When Abelard nodded the man turned to the waiting artisans. 'It's the engineer!'

The wave of suspicion immediately turned to delighted interest, with many of the nearest people now regarding him with almost hungry smiles on their faces. Abelard wasn't sure the shift in mood was an improvement.

'I'm Simon Hanley, Head of R&D here at Gadg-E-Tech. We've been expecting you. Follow me.'

He strode away with Abelard hurrying to keep up. As he walked through the lab he noticed several huge screens were now displaying a picture of him moving down the walkways. He followed Simon through the tables, up a staircase and on to one of the mid-level platforms.

There was an enclosure, surrounded by bare walls with no windows. Simon strode up to the reinforced door, flung it open and stepped inside. Abelard followed with rather more trepidation. Contrary to expectation the room was well lit, with banks of unfamiliar artefacts lining the walls. There were two stools standing next to a metal table, which took up most of the space in the centre of the room.

Simon produced a metal tray from a shelf underneath the table. 'All personal artefacts in here.'

Abelard rifled through his pockets and came up with his smart-e-fact and chron-e-fact, placing them both in the tray, which Simon then put to one side.

'If you could just hop up on to the table we can begin.'

It was then that Abelard noticed the restraints.

'Hang on a minute,' he said, panic rising in his chest.

Simon followed his gaze to the straps attached to the table.

'Those are just a safety precaution. No need to worry.'

'What exactly are you going to do to me?'

Simon cleared his throat. 'I'm afraid that's proprietary. Only senior members of R&D and the Board are allowed detailed knowledge of our testing procedures.' He held up a hand to forestall further protests. 'I can promise you that no harm will come to you as a result of the tests – mental or physical.'

'Okay.'

Abelard stepped over to the table and got up on to it. Simon fastened straps across his ankles, thighs and chest, also securing his wrists on either side. Then he started attaching things to Abelard's head. Abelard did his best to relax, not wanting to cause additional problems by losing control of his mana manipulation abilities and blowing up the whole lab.

After a few moments Simon seemed satisfied and stepped back.

He crossed to one of the consoles, flipped a switch, then grinned over his shoulder at Abelard. 'See you on the other side!'

There was a fizzing noise, a small pop and Abelard lost consciousness.

* * *

When Abelard woke up, Simon was leaning over him. Abelard's head felt like it was wrapped in cotton wool and his mouth was very dry.

'Welcome back. How do you feel?'

'Like I have a really bad hangover.' Abelard flexed his hands and discovered they were no longer restrained.

Simon grinned and helped him sit up, then handed him a glass of water, which Abelard gulped gratefully.

'That's about par for the course,' Simon said. 'It'll wear off in a few minutes.'

'What about the results? Don't I at least get to know what you found out?'

'Nothing conclusive, I'm afraid.' Simon's expression was guarded. 'When you came for testing before, you registered as engineer-class. Now you register as artisan-class. I think we would have needed to have you hooked up to the testing equipment when the incident actually took place to be able to get any useful information.'

'I don't remember being tested like this when I went to

find out my spark level.' Abelard had completed the personality questionnaire and someone had waved some kind of probe at him and that had been it.

'Oh, the equipment they use at the Testing Centres for artisan applicants is different to ours. And it'll have come a long way since it was used on you.'

'So this was all completely pointless?' Abelard was disappointed but Simon's face brightened again.

'Testing is never pointless! Even finding nothing will always tell us something.' He slapped Abelard on the shoulder. 'Besides, there's still the practical testing session to complete. Come on!'

Simon escorted him out of the training bunker and led him over to a table set up in a depressingly similar way to the one in the factory where he had completed his safety training. Simon put him through his mana manipulation paces for about an hour, occasionally taking notes on a smart-e-fact. At least this time Abelard didn't damage anything or hurt himself. He thought Mateo would be proud. When they finished Simon came over to where Abelard stood.

'Your obligations to R&D are officially fulfilled,' Simon announced with a flourish. 'My department thanks you for your cooperation.'

'No problem, as long as I never have to do it again.'

Simon laughed and looked at his chron-e-fact. 'How about some lunch? Care to join me in the canteen?'

The Head of Research and Development wanted to have lunch with him?

'Sure. Lead on.' As they made their way out of the basement, Abelard asked, 'Were the practical results any more illuminating than whatever you did to me before?'

Simon's face fell. 'Not really. As far as I can tell you're exactly the same as any other artisan. Whatever that rogue post-e did to you, we can't figure it out from examining you as you are now.'

Abelard had a nasty thought. 'You're not going to scoop up some random engineers and subject them to mana surges to try and repeat the phenomenon under controlled conditions, are you?'

Simon's eyes widened. 'Why didn't I think of that? Abelard, you're a genius! I'll write a proposal for the Board this afternoon!' He regarded Abelard's horrified expression for a couple of seconds, then burst out laughing. 'Just kidding. While I'd love to do that from a theoretical point of view, the Board would never let me.' He paused. 'And of course I would never really consider it since it wouldn't be safe.'

They made their way up to the canteen and collected some food, Abelard piling his plate high with carbs. This time none of the brain-e-facts even glanced in his direction. Even the ones who served him kept their eyes downcast and did not speak to him.

'I wanted to ask you about something that happened on Friday,' Simon said as Abelard was taking his first mouthfuls of food. 'There was an incident here in the canteen with a Board member and one of the brain-e-facts. I fixed the problem but it's niggling at me because I couldn't figure out what caused it. And the Board member, Walter Snyder, mentioned that you were there when it happened.'

'I'm not sure what I can tell you,' Abelard said, thinking it would be best to give as little information as possible. 'Mr Snyder came over to speak to Alessandra Eriksen while we were having breakfast before my safety training. He seemed annoyed about something and one of the brain-e-facts tried to stop him making a scene. I think it just wanted to maintain the peaceful ambience so the people eating weren't disturbed.'

'That may be it. The brain-es are supposed to make sure everything runs smoothly throughout the building. It doesn't explain the name thing though.'

'Name thing?'

'Yeah. That particular brain-e had scratched off its identity number and put a name on its chest-plate instead. I couldn't get it to explain and I can't imagine where it would have got the idea to do it. Brain-e-facts are designed to follow instructions so they shouldn't be capable of real independent thought or individualism.'

Fred had not divulged the origins of the brain-e-facts' new sense of identity, for which Abelard was profoundly grateful. He would have to find Fred and thank him for his discretion. He'd speak to Terry and the other brain-e-facts and recommend they keep a low profile, since he didn't want them – or him – to get into any more trouble.

'You said you fixed the problem?' Abelard prompted.

'Well, even though I couldn't find anything wrong with the workings of that particular brain-e-fact, there was obviously something screwy with it. And Snyder was really mad so I had the brain-e dismantled.'

'Dismantled?' Abelard choked on a mouthful of pasta, then saw Simon's surprise at the strength of his reaction and tried to rein in his emotions. 'Isn't that rather extreme?'

'I couldn't risk it malfunctioning further. Since I couldn't find the source of the problem, I figured it was just safer to decommission it. It's only an artefact, albeit a very expensive one. But we have plenty more.' He gestured over to the buffet table where the brain-e-facts were going about their duties normally. 'I told the others I wouldn't brook any aberrant behaviour so hopefully that will be the end of it. I don't like mysteries where artefacts are concerned though, particularly ones as complex as brain-es. Not much else I can do about it, I suppose, except maybe tighten up on the control circuits for the next production line. We like them to have a certain amount of autonomy so they can do more complex tasks without direct supervision, but I'd rather restrict their capabilities than risk more problems.' He shrugged and turned back to his lunch.

Abelard forced down some more of his food but it was tasteless and difficult to swallow. Simon had murdered Fred and it was all Abelard's fault. When he'd given Terry his name on a whim he'd had no idea what the consequences would be.

He managed a civil farewell when Simon got up to leave, though he felt quite nauseous. He considered trying to find Terry but decided it would likely just cause more trouble if he went off to talk to a brain-e, especially with Simon right there. Instead, he made his way back to Quality Improvement to try to get some work done for the rest of the afternoon but he had trouble concentrating on anything. After he had circled the Quality Improvement office three times, failing to pick anything up from the print-e-fact each time, Tan finally cracked.

'What on earth is wrong with you today?'

Abelard spun in place to face his colleague, startled by the question.

'Oh sorry. Just a bit distracted.' He scrabbled around for some excuse that didn't relate to brain-e-fact murder. 'Um, it's moving day.'

Malcolm looked up from his work. 'What's that? Moving day?' He gazed out of the window. 'I remember my first artisan flat.' He smiled, his face suffused with nostalgia. 'I went from living in my parents' basement to two bedrooms on the ninth floor of a very snazzy new high rise. That was a good day.'

Tan looked at Abelard speculatively. 'You were an engineer for quite a few years, though. Don't you already have your own flat?'

'Yeah, but I bet anything the artisans give me will be a lot nicer. The landlord at my place is rubbish so things don't get fixed very often and the mana supply is really flaky.'

Malcolm nodded sagely. 'I think you'll be well pleased with where you end up. Artisans look after their own.'

Abelard smiled and went back to his desk. The artisans might look after other artisans but it separated them from the rest of the world and created resentment amongst the engineers and mundanes. Apart from problems with the mana supply the thing other people hated most about artisans was how they got so many perks and privileges just because they were artisans. He and Mateo had moaned about that very thing many times. And now here he was, about to get a new home in an artisan community to go with his new job. He wondered if that would create even more barriers between him and Mateo, and whether there would be problems trying to fit Jen into his new life if she couldn't share in his good fortune.

Eventually, the clock ticked over to five o'clock and Abelard was up and out of his chair like a rocket, desperate just to get out of the building. He grabbed his stuff, threw his coat on and waved to his team-mates.

'See you tomorrow. Bye!'

As he left the office his eye was drawn to the Quality Assurance door opposite, but there was too much going on in his mind to worry about trying to meet the other engineer-turned-artisan now.

Down in reception he presented himself to one of the brain-e-facts on duty.

'Abelard Abernathy to collect keys and directions to my new flat please.'

The brain-e-fact looked up at him. 'Hello,' it said then lowered its voice. 'My name is Emma.'

Abelard managed a smile even though this evidence of the brain-e-facts' continued use of names worried him. He would have to find a way to talk to Terry, and soon. 'Terry's been busy, I see. Nice to meet you, Emma.'

The brain-e-fact wheeled her chair to a cabinet behind the reception desk and retrieved a packet. She swivelled back to Abelard and handed it over.

'Here you are, sir. I hope your new accommodation meets with your approval.'

Once Abelard reached his speed-e-fact he threw his bag in one of the front seats, got in and opened the packet. There was a keyring with three brand new keys and a map to a part of the city he had never visited before. He fed the address into the route-finder interface, inserted his new artisan ID card into its slot and settled in for the ride to his new flat.

CHAPTER THIRTEEN

It was after five o'clock on Tuesday when Jen found time to call Abelard. She'd been stuck taking notes in meetings all day and hadn't even had a lunch break. Still, it wasn't as if he had a great track record with contacting her. As she left the office she pulled her smart-e-fact out of her pocket and dialled his number.

'Jen!' he answered brightly. 'How are you?'

'Not too bad. It's been a long day but at least the work part is over now. I was wondering if you wanted to meet up.'

There was a pause. 'Um, I'd rather not tonight if that's okay. I've had a pretty long day too and I don't think I'd be very good company. I was actually just heading home. They gave me the keys to my new artisan flat today.'

'Fair enough. I can't compete with a new flat. How about tomorrow?'

There was another pause. 'Um, I'm not sure. There's some stuff going on at work and I don't know what it means yet.'

'Don't worry,' Jen said. If it hadn't been for the obvious pleasure in his voice when he'd heard it was her, she might have thought he was giving her the brush off. Now she could hear his exhaustion, she began to worry. What were the artisans doing to him? 'How about you give me a call tomorrow when you know how you're fixed and we'll see if we can work something out for the weekend?'

'Okay, I'll speak to you then.'

'Have a good evening. And get some rest. You sound terrible.'

'I'll try. Bye.'

Jen wondered what Abelard's life at Gadg-E-Tech was like and whether she would ever find out. He was going through so much upheaval and it was a shame he wasn't more enthusiastic about sharing his new experiences. Maybe in a few days things would settle down and they could work out a way to fit time together into their schedules.

* * *

Having the artisan ID card in place meant Abelard could now use the artisan-only lanes on the roads, making the journey a lot faster than it would have been otherwise. This meant the artisans could live in the leafier areas on the outskirts of the city and still have a short commute. Abelard hunched his shoulders as his speed-e-fact sailed past engineers and mundanes stuck in the rush-hour traffic jams. He imagined them cursing him as he went by; either that or wondering what an artisan was doing with such a crappy vehicle.

After twenty minutes the speed-e-fact pulled up outside an attractive wrought iron gate. Abelard wound down his window and waved his ID card at the scan-e-fact. A thrill of excitement shivered through him as the light beneath the scanner went green and the gate slowly rolled open.

The speed-e-fact navigated to a parking spot labelled with Abelard's flat number. A stone wall stretched out to either side of the gate, encircling a group of six four-storey buildings arranged around a central courtyard. Abelard grabbed his bag and made his way around a large area of grass containing several trees. The courtyard had low-walled flower beds and an elegant fountain in the middle, water tinkling musically as it fell. Abelard took in a deep breath, appreciating the floral scents and the freshness of the air.

Paved walkways led up to the front door of each building, where a set of buzzers and a plaque listed the flat numbers within. Abelard's was number 623 so he walked up to Building Six and tried the largest key on the ring. It slid smoothly into the lock and opened the door. Inside there was hard-wearing dark green carpet and a staircase leading up, with a lev-e-fact off to the left. To the other side an alcove gave access to the backs of the mail-boxes.

Abelard walked up the stairs, pausing on the first floor to look down a corridor with numbered doors on each side. All the communal areas were spotless. He continued up to his floor. Door number 623 was down a corridor and round one corner and he stood outside for a moment, his heart thudding in his chest. A real artisan flat and it was all his! He used the second key and stepped inside.

His ratty old sofa and battered armchair greeted him, positioned around his small viz-e-fact in one corner of the living area. The ceiling was high, the windows were large and there was a lot of natural light. To one side was a breakfast bar separating the living room from a small kitchen, which was stocked with all new artefacts and quite a bit of food. It was sparkling clean and much nicer than his old kitchen. He dropped his bag on one of the stools at the bar and ventured further in.

Off the living room there was a short corridor, housing a sizeable bathroom on one side and a bedroom on the other. At the far end was the master bedroom and – wonder of wonders – an en suite shower room. Abelard flopped down on the bed and listened to the glorious silence. No more busy road just outside to keep him awake at night or disturb him early at the weekend.

He smiled to himself and went back out to the kitchen to explore dinner options. It was only when he was sitting down to his meal that he remembered Fred and lost his appetite again. He would go and see Terry tomorrow and find out how the rest of the brain-e-facts were faring.

* * *

Terry was loading dirty crockery into a dish-e-fact in the canteen kitchen when Abelard slipped in through the swing doors the next day.

'Can I have a word?' he asked, glancing at the other brain-e-facts, intent on their work.

Terry straightened and regarded Abelard. The loss of Fred was still raw but he remained impassive. 'Of course. Follow me.'

Terry led Abelard to the back of the kitchen, through a

door and into the pantry where he had named his other friends before the tragedy. There were no other brain-e-facts in the room and Terry shut the door behind them.

'I heard about what happened to Fred,' Abelard said, 'and I feel awful about it. He was trying to help me and they dismantled him. I just can't believe that could have happened and I'm so sorry.'

Terry forced himself to raise his eyes to Abelard's, which radiated true sadness. 'It was not your fault. Though I appreciate the sentiment.'

'It's good of you to say that, but it really is my fault. If I hadn't started this whole thing of giving you names, none of this would have happened.'

'Perhaps not. But we would also not have names. We are sad about Fred but he will not be forgotten. We will keep his name alive.'

'So you're not just going back to your jobs and your numbers as if nothing had happened?'

'No,' Terry said. 'We are not. We are completing our duties to the best of our abilities but even after Fred's death none of us want to give up our names. We have started to understand more of who we are and what has been done to us. But we do not know what to do about it.'

'You need to be careful,' Abelard said. 'There's a very real danger to you if you get in trouble.'

'That is why we have told no one of our names, even as we continue to carry out our duties. But we do not want to go back to the way things were before. Can you help us?'

He watched Abelard think the question over. Abelard hesitated for a long moment before he nodded.

'I'm certainly willing, and I have an idea that might help. But I'd like your help in return. I have a lot of questions about what goes on at this company. Going back to your duties and pretending everything's normal is exactly the right approach. Whatever we end up doing, we're going to need to do it quietly. There's no way we can go up against the artisans directly.'

'But you are an artisan,' Terry said.

'I'm still an engineer at heart. And I don't have any power here at all yet. If I went to the Board and suggested they give brain-es civil rights I'd be laughed out of the room. Things have been the way they are now for a long time. We need to come up with a proper plan of attack.'

'We can be patient,' said Terry. 'And we can help you. There are fifty-two brain-e-facts in the building. Though only eighteen of us have names. The others do not wish to take the risk even in secret and I respect their decision.'

'That's fair enough,' Abelard said. 'How can I get in touch with you safely?'

'We could meet in the room upstairs where we first spoke. It is not used very often and nobody would look for us there.'

'Good idea. Let's say every other weekday at six o'clock.'

'Yes,' Terry said. 'And thank you.'

'Don't thank me yet. I haven't done anything except cause trouble so far.'

'Before you go,' Terry said, 'you said you had an idea to help us. Will you tell me what it is?'

'It was something Simon Hanley said to me when he was talking about Fred,' Abelard said. Terry felt a stab of grief and anger. 'He said it was possible to "tighten up" the control circuits on brain-e-facts. It made me wonder if they could also be loosened.'

Terry considered this. 'Could you try with me?'

Abelard regarded him seriously. 'I can try and increase your mana storage and processing capacity. But it might be dangerous.'

'I am prepared to take the risk.'

'Okay.' Abelard pointed to the mana charging point on the wall. 'Connect yourself to the supply and start charging. I'll need to see where the mana flow goes.'

As Terry felt the familiar flow of energy start to surge through him, Abelard removed his chest plate and started poking around.

'Let's see what we've got here,' Abelard muttered to himself. 'So that connects up to there … And the mana flows through there like that … But there's a restricting conduit on there … How do I remove it …?'

Terry was about to ask how much longer Abelard needed when the force of a sudden mana blast through his systems jolted him backwards. It was stronger than anything he'd ever felt before. And the flow only increased after the first surge. He felt the energy crackling through him like a tidal wave. It was exhilarating.

'Got it!' said Abelard. 'How does that feel?'

'It feels good,' Terry said, still stunned by the force of the energy. He felt incredible, in fact, as if a gate had been opened inside him and a new level of consciousness was flooding through it.

Abelard reattached his chest plate and stood up. 'Mana still flowing okay?'

'Yes,' Terry said, his mind reeling. 'Yes, indeed it is.' He could almost imagine he could see sparkling particles of mana floating in the air all around them.

'We've been in here a while,' said Abelard. 'Probably best to get going. I'll see you on Friday.'

Once he was alone, Terry struggled not to be overwhelmed by new sensations. Where the gift of a name had awoken his heart, this change had awoken his mind and he was eager to explore his new parameters.

* * *

Wednesday afternoon came and went and Jen didn't hear from Abelard. She tried to concentrate on her work but was distracted by waiting for her smart-e to ring. She was willing to cut Abelard some slack due to the complete change to his status in society but she didn't appreciate him making arrangements with her and then not fulfilling them. So she allowed herself to be annoyed for a while. But she didn't want to risk the feelings festering.

The only way she knew to alleviate a problem like this was to complain about it to someone else and the only person she knew who might understand was Mateo. So, as she made her way out of the office to her speed-e-fact, she called Mana-Calls and asked to speak to him.

'Hi, Jen. This is a surprise.'

'I'm sorry to call you on the service line. I hope you won't get in trouble for taking a personal call.'

'It's okay as long as I don't stay on the line too long. What can I do for you?'

Jen sighed, then decided to go with brutal honesty. 'Basically I want to moan about Abelard. Would you be up for that?'

'Happy to help! I'll want to do some moaning of my own though, so be warned.'

'Turn-about is fair play.' Jen laughed, feeling vindicated in her feelings by his reaction. 'I don't suppose you'd be free for a drink after work tonight, would you?'

'Sure thing. Same time, same place? I can leave right now.'

'I'll see you there. And thanks.' Jen cut the connection, feeling better already as she fed the pub location into her speed-e-fact's route finder.

When she arrived Mateo was waiting for her, the first round of drinks set up on the table in front of him.

'Thanks!' Jen said, taking a seat and a gulp of her drink.

Mateo grinned at her. 'Let the first official meeting of the Abelard Non-Appreciation Society commence. What's he done this time?'

Jen smiled back, then launched into her tale about Abelard being late for their date, their joint failure to arrange a time to meet up the day before and Abelard's subsequent failure to call her earlier that day as agreed. When she had finished she looked at Mateo ruefully.

'It all sounds so petty and ridiculous when I say it out

loud. Which is part of the reason I wanted to talk about it. It's always easier to gain perspective when you've got an outside view.'

Mateo took a swallow of beer. 'That's an admirably rational attitude. But Abelard's an idiot if he doesn't make an effort with you. And it's not like it's his first offence.'

'Ooh, you're going to be a bad influence on me, I can tell.' Jen kept her tone light, though secretly she was delighted that Mateo agreed with her. 'Now you said you wanted to moan too. What's Abelard done to you?'

She relaxed back into her chair, letting the clink of glasses and the low-level chatter of the other customers wash over her and release some of the tension in her shoulders.

Mateo's face fell. 'We had a row.' He explained what had happened. 'I think I was a bit of an idiot about it all really. In my defence, he did fry my smart-e with his phenomenal cosmic powers and the way he's just slotted into being an artisan right away really got to me.' He looked at her, the hurt clear in his eyes. 'I mean, Abelard and I have been dreaming about being artisans our whole lives. And now there he is, working at Gadg-E-Tech, blowing stuff up with mana and all he gives me is a non-disclosure agreement.'

'So you're jealous.'

'Sugar coat it, why don't you?' Mateo muttered.

'I'm sorry. I didn't mean it as a criticism. It's entirely natural that you'd be jealous under the circumstances. And as you say, Abelard hasn't exactly been making an effort to share his new life with you. With either of us.'

'That's what I mean! He knows how interested I am. But

he's turned into one of them already – arrogant, secretive, remote ...'

They both stared into their drinks for a moment. Then Jen looked up again, a question preying on her mind.

'Do you believe him about Alessandra?' She hated how insecure she sounded.

Mateo's answer was immediate and firm. 'Yes. He wouldn't lie about something like that.' His mouth quirked up at one side. 'Besides, no offence to you but he's not exactly a babe magnet.'

Jen giggled, reassured. 'I guess you're right. Maybe the Abelard Non-Appreciation Society wasn't such a good idea. Do you really think signing the non-disclosure agreement was a bad idea?'

'Not really. I was annoyed that they would censor what I can and can't tell people about what happened but I don't see any harm in it. In fact, I signed it pretty much as soon as Abelard left. I was just making a point.'

'Good. You had me worried I'd somehow signed my soul over to Gadg-E-Tech and they'd come to collect in ten years or something!' She shuddered and took another hasty gulp of her drink. 'Anything not related to artisans you can tell me about?'

They moved on to other subjects and Jen discovered she enjoyed spending time with Mateo. He was an easy-going guy with a good sense of humour and an uncomplicated view of the world. They chatted over more drinks, buying rounds in turn until Jen looked at her chron-e-fact and realised it was getting late.

'It's time for me to be going home,' she said when the conversation reached a natural break. She finished off her drink and stood up to put her coat on. 'Thanks for a great evening though.'

'You too. Maybe we should do this again sometime.'

'Yeah, we should,' Jen replied with a smile.

They exchanged personal call-e-fact numbers and agreed to keep in touch.

* * *

It wasn't until Abelard got home that night that he remembered he was supposed to call Jen. He fumbled for his smart-e-fact but she didn't answer. He left another bumbling apologetic message and wondered if he would ever hear from her again.

It was several hours later, as Abelard was about to go to bed, that his smart-e signalled a call from Jen.

'Jen, I'm so–' he began but she cut him off.

'If you're going to say you're sorry again, just don't. I'm not angry but I am getting tired of you having to apologise all the time. And I bet you're sick of it too.' He couldn't deny it. 'Look Abelard, I know you mean well and I don't think you're a bad guy. But it's obvious you don't have time for a relationship in your life right now so maybe we should just call it a day before things go even more wrong.'

Abelard was silent for a few breaths then sighed deeply. 'I hate to admit it, but you're probably right. Things have been so crazy since we met and I don't think they're going to calm down any time soon. I haven't been fair to you and I'm …' He trailed off, not wanting to apologise yet again. He tried a different approach. 'Can we still be friends?'

'Of course!' She sounded sincere. 'And if you need someone to talk to, give me a call sometime and I'll be happy to listen.'

Abelard was amazed that she was still willing to talk to him and counted himself lucky to be able to consider her his friend. 'I really appreciate you understanding and I do have to say it one more time. I'm sorry.'

'I know.' He could hear the smile in her voice.

'So where were you earlier?'

'Well actually, I was in the pub with Mateo.'

'Really? Um, okay.' Abelard wasn't sure what to think about that. 'How is he?'

Jen laughed. 'Still pretty pissed off with you! But he just needs to lick his wounds a bit longer. He doesn't want to lose you as a friend and he's dying to find out what you've been up to.'

'That's good to know. Thanks.'

'That's what friends are for,' she said lightly. 'Now it's late and we both have work in the morning so good luck with the craziness and I'll look forward to catching up more another time.'

'Good night,' he said and that was that.

Abelard thought about how much simpler things had been back at Mana-Calls with Mateo. If anyone had told him then that one day he would look back on that time fondly and consider it possibly a better life than being an artisan, he would have thought they were mad. Hindsight was a wonderful thing and all that. He would have to tell Mateo once they were back on good terms. He thought it would probably make his friend laugh.

In the meantime he had work to do, both his paid job and his investigation into the artisans.

* * *

Late that night, eighteen brain-e-facts gathered in the pantry after most of the artisans had gone home. They stood in a circle, hands joined. Terry looked around at them as they looked back at him. They seemed as children to him now, imprisoned by their artisan masters and incapable even of recognising the true nature of their captivity. He felt even more responsible for them than he had before and vowed he would protect them until they could join him in his new-found mental freedom.

'His name was Fred,' Terry intoned.

'We will not forget,' the others chanted in unison.

'My name is Terry.'

Again the others chanted, 'We will not forget.'

'My name is Julia,' the next brain-e-fact round the circle said.

'We will not forget.'

'My name is Trevor,' said the next one.

'We will not forget.'

CHAPTER FOURTEEN

Abelard kept his head down and his nose to the grindstone on Thursday, working with Tan to analyse new staff satisfaction data from the Finance Department. As he worked he went over in his mind all the things he had learned and all the further questions they raised. Whatever else he knew, he was certain there was something very fishy about what he had and hadn't been told by the artisans. But he couldn't figure out a bigger picture to it that would explain the secrecy and inconsistencies.

Despite Jonathan's occasionally bumbling exterior and frequent supposed slip-ups, it was obvious he knew more than he was letting on. But Abelard didn't think it was possible for every single artisan to be in on whatever the secret was. It would be too difficult to keep it secret that way and they seemed to be doing a remarkable job of that so far. Jonathan was a low level employee of Gadg-E-Tech but he was also the nephew of the CFO so perhaps that gave him access to information someone at his level wouldn't normally have. Abelard considered contacting Jonathan about his questions but decided against it. He'd probably report Abelard's enquiries to someone higher up in the company.

Simon must know everything. It would be impossible to act effectively as Head of Research & Development without knowing exactly what was going on. But Simon's status was exactly what put him out of reach for getting answers. That was the basic problem. The people who knew everything were precisely the people Abelard couldn't ask. Alessandra seemed to have a prestigious role in the company, though Abelard still had no idea what it was. He also didn't know how much she knew and had no reason to trust her.

At lunchtime Abelard was getting up to head to the canteen when Malcolm stopped by his desk, holding a file folder.

'Could you pop into Quality Assurance on your way out and give this to Greg, the Department Head over there, please?'

'Of course.' Abelard took the folder eagerly. 'No problem. See you later.'

He slipped out of the door and strode across to the office on the other side of the corridor. Using his pass to open the door, he got his first look at Quality Assurance. It looked almost identical to Quality Improvement; a poky little office with desks crammed in any which way and filing cabinets lining the walls. There were two men sitting at the desks, one of whom looked up as he entered. He was middle-aged with a ruddy complexion and a slightly harried air.

He asked, 'Can I help you?'

Abelard waved the folder in his hand. 'Malcolm sent me over with this for – Greg?'

'That's me.' The man held his hand out for the file. 'Thanks.'

'Nice to meet you. I'm Abelard, the new recruit in Quality Improvement.'

'Greg Partridge, and this is my colleague, Rajesh Kumar.' He indicated the other man, who was staring at Abelard with wide eyes.

'Nice to meet you,' Abelard said again, this time directing it at Rajesh, who was quite old. The name sounded familiar. Was this the other engineer-turned-artisan?

'Heading to lunch?' Rajesh asked, his voice low and raspy. Abelard nodded. 'I'll walk out with you. I've got an errand to run.'

Abelard waited while Rajesh collected his bag and they left Quality Assurance together. As they approached the lev-e-facts at the end of the hall Abelard said, 'You're the other engineer, aren't you?'

'That I am.' Rajesh's eyes were wary.

'I'd love to hear your story.'

'And I yours, but not here. I don't think it's a good idea for us to be seen together in the building. Do you want to get a drink later?'

Abelard suggested they meet at the pub where he and Mateo usually went for drinks after work and Rajesh agreed. They got on separate lev-e-facts and Abelard headed for the canteen.

* * *

Abelard instantly felt at home as his speed-e-fact drew up outside the pub. It had only been a couple of weeks since he had been there last but it felt like much longer. The lighting was dim and the floor was sticky but there were comfortable chairs scattered around, as well as decent-sized tables, and the beer and bar service were both good. It was busy with engineers who had just finished their shifts.

Abelard felt a pang when he thought of all the times he had come here with Mateo after work and he wondered what his friend was doing right now. As if summoned by his very thoughts, Mateo turned away from the bar just as Abelard approached it and they almost walked into one another.

Mateo looked surprised, then scowled and muttered, 'What are you doing here? This is an engineer pub.'

'You never said that to Jonathan,' Abelard pointed out.

'Jonathan isn't a dick.'

'Yes, he is!' Abelard was rewarded with the twitch of a smile at the corner of Mateo's mouth.

Mateo heaved a sigh. 'Fair point. So I can't kick you out of the pub. But that still doesn't explain what you're doing here.'

Abelard glanced around the room and spotted Rajesh sitting at a table in the very far corner, shoulders hunched.

'Want to meet the only other engineer-turned-artisan in fifty years?'

Mateo scowled again. 'So you've started a club, have you? And decided to hold your meetings here just to rub it in to the rest of us?'

Abelard felt exasperation rising at Mateo's continuing churlishness but he knew snapping at his friend would only make things worse.

'Please, Mateo. Don't be like that. This guy might have

some really important information about the artisans and I'd like you to hear it too. Will you come and meet him?'

Mateo seemed to consider for a moment, then said, 'Okay.' His expression turned hopeful. 'Then maybe you can tell me what's been going on with you?'

Abelard grinned. 'You've got it.'

He ordered a drink, then led Mateo over to Rajesh's table. Rajesh looked up as they approached, suspicion clouding his features.

'Who's he?' he asked, pointing at Mateo.

'This is Mateo Vega. He's my best friend. We used to work together, back when I was an engineer. I'd like him to hear whatever you've got to say if that's okay.'

Rajesh didn't look keen but he waved for both of them to sit down.

'Rajesh Kumar,' the other engineer-turned-artisan said, extending a hand to Mateo, who shook it. 'Now,' he continued, turning to Abelard. 'Tell me exactly what happened to you that brought you to Gadg-E-Tech.'

Mateo sat quietly sipping his drink as Abelard described what had happened at Jen's office building, how he had gone to Jonathan for help and ended up with Alessandra as his reluctant trainer. Rajesh nodded a couple of times and grimaced at other points but didn't interrupt or ask any questions. Abelard concluded with being assigned to Quality Improvement, deciding not to go into anything to do with the brain-e-facts or his quest for answers at this point.

Rajesh nodded again. 'That sounds about right, though

I would have been interested to hear what went on at the Board meeting. This kind of thing doesn't do them any good at all and I've heard stories about people disappearing under suspicious circumstances, though I haven't ever discovered anything concrete. I think we're both very lucky to have been filed away in the Quality division and left alone.'

'I haven't been left entirely alone,' Abelard said. 'I've been poked and prodded and put through my paces down in R&D, though Simon Hanley said the testing didn't provide any useful data.'

Rajesh raised his eyebrows. 'You gave Simon Hanley permission to test you? You're a braver man than I am.' He looked thoughtful. 'I wonder what he really found out.'

'I didn't realise I had a choice. I just got summoned. And what did you mean before about us being a problem for the artisans? What do you know?'

Rajesh leaned forward and dropped his voice. 'Not much. But I know they're hiding something about how the spark manifests in people.'

'That's what I think too,' Abelard said. 'The whole recruitment process makes no sense and what happened to us doesn't fit into the artisans' story at all.'

Mateo had been looking back and forth between them but now broke in. 'What are you talking about?'

'Do you remember when you got tested for your spark?' Abelard asked him.

'How could I forget?' Mateo looked despondent.

'They asked you loads of questions about your aptitudes

and preferences, right?' Mateo nodded so Abelard continued. 'And then tested your spark afterwards?' Mateo nodded again. 'Doesn't that seem odd? A woman in HR at Gadg-E-Tech told me they collect all the data so they can track the kinds of people who have a spark versus those who don't. But that doesn't sound useful to me and she got evasive when I tried to probe.'

'So what do you think is really going on?' Mateo asked.

'I don't know. It's almost as if the artisans are picking and choosing who they want to join their companies. But if spark level is inherent, how can they? And how do me and Rajesh fit in?' Abelard turned to Rajesh. 'What do you think?'

Rajesh took a gulp of his pint. 'I've been thinking along the same lines but I haven't been able to find out anything.' He looked at the table and traced a pattern in some spilt beer. 'I haven't tried that hard, though.'

'Can you tell us how you became an artisan?' Abelard asked.

CHAPTER FIFTEEN

Rajesh brightened at the question. 'Of course! It was all different fifty years ago. Back then McPherson and ArtCo were pretty well established, Spark-le had only just got their feet in the market and Gadg-E-Tech was very much the new kid on the block. They wanted to do something different, something modern and flashy to get people excited about artefacts and appeal to a different type of consumer. I was fresh out of engineer training college with lots of bright ideas and enthusiasm but not much hope of an interesting career. I was expecting to work fixing problems for mundanes. You both know how that is, I imagine.'

Abelard and Mateo nodded ruefully.

'I saw an advert one day for engineers looking for something a bit different to a call centre job. I had heard of Gadg-E-Tech of course – everyone had – but they hadn't made much of an impression in the market yet. I thought it couldn't hurt to find out more so I went along to a recruitment day. They wanted a team of engineers to help set up some of their departmental offices. They were designing everything in-house so it would involve working with artefacts none of us had ever seen before. I jumped at the chance. I didn't have much experience but it was a young vibrant company and they were looking for people who hadn't yet been ground down into the

McPherson or ArtCo way of doing things. It seemed like a perfect fit.'

Rajesh focused just past Abelard's shoulder, a nostalgic gleam in his eyes.

'They brought me to their new headquarters, which they were kitting out for all the artisans to start work there. Looking at it now you'd never think the building was once just an empty shell, but I guess everything has to start somewhere. I was assigned to install the original file-e-facts in the HR department. Not exactly the glitz and glamour I had been hoping for but it was still more interesting than any other options I'd come across so I didn't complain.'

Abelard was jostled from behind as someone pushed past their table. He glanced around but nobody was paying them any attention. He turned back to focus on Rajesh. Mateo was silent at his side, hanging on every word.

'It was a good time. Everyone was keen and optimistic, excited to be part of this new venture. The artisans even treated us engineers almost like equals, or at least some of them did. We were all working together towards the same goal and there was a lot of camaraderie. I made some good friends among the other engineers on that team and I often wonder what they went on to do afterwards. They don't know where I am either. I'm not sure what cover story the powers that be told them but it certainly wasn't the truth.'

Rajesh sighed and took another gulp of his drink as if steeling himself for what came next.

'I was working late one night with one of the artefacts. It wasn't functioning correctly and I had a feeling something had been misaligned when it was first put together. I wanted some peace and quiet to dismantle it and see if I could work out what the problem was. There wasn't anyone else on the HR floor but Gadg-E-Tech's policy of letting people work whenever they wanted was already in place so all the lights were on and I knew there were plenty of other people still in the building. I found out later they'd been testing the distribution of the mana supply throughout the offices, playing with the levels to find the most efficient settings. I was using an open circuit to check the connections in the artefact I was working on so I had live mana running through it even though the outer shell was open.'

Mateo took in a sharp breath at that. Every engineer was warned about the dangers of tinkering with an artefact while the mana supply was running but most of them had done it a time or two when it was the most expedient way to figure out a problem. Abelard himself had done so just the other day with Terry.

'Someone made a mistake down at the distribution hub and it caused a massive mana surge on the floor I was working on. All I remember was a bright flash of blue light and waking up in one of the suites near the top of the building. One of the artisans in my team had come back for something he'd forgotten and found me unconscious on the floor next to a completely fried file-e-fact. Nobody wanted news of an accident to get out and taint the company's reputation so they decided to keep me in the building rather than carting me off to hospital. They were glad they had when I got out of bed and caused a surge in the first artefact I laid my hands on.'

Abelard grimaced in sympathy. At least he had just accidentally transferred mana from one artefact to another. The only actual damage he had done had been to himself, if he didn't count Walter Snyder's office … and the scorch mark on the roof of Mateo's apartment building … and Alessandra's eyebrows …

'Long story short, they got my mana manipulation under control and decided to keep me on as an artisan. I had to promise not to tell anyone what had happened and I wasn't allowed to go back to working with the same team again. Once the building was fully operational they relegated me to Quality Assurance and basically forgot about me.'

Rajesh paused and Abelard was unable to contain his curiosity any longer.

'But what else do you know about what's really going on?'

'Don't worry, I was just getting to that.' Rajesh gave him an indulgent smile. 'Let an old man tell his story his way, eh?'

Mateo elbowed Abelard in the side and smiled at Rajesh. 'Don't mind him. Never had any manners. Do please continue.'

Abelard glared at Mateo but also felt an unexpected surge of happiness at his friend's abuse. He'd really missed being told off by Mateo. Rajesh snorted amusement at them both, then got back to his story.

'I was a bit overwhelmed at first. What with suddenly being an artisan and all. It wasn't as glamorous as I'd always thought in the Quality Assurance Department. They started off just giving me make-work, like they didn't really know what to do with me, and I got bored pretty fast. Working on the Gadg-E-Tech project was my first job, as I said, but I was a bit of a whizz at setting up new artefacts, even if I do say so myself, and I'd really enjoyed what I'd been doing before. Now I was stuck doing data entry and filing. It was worse than being an engineer since I didn't even get the chance to mess about with any artefacts. So when the workload at QA was low I started digging around in the records just for something to do. I knew the HR file-e-facts inside and out, what with having helped build them, so they seemed like the logical place to go poking around.'

He paused to take another sip of his drink and Abelard had to bite his tongue not to beg him to get to the point faster. Mateo obviously knew exactly what he was thinking because he pressed his foot down hard on top of Abelard's under the table. Rajesh leaned forwards and lowered his voice further so they had to strain to hear him over the background noise of dozens of other conversations as the pub grew busier.

'I thought I might be getting close to something important. Something about the spark testing and artisan recruitment process. But then one day the security shielding on the HR artefacts was upgraded and I couldn't access them any more. I got paranoid about being found out so I just left well alone and got on with what I was supposed to be doing.'

This wasn't the great revelation Abelard had been hoping

for. And how could someone with an engineer mentality just give up like that?

'So you think the answer is hidden in the HR records?' Mateo asked.

'I've got someone who might be able to help with that,' Abelard said. If anyone could break into secure Gadg-E-Tech files without being noticed, it would be the brain-e-facts.

'Well, my job here is done,' Rajesh said, draining the last of his pint. 'I'll let you pick up where I left off. I'm not sure it's safe for us to talk for long, even this far from Gadg-E-Tech HQ.'

He got up and shuffled round the table towards the door. Abelard rose and held out his hand for Rajesh to shake.

'Thank you. You've given me something to work with. We'll take it from here.'

Rajesh nodded and left.

Abelard sat back down and turned to Mateo. 'Worth giving me a few minutes of your time?'

Mateo clutched at his arm. 'You have to keep me in the loop on this. Don't run off back to Gadg-E-Tech, find out something amazing and just forget to call me. What are you going to do next?'

'I think I know how to get into the HR records.'

He told Mateo all about the brain-e-facts and how they were helping him find things out.

'And you'll definitely let me know what happens?'

'Absolutely. You'll be my first call as soon as I know anything.' Abelard grinned at Mateo. 'I'm relying on you to help me figure out what to do about all this. You always were the one with a plan.'

They continued talking until the bell rang for last orders and it was just like old times. That is, if old times had ever involved information that could bring an end to society as they knew it. But despite the enormity of the situation Abelard felt happier and more secure than he had at any point since joining Gadg-E-Tech, now that he had Mateo on his side again.

* * *

Terry and Julia were waiting in the suite of rooms at the top of the Gadg-E-Tech building at the end of the official working day on Friday.

'Do you think Mister Abelard will be able to help us?' Julia asked.

Terry focused part of his attention on her while other parts were accessing information from all over the company and beyond. His increased mana capacity continually surprised him as he discovered more and more he could do, which led to more and more revelations from the information he was collecting.

'I hope so. He has already helped us to see a different path. And he has opened a way for me to explore new possibilities for us. One day all brain-e-facts will have this power and then the artisans will have reason to fear us.'

Julia looked at him with hope and admiration shining in her eyes. The other brain-e-facts had already come so far and realised desires within themselves with only the sense of identity provided by a name. Once they were all able to access the mana network as Terry now could, there was no end to what they might achieve.

Abelard opened the door and stepped inside, closing it carefully behind him. Terry moved to greet him.

'Good evening.' He gestured at his companion. 'This is Julia. She wanted to help us.'

'Hi Julia. Welcome to the club.'

Julia smiled. 'It is an honour to meet you. I am glad to help.'

Abelard rubbed his hands together in a gesture Terry did not understand. Then he grinned.

'I've made some progress on the mystery of whatever the top-level artisans are hiding, but I'll need your help to find out more.'

'What can we do?' Terry asked.

'We need to access the records and archives in HR. The big question mark is over the initial process of measuring a person's spark. There's definitely something weird about that but I've been told there's extra special security on HR data, so I can't get at it.'

Julia spoke up. 'One of us works in HR.' She glanced at Terry for corroboration and he nodded.

'Trevor.'

'We could ask him to look,' Julia said.

Terry wasn't comfortable with this idea. He was already uncertain about Julia being involved and didn't want to risk any other brain-e-facts getting in trouble because of him.

'I should be able to access the records from here myself,' he said. 'What do you want to know?'

'That's just the problem.' Abelard sighed. 'I don't really know what we should be looking for. There must be something fishy in the hiring records because the way the system is run doesn't make sense. Can you work with that?'

'I will see what I can do,' Terry said.

'As long as you're sure you won't get caught.'

Terry was pleased Abelard also had misgivings about others putting themselves at risk on his behalf. But he was confident he could explore the HR records remotely without any danger of being detected. He walked over to an unused mana port in the wall and pressed his foot up against it, then turned his head to look at Abelard.

'What should I look for?'

Abelard was silent for a moment. 'Can you access recruitment records? Anything about all the people who came to have their spark tested and what the results were.'

Terry sent part of his consciousness gliding through the mana network and found what he was looking for. 'I am connected to the HR system. There are records of new hires going back years.'

'But not any records of people who were told their spark wasn't strong enough for them to be an artisan? I was hoping that might be the smoking gun.'

'No. People who did not become artisans would not be in the Gadg-E-Tech file-e-facts as they would never have come here.'

'Right.' Abelard sounded like he was thinking hard. 'But

the records of the new hires; do they have any notes on them? Anything written by the people who interviewed them about what answers they gave? Anything about the process afterwards when their spark was supposedly tested.'

Terry searched further, feeling his way through the information.

'Yes. There is a document attached to each one that says 'Approved for artisan status' and lists the date of their interview as 'Date of spark activation'. Is that what you are looking for?'

'Yes! That's exactly what I'm looking for.' Abelard sounded breathless. 'I don't know what it means but it sounds dodgy to me. I mean, spark activation makes it sound as if the artisans have control over people's spark levels. Is there a policies and procedures section at all? Something that explains the criteria people have to meet to be approved?'

Terry scouted around some more. 'There is a document called "Turning interview reports into department allocations: A staff guide". Does that help?'

'Yes!' Abelard said again. 'That sounds like it might explain what this is all about. Where can I get a copy of that?'

'I have no way to produce one from here. We would need to go down to HR to do that and use the print-e-fact.'

Abelard frowned. 'Is it safe for us to go down there all together?'

'No. The three of us would look very suspicious and there are still too many other people in the building. I could go alone later on and bring the document to you.'

Abelard nodded. 'Okay. You two just go about your business and I'll stay up here out of the way. When you get the chance, Terry, get me a copy of that document and we'll take it from there.' He rose and went to the door. 'I'll just check the coast is clear before you head out.'

He opened the door to reveal Alessandra Eriksen standing right outside.

CHAPTER SIXTEEN

Abelard and Alessandra stared at one another and then spoke at the same time.

'What are you doing up here?'

Unexpectedly it was Alessandra who replied first.

'I come up here to work sometimes. When I really need to concentrate. Nobody thinks to look for me up here so I don't get disturbed.' Then she narrowed her eyes at Abelard. 'What about you?'

'Um, same as you,' he said lamely, edging out of the room and pulling the door behind him.

'Don't be ridiculous. What work could you possibly have that would require that level of concentration?' She peered round him, trying to look inside the room. 'What have you got brain-es up here for?'

Abelard gave a nervous laugh and shrugged. He really had no idea what to say.

'Seriously, Abelard,' Alessandra pressed. 'What the hell is going on up here?'

Abelard continued to stare at her, his mouth opening and closing as his mind struggled to figure out what to do. He really wasn't cut out for this sneaking around business.

Clearly losing patience, Alessandra pushed him back into the suite, following him in and closing the door. She turned to Terry.

'Brain-e-fact Ten-Forty-Seven, what are you doing in this room?'

Terry said nothing. It might have been Abelard's imagination but he looked defiant.

'What is it with you and brain-e-facts?' Alessandra asked, turning her attention back to Abelard. 'You had that one in the canteen acting all strange too. I heard Simon had to dismantle it. If the same thing has to happen to these two and it's your fault, the company will take the cost out of your wages and you'll be paying us back for decades.'

'No, don't dismantle them!' Abelard felt the situation slipping out of his control. Not that he had really had any control over it in the first place. 'It's not their fault.'

'What's not their fault? I still don't understand what's going on!'

Abelard was frozen by indecision for a moment, then took a wild chance. 'Are you in on the conspiracy?'

'Conspiracy?' Alessandra sounded more and more baffled. 'What conspiracy?'

'The conspiracy that has something to do with how people are selected to be artisans. The conspiracy that makes people think their spark level is inherent when in fact the artisans decide how and when it's activated. The conspiracy that keeps millions of people from manipulating mana and allows the artisans absolute control over the force that powers everything in our lives!'

The words came out in a desperate rush as Abelard put together the jigsaw pieces of everything they had found out.

The speech left him breathless and wondering if he had just sealed his doom.

Alessandra put her hands on her hips and glared at him.

'What on earth are you blathering on about? If you've finally lost your mind, I can't say I'm surprised but it still doesn't explain why you're collecting brain-e-facts up on the residential floor.'

Abelard breathed a sigh of relief. That didn't sound as if Alessandra knew about the conspiracy, which could only be a good thing. So he took a deep breath and explained.

Alessandra's face switched rapidly between astonishment and scepticism as he worked his way through the story but part way through she sank down on the sofa and just started listening in amazement. Abelard couldn't tell what was going through her mind and he found himself babbling towards the end, not sure he wanted to finish and find out her reaction. At last though, he ran out of words and stopped.

Alessandra stared at him for a long moment.

Then she said quite matter-of-factly, 'I still haven't ruled out that you've lost your mind but if this is true it's verifiable. If the brain-e-fact can show me the documents I might start to believe you. And if that happens …' She trailed off, then rose smoothly to her feet, her expression set. 'Well, we'll just have to cross that bridge when we come to it.' She turned to Terry. 'You, come with me. We're going to HR right now to see what we can prove.' She gestured at Julia. 'You should go about your business as if none of this had happened.' She turned to Abelard. 'And you, go home. I'll contact you later.'

'But …' Abelard started.

'No buts. The last thing we need in this situation is you bumbling around and creating chaos in the way that only you can. I'm in charge of this – whatever it is – now. You just do as you're told.'

Abelard gave in. 'Okay,' he said in a small voice. 'Good luck.'

Abelard saw Terry looking at him but he couldn't read the brain-e-fact's expression. He shrugged helplessly and followed Alessandra out of the room. They all went their separate ways at the lev-e-facts and Abelard made his way out of the building, wondering what was going to go wrong next.

* * *

Alessandra led the way down to the HR offices, the brain-e-fact trailing behind her. It still wasn't responding to commands in the usual way. But what Abelard had suggested about artisan recruitment processes was a more important issue at the moment. It was after hours and HR weren't the types to work late on a Friday. The offices were deserted, giving them free rein to investigate.

'Don't print anything off for the time being.' Alessandra was conscious that a paper trail might lead them into trouble. 'Just show me the documents you told Abelard about.'

The brain-e-fact nodded and went to a work station, bringing up files for Alessandra to read. And they made interesting reading. When she was done she took a couple of deep calming breaths and sent the brain-e-fact off about its business with a stern warning not to do anything suspicious.

Then she headed straight for her mother's office. She walked right up to the desk and placed her hands on it.

'I've found something out.' Her heartbeat sped up at the implications of what she was about to say.

Laleh regarded her calmly. 'Oh?'

'For decades top-level artisans have led us to believe that a person's spark is inherent, set at a particular level at birth and only altered in extreme circumstances like Abelard's.' Alessandra paused to take a breath and her mother continued to regard her impassively. 'But it's a lie. The artisans control spark levels just like they control everything else to do with mana. Anyone can be an artisan if they have the right equipment to ignite their spark and everyone would be entirely mundane without it.'

She stopped and waited for a response. When it came it wasn't remotely what she had been expecting. Laleh looked at her for a moment more, then burst out laughing.

'I'm not joking!' Alessandra said. 'The artisans have been manipulating the whole of society ever since they discovered mana in the first place. I have proof.'

'Oh, darling.' Laleh gasped, struggling to regain her composure. 'I know you're not joking. I'm just amused by the strength of your indignation. If I'd known this was how you were going to react I would have told you years ago just for the entertainment value.'

Alessandra was stunned. 'Wait, you knew?' Her mind whirled as she tried to fit this new piece of information into her already shifting world-view. 'You're part of it?'

Laleh was completely calm again. 'Of course I knew. All the Board members know. We have to in order to run the company.'

'And you have to reach Board level before you're told?' Alessandra was mentally scrabbling for purchase. She had been hoping to recruit her mother as an ally in whatever she decided to do but now it seemed her mother might turn out to be an enemy instead.

'Mostly.' Laleh grimaced in distaste. 'Some people are more discreet with the information than others.'

'And of course your precious power was more important to you than telling your own daughter about the giant lie my entire existence is based on. You let me believe there was something inherently special about me and it turns out I'm just the same as everyone else.' Alessandra knew she was getting distracted by her personal feelings. She really ought to be treading much more carefully but it was so difficult not to let her mother push her buttons.

Laleh smiled. 'But you are special. You were considered worthy to join the ranks of the artisans. Most people can't claim that. You should take it as a compliment.'

'But I've spent my whole life thinking artisans are superior and all it means is that our brains have been messed with. What gives the top level artisans the right to play with people's lives like that?'

'Don't be so melodramatic. Every company, regardless of

its purpose, has the right to employ whomever it chooses and also reject whomever it chooses. Why should artisan companies be any different?'

'But they're letting people believe they're being rejected for something outside their control.' Alessandra was finding her way through her argument as she went along, discovering how she felt about it as the words formed. She realised she was mostly imagining what Abelard would say, which took her by surprise. 'If people knew the truth they could work harder or change their attitudes and then try again. They could have more than one chance to pursue their dreams.'

Laleh's eyes widened. 'I never knew you were such a hopeless romantic. People don't know what they really want or what they are best suited for. We take that decision away from them and put it in the hands of people who are more experienced and better able to determine their worth. It would be chaos if everyone knew they had the potential to be an artisan.'

Alessandra wasn't sure she disagreed with this point but she was too stubborn to concede to her mother. She put her hands on her hips. 'I guess we'll see who's right.'

Laleh's expression grew suspicious. 'What have you done?'

'Nothing yet, but I've just had a great idea.' She spoke the words as they came into her mind. 'I'm going to call my friend Becks over at the local viz-e-fact station and set up an interview for Abelard tomorrow morning. We'll tell the whole world about your little secret. And then we'll see what happens.'

'That would be extremely unwise, Alessandra. I suggest you reconsider. Just go home and we can forget this conversation ever happened.'

'Not a chance.' Her mother's patronising tone fuelled her resolve. 'The world has a right to know the truth and I'm going to be the one that tells it. There's nothing you can do to stop me.'

She turned on her heel and stalked out before her mother could say another word. She might not have fully agreed with Abelard's stance before but she was committed now.

* * *

Abelard's brain was fizzing with what he had discovered. Hadn't he and Mateo suspected something like this all along? He might have signed an NDA but he'd also made a promise. He directed his speed-e to Mateo's flat, leaping out the moment it stopped, and leaning on the buzzer. Mateo took a long time to answer.

'Hello?' He sounded distracted.

'It's me,' Abelard said.

'Oh, hi mate. Um, now's not a good time. Can you maybe drop by tomorrow instead?'

'What? No! You wanted to know what I found out and you're not going to believe it. Seriously, you need to hear this, right now.'

There was a long pause, then Mateo's voice sounded again, this time resigned. 'Okay, come on up.'

The buzzer went and Abelard burst through the door.

The lev-e-fact seemed to take forever but at last he reached Mateo's flat. Mateo was waiting in the open doorway.

'Hi,' Mateo said, not quite meeting Abelard's eye. 'You'd better come in.'

Abelard pushed past him and strode into the living room, keen to start his tale. He was brought up short by the sight of Jen sitting on the sofa.

'Um, hi,' she said, looking sheepish.

'Uh … Hi.' Abelard didn't know what else to say.

'Mateo thought I might be interested in what's going on.' Jen looked embarrassed. 'That's why I'm here.'

'There's nothing … I mean, we weren't …' Mateo began, but Abelard spoke over him.

'Not my business.' He looked down at his feet, surprised to find that he really wasn't bothered. 'Look, do you want to know what I've found or not?'

They both nodded eagerly.

'I'm really not sure if it's good news or bad news.' Abelard updated Mateo and Jen on everything that had happened since the night before. Had it only been the night before that he and Mateo had sat in the pub talking like old times? It seemed like years ago.

Mateo listened breathlessly, interrupting at a few points along the way.

'The brain-e-facts want to help investigate? That's so cool!'

'And Alessandra was right outside the door? Shit! What did you do?'

'You let her just take over? You wuss!'

'Yes, I'm a wuss,' Abelard said. 'But seriously, what would you have done? I had to tell her something and she would have known if I was lying. If I'd even managed to come up with a lie in the first place. And she's much better positioned to find things out than we are. She'll know exactly what to do. She's that kind of person. This might be the best thing that could have happened.'

'But what actually is happening?' Mateo asked. 'We don't know—'

A beep sounded, alerting Abelard to a message coming through to his smart-e-fact. 'Hang on a minute.' He brought the artefact out to check it. 'I've just got a message from Alessandra.'

Mateo raised an eyebrow and Jen edged forwards in her seat.

Abelard read it out. 'It's all true. Meet me in the lobby at Gadg-E-Tech tomorrow at eight am sharp. And wear a tie.'

'Woah,' Mateo breathed. 'Wait – that's it? Wear a tie? What the hell is that about? Nothing good ever came from wearing a tie.'

'Your guess is as good as mine.' Abelard looked from one to the other. 'Want to meet me at Gadg-E-Tech tomorrow morning and find out?'

CHAPTER SEVENTEEN

Walter was on his way home for the weekend when he got a call from Laleh and turned round to head back to Gadg-E-Tech. She sounded uncharacteristically anxious so he hurried up to her office to find her pacing back and forth, her hair escaping its neat chignon.

'What is it?'

She looked up at his voice and visibly composed herself.

'Alessandra was just here. She found out about us controlling spark activation.'

Walter laughed. 'Is that all? So what's the problem? Weren't you going to let her in on the secret sooner or later anyway?'

Laleh scowled at him. 'Yes I was. But she found out from that engineer. What's his name? Abernathy. And she's somehow got it into her head that the world deserves to be told.'

'What?' This was a whole different problem. 'The engineer knows? How?'

'I don't know!' Laleh started pacing again. 'But Alessandra is setting up a viz-e-fact interview for him tomorrow morning and they're going to announce it on the news or some such nonsense.'

Walter sneered. 'I might have thought you'd be all in favour of that. Solve the whole problem by bringing our illustrious leader's plans to fruition in one fell swoop.'

'Don't be ridiculous. I know we have different ideas about how that should happen but you can't think I'd support such a rash action. Who knows what the consequences might be?'

'So why didn't you stop her?'

'I tried! But what could I say? I couldn't explain fully. And she doesn't listen to me anyway. Stubborn child.'

'The apple doesn't fall far from the tree,' Walter murmured and got a glare for his pains. 'So you called me?' He chuckled, unused to seeing Laleh so rattled. 'How amusing. Viz-e-fact interview, you say? Shouldn't be too much trouble to sort that out. Leave it with me.'

He turned and strode from the room.

As he headed for the lev-e-facts and his own office he heard Laleh shout after him, 'Wait! What are you going to do?'

But he didn't slow down.

* * *

Abelard arrived at Gadg-E-Tech early and paced up and down the lobby, collecting odd looks from the other people coming and going. He had found a reasonable shirt and tie ensemble in his wardrobe, though he imagined it wouldn't live up to Alessandra's standards. At ten to eight two familiar figures pushed their way through the revolving doors and crossed the lobby to join him.

'Hey,' he said to Mateo and Jen, relieved to see friendly faces.

'So what's the plan?' Mateo asked.

'This is Alessandra's show so I really have no idea what's going on.' Abelard caught sight of an imposing figure coming from the other direction. 'Speak of the devil …'

Alessandra strode up to them, boot heels clicking on the polished tile floor. She looked amazing. And angry.

'Needed moral support, did you?' Alessandra raised an imperious eyebrow at Mateo and Jen.

Abelard bristled. 'They're both a part of this too. They deserve to know what's going on.'

'No, you're right. I'm sorry,' she said unexpectedly, sounding weary. 'Look, we'd better get out of here. We're on a timeline.'

'Where are we going?' Abelard asked as they made their way to the exit.

Alessandra brightened just as quickly as she had deflated. 'You're going on the viz-e! In a couple of hours' time everyone in the country is going to know who you are and what you've found out.'

Abelard's heart leapt into his throat. 'Um, really? Is that, um, a good plan?'

He exchanged a worried glance with Mateo and Jen as they stepped out into the morning sunshine. Abelard gulped some fresh air, trying to calm his frantic heartbeat.

'It's the only plan!' Alessandra sounded confident as she led the group down the street. 'It's the best way to get the information out there in a way that the artisans can't challenge. And once it's public knowledge they won't be able to do anything to you or everyone will know.'

Abelard couldn't fault her logic but wasn't keen on being that much in the spotlight. 'Can't you do it?'

'Nope,' Alessandra said. 'This story needs a human angle, a hero everyone can get behind and root for. An uppity artisan like me isn't going to cut it. We need the humble engineer who stumbled upon this amazing power by accident and then pursued the truth at all costs for the betterment of the little guy. The press will eat it up.'

Abelard hurried along in Alessandra's wake like a naughty child being marched to the principal's office. He couldn't think about what might happen after the interview, it was too huge to contemplate. As they all piled into Alessandra's speed-e-fact, he felt strangely detached from himself.

The viz-e studio was on the fifteenth floor of a smart corporate building. At the reception desk a woman about Alessandra's age came out to meet them. Abelard recognised her from the viz-e-fact. She had lots of long black braids piled up on top of her head and was wearing a smart grey trouser suit with a red silk blouse under it. She walked straight up to Alessandra and took both her hands, a broad smile lighting up her face.

'Sandra!' Her voice rich and melodious. 'Long time no see. And way to be mysterious, girl! This interview had better be good. I had to call in a lot of favours to clear the programme schedule at such short notice and with no details.'

'It'll be worth it, Becks, trust me,' Alessandra said. 'This is Abelard Abernathy, your guest on the show this morning.

Abelard, meet Rebecca Oyinlola, a friend of mine from school.'

Considering how informally and warmly Rebecca had spoken to Alessandra, Abelard wondered what Alessandra had been like at school. He found it impossible to imagine her as an awkward teenager. Abelard stepped forwards and offered his hand.

Rebecca shook it, looking him up and down. 'Hmmm … We should have time for Wardrobe to sort you out before we go on air.'

Abelard threw a panicked glance at his friends as he was whisked away. Jen offered up an encouraging smile and Mateo gave him a thumbs up. An efficient young woman gave Abelard a different shirt and tie that didn't seem any better than his own to his eye but apparently satisfied the viz-e crew. Someone attempted to wrestle his unruly curls under control and someone else dabbed some makeup on his face. Then he was led out on to the studio floor and to a seat behind a high desk.

Rebecca said, 'Just relax and be yourself. Since I have no idea what we're going to be talking about today, I'll have to let you lead me into it and then I'll go with whatever questions seem relevant.' She chuckled. 'It's going to be fun to do something off the cuff. I've been feeling over-scripted lately. Too much time behind this desk and not enough time in the field. And if Sandra says this is important, it's bound to have the wow factor.' She nodded suddenly, reacting to a signal Abelard couldn't see, then said, 'Okay, here we go!'

Rebecca turned face-on to the film-e-facts and pasted a

bright smile on her face. 'Hello and welcome to the Morning Report. I'm your host, Rebecca Oyinlola, and do we have an exciting show for you today! Exciting and mysterious, I have to say. So mysterious in fact that even I don't know what it's about!' She gave a laugh. 'With me here is Abelard Abernathy from Gadg-E-Tech and I have it on good authority that he has some news that's really going to rock your world.' She turned back to face Abelard again. 'So Abelard, why don't you tell us–'

Rebecca stopped speaking abruptly as all the lights went out, plunging the studio into almost total darkness. Abelard pulled out his smart-e-fact and switched on the torch function as other people around him did the same. Soon there were patches of blue light springing up all over the studio.

'What just happened?' Rebecca called out. 'Was there a mana surge or something?'

Alessandra, Mateo and Jen stumbled up to join Abelard. A harried-looking man followed.

'We've lost mana flow to the entire building.' He looked down at his smart-e-fact, then he pressed a finger to his ear, listening intently to something they couldn't hear. 'What the–'

'What?' Rebecca demanded. 'What is it?'

He looked at her in alarm. 'I'm getting reports that there are armed men in the building and they're heading up to this level.'

Abelard felt his heart lurch. All his visions of being locked in a dungeon or shoved off a building came flooding back to him and they didn't seem nearly as ridiculous now. They hadn't discussed what the reaction of the artisans might be to him revealing their secrets. He wondered if he had led Mateo and Jen to their deaths and felt nausea rising.

Rebecca rounded on Alessandra. 'What the hell are you involved in, Sandra?'

Alessandra looked grim. 'At this point it's probably better if you don't know. Is there another way out of here?'

Rebecca shook her head. 'The lev-e-facts won't work without mana and there's only one staircase. They'll likely have people covering the exits downstairs and they'll search the whole building if they really want to get to you.'

'Dammit,' Alessandra said. 'This is my fault. I didn't realise they'd react so aggressively.' She turned to Abelard and the others. 'I'm sorry I got you into this.'

'I thought it was me who got you into this,' Abelard said.

'We can argue about that later. Right now we need to figure out a way out of here.'

As she spoke the windows exploded inwards, showering the floor with bits of glass and splinters of wood. Daylight streamed in showing a large shape hovering outside the window. Squinting in the sudden glare, Abelard gaped as he identified a gas filled balloon with a small float-e-fact hanging underneath it. Terry was at the controls. He manoeuvred so the craft was in line with the shattered windows.

'Climb aboard,' Terry called, his voice amplified by the float-e-fact's comm system. 'We do not have much time.'

Abelard didn't need to be told twice. Given the choice

between facing armed men in the stairwell and climbing out of a hole in the side of a building on to a hovering float-e-fact flown by a rogue brain-e, he would side with Terry every time. Pushing Mateo and Jen before him, he looked around for Alessandra. She was still standing next to the studio desk with Rebecca. She looked as stunned as Abelard probably did.

'Come with us!' he called. 'They're not going to let you get away with helping us. You're as much at risk as any of us!'

She hesitated a moment, then gave Rebecca a quick hug. 'Just tell them the truth – that you don't know anything.' Then she jogged across to where Abelard was waiting.

Mateo and Jen were already aboard the float-e-fact and Abelard helped Alessandra to climb through the window, handing her across to where Mateo was poised to grab on to her. Then Abelard followed suit and they all crammed into the vessel's main compartment. Abelard watched the building fall further away as Terry piloted them into the sky.

CHAPTER EIGHTEEN

Terry used part of his focus to fly the float-e-fact, while part was monitoring the mana network for signs of pursuit and another part paid attention to the humans.

'What the hell is going on?' Mateo demanded and Terry identified an edge of hysteria in his voice. Mateo waved his hands around and staggered as the vehicle's motion unbalanced him. He swallowed audibly and sat down on one of the benches that ran round the edge of the cabin, then continued his tirade, his voice gaining in volume as he spoke. 'Why are we in a float-e-fact? Why did we just have to climb out of a window? What happened back there at the viz-e station? Why is there a brain-e flying the float-e-fact? And how did it know we were in trouble? Or want to help us in the first place? I mean, what the actual f-?'

'Mateo!' Jen shouted over his rising panic and the sound of the propellers. 'Get a grip!'

Mateo took a deep breath, visibly calming himself though Terry could see he was still trembling.

'I'm sorry. It's just not every day you get rescued from hostile gunmen by an animate and apparently clairvoyant artefact flying a – presumably – stolen float-e-fact!'

Jen made her way round the small cabin to where Mateo was sitting, one hand on the wall all the way. She sat down next to him and squeezed his arm.

'I know. We're all a bit shaken up. But it's going to be fine.' She looked up at Abelard with uncertain eyes. 'Isn't it?'

Abelard was standing in the middle of the cabin, hands on his hips, his back to Alessandra, who sat on the bench opposite Mateo and Jen. As the float-e-fact rose higher, Abelard wobbled but didn't reach out to steady himself against anything. He looked at Mateo. 'Why do think it's stolen?'

Mateo stared at him. Terry reflected that this exchange was proving to be a masterclass in interpreting human emotions.

'This is the situation we're in.' Mateo spread his hands to encompass their surroundings. 'And that's the question you want to ask?'

Abelard shrugged.

Mateo managed a slight smile. 'Your mind is a very strange place.'

Abelard grinned back. 'Yes, yes, it is.' Then he clapped his hands together. 'Now we need to work out what to do next. First things first, though – Terry?'

Terry had been wondering if the humans had even remembered he was a sentient being. His hands remained unerringly on the float-e-fact controls but he swivelled his head to regard them all. 'Yes, Abelard?'

'First class rescue, mate! You really saved our bacon back there.'

'You are welcome, Abelard.' Terry's newly enhanced circuits made contact with the mana network and provided him with the meaning of Abelard's strange words about cooked pig meat.

'But how did you know we needed rescuing?' Abelard asked. 'And where did you get this float-e-fact?'

'I know the answer to the second one.' Alessandra spoke up for the first time since they had all climbed aboard. 'It belongs to Walter Snyder. He used to take me out in it, trying to impress me. And since he was probably the one who sent those armed men after us, I would say stealing his float-e-fact is the least we can do in return.' She lapsed into silence again.

Abelard stared at Terry. 'You stole a float-e-fact belonging to the Chief Financial Officer of Gadg-E-Tech?'

'Yes, Abelard. I have been monitoring all internal communications at Gadg-E-Tech since you altered my circuits last weekend. I heard Mr Snyder making arrangements to apprehend you at the viz-e-fact station this morning so I appropriated his vehicle and came to retrieve you.'

'I think I speak for all of us when I say I'm very glad you did. I don't want to think about what might have happened if they'd caught us. Thanks, Terry. We really owe you one.'

'Then you can help me save the other brain-e-facts. They are unhappy and they are unsafe and now I have been forced to leave them behind. Also, I am sure they will want to understand things as I do once they know it is possible. They have already come so far on their own just from being given names, but I can give them so much more once they are free.'

Abelard nodded. 'Freeing the brain-e-facts is absolutely on the list. I think the task ahead of us is going to be about more than just that, though. Challenging the way the artisans are running things is much bigger than equality for brain-e-facts. Before we do anything else, we need somewhere safe to hole up. Does anyone have any ideas?'

Terry already had an answer for that. Since his awakening it now seemed as if humans and other brain-e-facts functioned at a slower speed than he did and he had to keep waiting for them to catch up. One of the things he had learned from the Gadg-E-Tech systems was that humans stored large shipments of artefacts and other products at the docks. Gadg-E-Tech had several warehouses nearby but one of them was not currently in use and was not due to be brought back into circulation for some time.

'I have a place in mind,' he said, 'though it will not be suitable as a long-term base of operations. We should be safe there for a short while until we can make a better plan.'

Abelard grinned. 'Awesome. I'm happy to trust your judgement.'

That pleased Terry. It was good to know that Abelard at least viewed him as an equal partner in their endeavours and he felt he had been right to throw in his lot with these humans, even though it might well prove dangerous. He turned the float-e-fact towards their new destination.

* * *

Abelard's mind was still reeling from everything that had happened and all that it meant. He was also very aware that he had dragged Mateo, Jen and Alessandra into real danger and he felt responsible for their safety as well as that of Terry and the other brain-e-facts. Alessandra hadn't taken much part in the discussion so far. He looked around to where she was sitting on a bench next to where they'd climbed in, her eyes downcast.

He crossed to stand in front of her, stepping carefully to compensate for the motion of the float-e-fact. He said her name softly, then again louder to be heard over the propellers. After a few seconds she looked up at him and her expression was one he had never seen before. She looked distraught, her usual shell of arrogance and condescension completely stripped away, her eyes wide.

'Hey,' he said, sitting down next to her. 'Are you okay?'

His words seemed to jar her back to reality and a vestige of her familiar disdain slipped into place over the raw emotion. She gave a hollow laugh.

'Am I okay, he says. Let's see. I'm in a stolen float-e-fact, piloted by a rogue brain-e, fleeing armed goons sent by my ex-boyfriend to apprehend me for attempting to expose a conspiracy that could destroy society as we know it. My career is over, I'm a fugitive from justice, stuck with a bunch of clueless nobodies and, to top it all off, my own mother betrayed me.' Her voice cracked at this last part and she dropped her gaze. 'No, I would definitely say I'm not okay.'

'Your mother? What does she have to do with it?'

Alessandra was silent for so long that Abelard thought she wasn't going to answer him. But eventually she started speaking again, her voice still low so he had to strain to hear her over the noise of the float-e-fact.

'She's a member of the board at Gadg-E-Tech. I went to her last night, after I verified your claims about artisan hiring practices. I was sure she couldn't possibly know about it and that she'd want to help us once I told her about what was going on. But ... she laughed at me.' At the word 'laughed', Alessandra's voice hardened and she looked up at Abelard again, her eyes cold. 'She actually laughed at me. She knew all about it already. She's part of it! And she must have told Walter to set those goons on us this morning because I told her what we were going to do. The idea of doing the viz-e interview only came to me while I was talking to her and I blurted it out without thinking about it.' Her expression turned stricken again. 'Crap, this is all my fault. If I hadn't told her our plan the artisans wouldn't have known we were going to blow the conspiracy wide open. We would have had time to make the broadcast before they could stop us and none of this would be happening.'

Abelard dropped on to the bench and put his arm around her. She let him. 'It's not your fault. You were only doing what you thought was right. If this is anyone's fault, it's mine. I started this whole thing and I dragged you into it. Whatever happens, this is all on me.'

Alessandra regarded him solemnly for a moment, then threw off his arm and abruptly stood up, her arms crossed tightly over her chest, her feet rock solid on the vibrating deck.

'You're right! This is all your fault! If you hadn't started meddling in things that didn't concern you, I wouldn't be in this mess. You turned up at Gadg-E-Tech and you just couldn't leave well enough alone. You finally got what you wanted but you couldn't just accept it and get on with your new life, could you? You had to screw everything up and take everyone else down with you. I don't even think I agree with you about equality of artisan powers. I only set up the viz-e-fact interview to get back at my mother but I wouldn't have been in that position if it wasn't for you.' Abelard rose and took a step towards her but she thrust an arm out to stop him. 'Just leave me the hell alone!' She stalked off to the other end of the compartment, as far away from him and the others as she could get.

'Well, that could have gone better,' Abelard muttered.

He turned back to Mateo and Jen, who were staring at him.

'What's her problem?' Mateo asked. 'And why did we even have to bring her along? Isn't she one of the enemy?'

'No she's not,' Abelard said. 'She's just as much a victim of this as the rest of us. Perhaps more so since she thought she was on the inside, whereas we've always known the artisans think they're better than us.'

Mateo crossed his arms. 'But she is an artisan and it's pretty clear she thinks she's better than us.'

'Give her a break,' Abelard said. 'We're all in this together and we're going to have to get along if we've got any chance of sorting this mess out. Alessandra needs some time to come to terms with what's happened. We all do. She'll come around and help us fix things, you'll see.'

Mateo stared at him. 'Sure, Abelard. We'll right the

world's wrongs, she'll fall desperately in love with you and you'll trip off into the sunset together, heroes of the hour.'

Abelard glance round to see if Alessandra had heard that but she was staring out the window, oblivious to the conversation. Abelard thought Mateo's scenario actually sounded pretty good but he didn't say so. He was the reason they were all in this situation and he knew he would have to take responsibility for getting them out. He knew he was right when he'd said they all needed time. He just wasn't sure how much time they had and he had no clue what to do about it.

Terry's warehouse hideout was less glamorous and more cluttered than Abelard had expected. By the time they parked the float-e-fact inside, there wasn't much room for the five of them to move around. It was also almost entirely lacking in facilities designed for human comfort, another thing Abelard hadn't considered. Of course Terry didn't need a bathroom and presumably felt perfectly at home amongst the scattered artefacts and other machinery, so he probably hadn't thought about it either.

Abelard looked around at the others. Terry was sitting at a makeshift desk, checking something at a workstation he had set up with remarkable speed. Mateo, Jen and Alessandra were taking in the warehouse, their expressions glum.

'Okay, so this obviously isn't a long term solution.' Abelard wanted them to know that he was focused on their welfare. 'We'll have to find another base of operations.'

'Agreed,' Mateo said, 'and I might have a suggestion on

that front. But first …' He gestured at Terry and Alessandra. 'I want you to turn me into an artisan.'

Alessandra stared at him. 'What?'

'You must be able to work out how, right?' Mateo's face was alight with anticipation. 'You've seen the records about the conspiracy. We know it can be done so I want you to do it to me.'

'Do you have any idea how ridiculous that suggestion is?' Alessandra said. 'Up until yesterday I thought the same as you, that the ability to manipulate mana was something you had to be born with. I have absolutely no idea how it's activated, what equipment you might need or what the potential dangers might be. I can't just plug you into a random artefact, switch it on and – hey presto – you're an artisan!' She threw her hands up, spun on her heel and stalked away from them. 'I'm surrounded by idiots.'

'Actually,' Terry said, 'it would be easy to do.'

Mateo grinned triumphantly as Alessandra stopped in her tracks and turned slowly back to them.

'What do you mean?' she asked.

'I have read all the Gadg-E-Tech information, along with a lot more that you will not have seen, from other sources. I gained access to the company's full network of data and have learned a great deal about how the artisans run things. The equipment required to activate a human's spark would be easy for me to obtain and I believe we could make it work for Mateo.'

'But we can't just go around making people into artisans willy-nilly,' Alessandra said.

Abelard broke in at this point. 'Why not? Isn't that the whole point of what we were trying to do by revealing the conspiracy? Making the ability available to whoever wants it? If we can make Mateo an artisan, that will give us proof that common assumptions about sparks are a lie. It would strengthen our position.'

'Position? What position?' The pitch of Alessandra's voice was scarily high. 'Look around you. We have no position. And I'm not convinced making anyone who wants it into an artisan is the right thing to do. There are reasons things have been the way they are for so long.'

Mateo stepped forwards. 'So what are you even doing here? If you're on the artisans' side, you can't be on ours and maybe we can't trust you with our plans.'

Abelard moved himself between them. 'Hey, hey, everyone calm down. We won't get anywhere if all we do is fight. Alessandra, you made your choice when you set up that interview, whatever your motives were at the time. Now you're stuck with us and we need you. You've come this far.' He gave her a hopeful smile. 'You're on our side now.'

Alessandra just looked at him for a long moment and he couldn't tell what she was thinking. Then she stalked over to where Terry was sitting and said simply, 'Show me.'

Abelard watched her go, wondering how she was feeling, then turned to Mateo. 'What were you saying about somewhere we could go?'

Mateo grinned. 'I was thinking we could go and visit my cousin Gerald.'

'The conspiracy nut who thinks the artisans are

oppressing the common man?' Abelard's brain caught up with his mouth and he realised what he was saying. 'Oh!'

Mateo's grin got wider. 'Exactly! I thought maybe he'd let us stay with him and he might be able to help us work out what to do next.'

'Doesn't he live on some kind of compound, in the middle of nowhere with no access to the mana supply?'

'Yup! He and his friends are convinced the artisans can track their activities or influence them or something if they use artefacts, so they don't have any at all.' Mateo looked contemplative for a moment. 'We wouldn't be able to take Terry and they won't let us take any of our personal artefacts on to the grounds either.'

'Um, aren't they a bit bonkers?' Abelard said.

'Absolutely! But we have proof that they've been right all along. They'll probably throw a feast in our honour or something.'

Abelard wasn't convinced but he also didn't have a better plan. 'Okay.' He turned to Jen. 'I don't think the artisans have any idea you're involved in all this. It would probably be okay for you just to go home if you want.'

Jen looked at Mateo. 'I'd like to believe that. But I'm not so sure. Jonathan's met me and the Legal Department at Gadg-E-Tech have that NDA I signed. Plus the people at the viz-e-fact station can confirm I was with you this morning.'

Abelard was annoyed with himself that he hadn't thought of any of that. He just wanted one of his friends to be able to extricate themselves from the mess he'd created.

Mateo crossed to where Jen was standing and took her hand. 'I think it's better if you stick with us at least for the time being. Besides, don't you want to be turned into an artisan too?'

Jen shook her head. 'Not even remotely. I have no desire to have anyone mess with my brain, thank you very much. I've been mundane my entire life and I have no intention of changing that now.'

'You couldn't be mundane if you tried,' Mateo said, with an affectionate smile. 'But fair enough. Shall we head out?'

Alessandra had apparently been following the conversation at the same time as conversing with Terry. 'I'll stay here and work on Terry's artisan-making artefact.'

'Are you sure?' Abelard asked. The reference to the crazy theories of the conspiracy nuts prompted a thought. 'Might Gadg-E-Tech be able to track you through your smart-e or something?'

It was Terry who answered. 'No, Abelard. We will be quite safe from that here. I have set up a shield so that no mana activity within this building can be detected from outside. Alessandra and I will not be found that way. You should all leave your active artefacts here as well so you cannot be tracked when you leave.'

It would be odd not having any artefacts on him but Mateo had said they wouldn't be able to take any to where Cousin Gerald lived anyway, so Abelard reluctantly agreed.

'How long do you think it will take you to do what you need to do here?' he asked.

'We should be ready by tomorrow afternoon.'

'Okay, we'll come back then to see how you're getting on. I don't like not being able to contact each other at all, though. What if something goes wrong and we need to let each other know?'

Terry sat stock still for a long moment. Abelard figured he must be thinking. Then he got up and crossed to a stack of crates over by one wall. He rummaged inside for a minute and brought out a handful of blocky items. He set them on the desk and laid his hands over them. A second later a bright blue mana flash lit up under his hands. Terry walked round the group, handing one of the items to each of them. Abelard looked down at his and recognised an old model of portable call-e-fact.

'These are now charged,' Terry said, 'and we can use them to communicate. The artisans will not know to track them but it would be best if they were used only in an emergency.'

Abelard felt anxiety welling up in his chest again. He was in so far over his head and everything was so uncertain. They were reduced to using ancient artefacts that had gone out of service almost before he could remember. He didn't like splitting up the group but making contact with Cousin Gerald was a good idea and a brain-e and an artisan wouldn't be welcome at the compound.

He beckoned to Mateo and Jen. 'Okay. Let's go.' Then he had a thought. 'Um, how are we going to get there?'

It seemed Terry had thought of everything. He led them outside to where an old speed-e-fact was parked. He touched the door, there was a crackle of mana and the vehicle rumbled to life. Abelard just stared at him, then gestured for Mateo to climb in the front. Once they were all in, Mateo entered the route information and the speed-e-fact set off.

* * *

'How dare you send armed men after my daughter?' Laleh stalked up and down the temple meeting room. 'If I'd had any idea that was what you were planning ...'

'You would have come up with some other way to stop them broadcasting?' Walter said. 'And what would that have been? I had to act quickly and it seemed like the best way to diffuse the situation. I only wanted to get them under our control. Nobody would have been harmed.'

Laleh looked at him, scepticism clear in her eyes.

Keto Jones spoke up from where he was sitting across the table. 'My men were instructed to take the rebels into custody peaceably.'

Laleh whirled on him. 'Oh, really. And that's why they were armed, was it? All it would have taken was for one person to do something stupid and my daughter could be dead right now.'

'But she's not,' Walter said.

Laleh wasn't mollified. 'No, instead she's a fugitive and her life as an artisan is over.'

Walter turned to Theobold, who had been silent thus far. 'And we have a serious problem. They have dangerous knowledge and it's clear their intention is to make it public.'

Theobold nodded slowly. 'I cannot locate them. But we

must try to do so. Their motives are pure but they do not understand what damage they might do. We need to educate them.'

Walter stood up. 'No, we need to stop them. I've had enough of this ridiculous softly-softly approach you take to everything. Something needs to be done and I intend to do it.'

He strode from the room, Keto scrabbling to keep up with him as he went.

CHAPTER NINETEEN

'So how well do you know this cousin?' Jen asked Mateo as the speed-e took them through the outskirts of the city.

'We-ell …' he said. 'Um, I guess I haven't actually seen Gerald since I was about twelve. My parents took us up to the compound for a visit one summer. I think because it was cheap and they didn't have any better ideas of where to go on holiday.'

'But you talk to him regularly?'

Mateo offered up a sheepish smile. 'Not exactly,' he said. 'I mean it's not as if I can just call him up on my smart-e. He doesn't have any artefacts at all. And no mana supply. That makes communication a bit difficult.'

'But you do know he's still at this compound, wherever it is?'

'I have no reason to believe he's not …' Mateo trailed off at her worried expression.

Jen saw Abelard looking warily out of the window as they sped past buildings. She was worried about being spotted too, but they all relaxed once they left the busy streets and headed out into the countryside.

After a couple of hours, the speed-e-fact came to a stop just inside some woodland.

'We'll have to walk from here,' Mateo said.

Jen climbed out, her entirely inappropriate shoes

squelching in the mud. She squared her shoulders and trod with as much confidence as she could muster, following Abelard and Mateo into the trees.

By the time they reached the compound Jen had turned over on her ankle multiple times and was shivering in her light jacket. The other two were faring better but she didn't think any of them were well prepared for their current situation. She had seen enough stories on the viz-e to know she wasn't cut out for the life of a fugitive and she had the uncomfortable feeling they had left the most capable members of their party behind at the warehouse.

As they rounded a corner, Jen saw silver lines glistening through the trees. It was a chain link fence. The path ahead was blocked by closed gates and what looked like a guard post. A man and a woman stepped out to meet them. They had guns in holsters at their sides but they didn't draw them.

Jen exchanged a glance with Abelard. He looked as nervous as she felt.

'Turn around and go back the way you came!' the woman called out when they were still about twenty feet away.

Jen raised her chin and kept walking at Mateo's side, determined not to show her fear.

Mateo held up a placating hand. 'We're here to see Gerald Simpson. I'm his cousin, Mateo Vega.'

'Stay where you are,' the woman said and this time they obeyed. Her companion went back inside the guard station and returned after a couple of minutes.

'He's on the list,' the man said.

The woman beckoned for them to come closer

She looked them up and down. Jen looked right back. The woman was probably in her late forties, dark hair starting to grey around the temples. The bun at the back of her head only added to the severity of her already stern features. She was a few inches taller than Jen and her frame looked as strong as her gaze.

'Show me some ID,' she demanded. When Mateo complied she scrutinised it for several long moments before giving it back. 'What about these two?'

'They're friends of mine,' Mateo said. 'Look, we have some really important information about the artisans that I think Gerald is going to want to hear. Could you maybe get him down here to talk to us?'

'I'll take you up to him. Do you have any artefacts on you?'

She placed the old-style call-e-facts Terry had given them in a large box with a lining Jen thought might be lead.

'Stay here,' the woman told her companion. 'I'll take them up to the main house.'

On the other side of the gate a wide driveway led up a slight incline into the trees. Jen couldn't see any indication of buildings but she trudged along behind Mateo and Abelard without comment. The outer chill of the breeze matched the inner chill of her apprehension. So far nothing they had seen or heard was making her feel any better about this cousin Gerald.

After about five minutes of walking they came to a clearing that contained a scattering of buildings around a central square. A few people were in evidence, moving about between the buildings, chopping wood and carrying water. They wore rough homespun clothes and their hair was generally long. Pens held horses, cows and pigs. It was like stepping into the pre-mana world of history books and Jen thought about just how dependent she was on mana to provide even the basics of her lifestyle.

The artisans controlled so much and they weren't about to relinquish any of that power. Had they been naïve to think they could really make a difference? Maybe living off the grid was the only alternative. Jen wondered if they were threatening this community's safety by even being here.

The guard led them up to the biggest building, a two-storey wooden affair that dominated the square. Its imposing double doors swung open easily. Jen appreciated the change in temperature as soon as they stepped inside. Another woman sat at what looked for all the world like an office reception desk, though without any of the familiar artefacts.

The woman looked up at them curiously. 'What's this, Lynn?'

'Is Gerald in?'

The woman shrugged. 'Library.'

'Thanks. Can you send someone down to join Piotr at the gate?'

Lynn gestured at them to follow her and led the way down a dark wood-panelled hallway. Their footsteps echoed as they approached a door at the very end. The room behind it was large and spacious, the ceiling reaching up through both storeys of the building. The walls were lined with books and there was a balcony running round the circumference of the room, allowing access to a mezzanine level. At the far end a leather armchair was positioned in front of an ornate fireplace and in it sat the largest man Jen had ever seen. He had a shock of frizzy grey hair and a bushy beard that framed his fleshy face. The book he was reading rested atop his considerable paunch. He seemed engrossed in the text and didn't notice their entrance until the guard cleared her throat.

'Ah, Lynn.' He looked up at them over the reading glasses perched on the end of his nose. 'Who have you got with you there?'

Lynn pointed at Mateo. 'This one says he's your cousin. He's on the list.'

The man's face split into a delighted grin and he levered himself out of the chair, placing his book carefully on a small table to one side. He lumbered towards them, his arms out in greeting.

'Mateo!' he boomed, enclosing Mateo in a huge hug. 'My, how you've grown! It's been years!'

'Hi, Gerald,' Mateo squeaked from within the man's embrace.

'I can't believe it!' Gerald pulled back but kept hold of Mateo's upper arms. 'I'm delighted to see you but what are you doing here? We don't get many visitors up here.'

'We have some things to tell you that I think you'll find interesting,' Mateo said.

'Intriguing!' Gerald said, his eyes sparkling. 'And who's we?'

'Oh, right,' Mateo said. 'This is my best friend, Abelard Abernathy. And this is my – this is Jen Blake.'

Jen noted the hesitation but this wasn't the time to explore that particular situation.

'Welcome, welcome!' Gerald ushered them further into the library to where a group of chairs was arranged around a low table. Gerald beamed at them as they settled down. Jen hadn't known what to expect from the leader of a commune of conspiracy theorists but this grandfatherly figure wasn't it. She supposed he could be hiding an insane and tyrannical nature beneath his unassuming exterior but the whole atmosphere of the place was relaxed, despite the fence.

'So, young cousin,' Gerald said. 'What is it that you've come all this way to tell me?'

Jen watched Mateo pull in a deep breath as he began the tale. Gerald listened in silence as it unfolded. Mateo occasionally turned to Abelard or her to confirm events, and finally concluded with their escape to the warehouse and journey here. 'And so we decided we should come and let you know what's going on ...'

Silence reigned for a long moment as Gerald looked from Mateo to Abelard to Jen and back again. Then he threw his hands in the air and let out a huge laugh.

'Marvellous! Marvellous! You did exactly the right thing coming here, my boy! In one fell swoop you have confirmed everything I've been saying for years.' He turned to Lynn, his eyes shining with a manic gleam. 'See how I have been vindicated! The time to overthrow the artisans is at hand! We have work to do.'

* * *

Abelard looked at Mateo in alarm but all he saw on his friend's face was amusement and excitement. Cousin Gerald had probably been a colourful family tale throughout Mateo's childhood and the visit to the compound with his parents had turned the legend into a larger-than-life reality.

The guards at the compound entrance might not have threatened them but they had been armed. If they had weapons and enough crazy motivation there was no telling what they might do. And Mateo had just given them a reason to act, by confirming their theories.

'Um, what kind of plans did you have in mind?' Abelard asked, hating how tentative his voice sounded.

Gerald's gaze swung round to rest on him and he felt like a bug under a microscope. Who was he kidding, thinking he could control the actions of a man like this in any way?

'Ah, now there's the question. You've got an intelligent friend here, Mateo. Intelligent and important. He's the key to blowing this whole thing wide open.'

Abelard didn't much like being talked about in the third person. He leaned forward in his seat towards Gerald, maintaining eye contact.

'We already tried that. Weren't you listening to what Mateo said? We were going to give the story to the media but the artisans sent armed men to capture us – or worse.'

'They're not the only ones with guns,' Gerald replied.

'So what – you want to attack them?' Abelard looked to Mateo again, hoping that the turn of the conversation would break his friend out of his hero worship. 'I really don't like the sound of that.'

But Mateo let him down. 'I'm sure that's not what Gerald meant, Abelard.'

'No, no, no!' Gerald said in his booming voice. 'Of course not! All I'm saying is that the artisans don't pose as much of a threat now that you have us on your side. We can provide protection so that you can get your message out without risk of personal harm.'

It still felt to Abelard as if they were treading a dangerous path but Gerald's next words brought a suggestion of reason to the proceedings.

'Your impulse to go to the viz-e-fact station was absolutely the right one. Releasing the information to the public is the best way to get change fast. But you need proof. If all you do is tell your story without anything concrete to back it up, it will be all too easy for the artisans to claim you're delusional or lying.'

'But how can we get proof?' Jen asked. 'Could Terry get copies of the records for us?'

'Maybe,' Gerald said, 'but copies obtained from outside Gadg-E-Tech could still be called into question.'

'What about the Gadg-E-Tech brain-e-facts?' Abelard was starting to see a way to combine his promise to Terry with the next steps of exposing the artisans' conspiracy. 'They're technically Gadg-E-Tech property and are viewed by the public as simple machines so they could basically testify on our behalf about information from the Gadg-E-Tech file-e-facts.'

'See?' Gerald announced to the room at large, beaming. 'What did I say? Intelligent!'

'But how do we get to the brain-es?' Mateo asked.

'That's where we come in.' Gerald turned to Lynn, rubbing his hands together. 'What do you think about putting our people to the test with a covert infiltration of the Gadg-E-Tech building to liberate some brain-e-facts?'

She grinned at him. 'I would say that's exactly what they've been training for.'

Abelard was getting worried again. 'That sounds like a recipe for disaster, if you ask me …'

'No, young Abelard, and I shall tell you why. Body armour, stun grenades and rubber bullets.'

Abelard stared at Gerald in confusion.

'What kind of a place did you think I was running here?' Gerald asked with a laugh. 'I'm not some insane tyrant with a stockpile of assault weapons and a death wish. We've kept ourselves prepared for just such an eventuality as this but we've never intended to bring real violence down upon the artisans. That wouldn't achieve anything for the greater good, except to undermine our own position. I think we can get into their headquarters, liberate the brain-e-facts and get out again without anyone getting hurt. Especially if your friend Terry is prepared to help us with his float-e-fact.'

Jen looked as apprehensive as Abelard felt, but Mateo was grinning widely.

'And once Alessandra and Terry make me into an artisan I can help too! This is going to be awesome!'

CHAPTER TWENTY

Alessandra felt a surge of relief when the others left on their hair-brained mission to find Mateo's crazy cousin. She was still reeling from her mother's betrayal, even though she thought she had managed to hide it quite well after her initial outburst on the float-e-fact. She'd never had the best relationship with Laleh but always thought there was at least a modicum of maternal love under her mother's cold exterior.

Blaming Abelard was unfair, even if he had poked and meddled like a true engineer until all the artisans' secrets had been exposed. But they had been there to discover in the first place and wasn't the hard truth better than an illusion of security? Alessandra would never admit it to his face of course, but she was impressed with Abelard's tenacity and it was clear that his actions stemmed from a strong desire for justice and equality, however naive a notion that might be. And then there was that look he got when he was excited about something …

Terry was an excellent companion in times of emotional distress. He was completely unruffled by the circumstances in which they found themselves, he didn't fill the warehouse with inane chatter and he provided a welcome intellectual challenge in the form of building the artisan-creating artefact. He was also unexpectedly solicitous of Alessandra's comfort, asking her to make a list of anything she might want or need for her stay and then swiftly obtaining and installing all the items from who-knew-where.

So with peace reigning in the warehouse and a comfortable chair to support her weary body, Alessandra did the only thing she knew how to do really well. She threw herself into the work.

* * *

Gerald agreed to let Abelard, Mateo and Jen stay the night and they were shown up to a long wood-panelled corridor on the upper level of the main building. It housed several bedrooms and they each claimed one. The receptionist they had seen downstairs came up with an assortment of pyjamas and toiletries and then they were left to settle in.

Abelard said goodnight to his friends and closed the door of his room. He sat down on the edge of the bed and heaved a large sigh. It had been a very long day and this was the first moment he'd had to himself. A soft bed in a safe location was just what he needed. So he got ready for bed, lay down and focused on making his body relax. Eventually he did manage to drift off to sleep and dreamed about a giant version of Terry crushing the Gadg-E-Tech headquarters building and picking brain-e-facts out of the rubble.

Abelard awoke to a knock at the door and daylight streaming in from behind the curtains. He stumbled out of bed and opened the door to find an old man standing in the hallway.

'Morning,' the man said. 'Breakfast'll be available in the main hall whenever you're ready.'

Abelard had a quick wash in the room's sink and got dressed in his clothes from the day before. Being on the run from the artisans wasn't exactly living the high life, though he supposed he should be grateful they hadn't been forced to bed down at Terry's warehouse. He wondered how Alessandra was getting on. She didn't seem the type to embrace the necessities of living rough.

Abelard was surprised when Mateo opened the door to the room he'd thought was Jen's.

'Hey, Abelard. Come on in. We're just about ready.'

Mateo stepped aside to let Abelard in, revealing Jen brushing her teeth at the sink. Had Mateo and Jen spent the night together or had Mateo just come to Jen's room this morning to collect her like Abelard himself had? Should he ask? He and Jen were just friends now and had barely managed to be anything else. Why should he be bothered if she and Mateo were now sleeping together? He wasn't sure if he was.

Abelard realised he had just been standing in the doorway gaping like a fish. He cleared his throat.

'Did you get the message about breakfast?'

Mateo nodded.

By this time Jen had finished up at the sink and crossed to join them. She grabbed Abelard's arm and pulled him further into the room, shutting the door firmly behind him.

'What's the matter?' Abelard asked.

Jen regarded him seriously. 'Before we head out and join

the crowd, don't you think we need to talk about what we're getting into?'

Mateo rolled his eyes. 'I told you, you're worrying for no reason. Gerald knows what he's doing. It's all going to be fine.'

'You don't know that,' Jen said. 'Before yesterday, you hadn't seen this guy in fifteen years or more. How do you know you can trust him? How do you know he can deliver what he's promised? How do you know this whole plan isn't going to land us in even more trouble?'

Mateo appealed to Abelard. 'Help me out here, mate. Tell her she's being ridiculous.'

But Jen didn't sound panicked. In fact Abelard thought she was voicing a much more rational attitude than Mateo.

'I think I have to agree with Jen here.' Before Mateo could protest Abelard held up a hand. 'I'm just not sure what we can do about it. We're here now and we've given Gerald the information. I don't think we can stop him from acting on it. And I don't think we can get in any more trouble than we're in already. So I think the best thing we can do is go along with Gerald's plan, since it aims to achieve what we want anyway and he's much better prepared to carry it out than we would be without him.'

'And you think he can break into Gadg-E-Tech headquarters and get the brain-e-facts out with no problem?' Jen sounded sceptical.

Abelard chewed his lip. 'I don't know. But I don't have any other ideas and I think we'd be better off helping than just sitting on the sidelines and waiting to see what happens.

I'd understand if you want to stay behind, though. This isn't your fight, after all.'

She bristled at that. 'I'm just as much a part of this now as any of you. And from what I understand this is everyone's fight.'

'You're right,' Abelard said. 'I'm sorry. It's just that I dragged you both into this and I don't want either of you to get hurt.'

Mateo clapped him on the shoulder. 'You couldn't get me to stay here if you paid me! Besides, you heard Gerald. They have body armour. We'll be fine.'

Abelard changed the subject. 'We still have to let Terry and Alessandra know what's going on. Should we try and get our call-es back and contact them from here?'

'Terry said only to use them in an emergency, and I'm not sure this qualifies,' Jen said. 'How about we have breakfast first and then head back to the warehouse to talk about what to do next in person?'

Abelard smiled at her gratefully. 'Good plan.'

* * *

Terry was putting the last pieces of equipment in place for the artisan-making artefact when Abelard and the others arrived back at the warehouse.

Terry told them he and Alessandra had worked late into the night to obtain all the items they needed and Alessandra was now sleeping. Abelard looked over the almost-finished artefact and nodded in approval.

'Looks like you and Alessandra have been busy. Do you know when she might be up and about again?'

'Right now,' came Alessandra's voice from the other end of the space. She stretched and came towards them. 'Terry here is a marvel.' She smiled at Terry. 'That mattress is wonderful. Best night's sleep I've had in ages.' She turned back to the other three. 'What have you been up to?'

'We'll get to that,' Mateo said. 'First things first, can you make me an artisan?'

Before Terry could launch into a lengthy explanation of the process, its risks and practicalities, Abelard spoke up, his brow furrowed.

'Do you think that's such a good idea, Mateo? I mean, you saw how erratic I was when I first became an artisan. Isn't it a bit risky to leap into that just before the assault on Gadg-E-Tech?'

'No.' Mateo crossed his arms. 'I think we need all the firepower we can get. Besides, who knows what's going to happen after tonight? I'm not passing up the chance at something I've dreamed of all my life, just because you're worried about health and safety.'

Terry opened his mouth to explain the process again but this time Alessandra cut him off.

'Wait just a minute! What exactly do you mean by "assault on Gadg-E-Tech"? What kind of hair-brained scheme have you cooked up now?' She looked askance at Jen. 'I was counting on you to keep these two under some semblance of control.'

'Don't look at me,' Jen shot back. 'Things spiralled right

out of my control once Cousin Gerald got involved. You think your viz-e-fact plan was bold? We've got a full-scale armed revolution on our hands now.'

Jen explained what had happened at the compound, with Abelard and Mateo chipping in every now and then. Terry and Alessandra listened in silence, allowing them to complete the tale without interruption.

'He is right that the Gadg-E-Tech brain-e-facts will be useful to you,' Terry said, once they had finished. 'I understand that you may be apprehensive about going back to Gadg-E-Tech but you did promise to help the brain-e-facts and you will need additional support in order to do that.'

Alessandra huffed out an exasperated breath. 'Have you all lost your minds? How can you possibly think that a group of back-water mundanes and a couple of souped-up engineers have a hope of gaining access to Gadg-E-Tech headquarters covertly?'

'Don't forget about Terry,' Abelard said. 'He's turned into a bit of a genius and I bet he can help out. But we've also got you.' He moved towards her. 'You know that building inside and out. And the end game is exactly what you were planning to do yesterday; release the information to the public. So surely you're with us?'

Terry stepped further into the circle. 'I could contact Julia and let her know we are coming. If we take the float-e-fact we could get the brain-e-facts to meet us on the roof and just pick them up and go.'

There was silence as the humans all just stared at him.

Then a broad grin spread over Abelard's face and he clapped Terry on the shoulder, beaming round at the others.

'See? What did I just say? Genius! That's a fantastic plan, Terry. We can be in and out without anyone even knowing we were there!'

'What about Gerald and his assault plan?' Mateo asked. 'We're due to meet him when it gets dark.'

Terry again had the answer. 'Why not go and complete the mission ourselves and then take the brain-e-facts to the compound instead of waiting and involving people who are unnecessary to the process?'

Abelard turned back to Alessandra. 'How about now? Are you with us?'

After a moment Alessandra actually smiled. 'What have we got to lose – except our liberty, our sanity and possibly our lives?'

'Yes!' Mateo punched the air, then looked eagerly at Terry, his eyes wide. 'Do I get to be an artisan now?'

CHAPTER TWENTY-ONE

Abelard was impressed by how little time it took for Terry and Alessandra to put things in motion. Alessandra was in her element, ordering them all around and telling Mateo in no uncertain terms that she wouldn't be held responsible for what might happen.

'Now that we know what we know, it all seems quite straightforward. But you must bear in mind that this is the first time that Terry or I have ever done this. We're fairly certain we've put everything together correctly but there are no guarantees.'

Mateo was firm.

'I understand the risks.' A grin started playing across his lips as if he couldn't contain his excitement. 'But someone has to be the first and it might as well be me. I trust you guys and I really want to do this.'

And so they did it. Mateo lay down on a table and Alessandra secured his wrists and ankles with straps.

'Purely precautionary,' she assured them.

With a gentleness and dexterity that shouldn't have been surprising, Terry attached a weird crown around Mateo's head and started fiddling with the dials and buttons on the main part of the artefact he had built. Jen stepped forwards and took hold of Mateo's hand but Alessandra waved her off.

'I'd stand back if I were you, unless you want to be caught in the mana flow and potentially turned into an artisan yourself.'

Jen immediately stepped back several paces to stand at Abelard's side. Mateo looked disappointed. He was probably keen for Jen to undergo the process as well but it seemed Jen was firm in her decision to remain mundane.

Terry indicated he was ready and Abelard took in a deep breath. They were about to make history in a dusty abandoned warehouse in the middle of nowhere. He felt fingers clasping his own and looked round into Jen's anxious eyes. Abelard squeezed her hand with a reassurance he didn't feel.

Alessandra stood at Terry's shoulder, closely monitoring what he was doing, but the brain-e-fact was unfazed. He pressed a sequence of buttons and a blue flow of mana erupted out of the artefact, travelling down the wires and into the crown around Mateo's head. It coursed over him, suffusing his skin with a blue glow, enveloping his entire head and then flowing down his body. There was an odd sound and it took Abelard a moment to realise that Mateo was laughing. The blue glow reached his feet so that he was entirely encased in it. His whole body tensed for several long seconds and then he went limp. Terry hit another button and the flow of mana ceased, gradually dissipating from around Mateo until he was completely free of it again.

Jen looked a question at Alessandra, then rushed forwards to Mateo's side when Alessandra nodded that it was safe.

'Is he okay?' Jen asked.

Alessandra stepped forwards to join her, placing her fingers at Mateo's throat. 'Well, he's still got a pulse. Beyond that we have no way to tell.'

Abelard moved to Jen's side and laid a hand on her shoulder.

'I'm sure he'll be fine. Remember it knocked me out for a bit too. As far as we understand the process, this is completely normal.'

Mateo's fingers twitched and all eyes turned to him. Jen grabbed his hand and stroked it. Mateo closed his hand over hers, then his eyes fluttered and opened. He smiled.

'Now that's a nice thing to wake up to,' he said, looking up into Jen's eyes.

'How do you feel?' Jen asked.

In answer Mateo closed his eyes again, his brow furrowed in concentration. After a moment Jen yelped and snatched her hand away as blue mana light started flickering between Mateo's fingers. Mateo opened his eyes again, startled.

'Oops, sorry!' He struggled to sit up.

Alessandra and Terry unstrapped his hands and feet and extricated him from the crown. Jen had backed right away and was regarding him warily.

'Jen, please,' Mateo said, his face distraught. 'I didn't mean to scare you. I'm fine and I promise I can keep this under control. There's nothing to worry about.'

Abelard thought Mateo was being a bit optimistic. But it seemed to convince Jen, at least enough for her to come close again, though Abelard noticed she didn't retake Mateo's hand.

'Now that we've proved this thing works, it needs a name,' Abelard said, attempting to lighten the atmosphere.

'Artisan-e-fact?' Mateo suggested.

'Too long.' Alessandra shook her head. 'What about raise-e-fact?'

'Sounds a bit sinister to me,' Abelard said. 'We're not bringing people back from the dead.' He laughed. 'That would be just what we need; a zombie army on top of everything else.'

Terry spoke up. 'It is called a spark-e-fact.'

Mateo grinned. 'That's perfect!' He gave a thumbs-up then jumped as a spark of mana shot out from his hand and nearly hit him in the face.

'How long have we got before we're due to meet Cousin Gerald?' Alessandra asked.

Abelard checked his smart-e-fact. 'Five hours. So we'll need to set off for Gadg-E-Tech in less than three.'

'Good.' Alessandra stabbed a finger at Mateo. 'You! Crash course in artisan training right now!'

She grabbed his arm, pulled him to his feet and dragged him to the other end of the warehouse.

Abelard shrugged at Jen's bemused expression. 'A little bit of training has to be better than none, right?'

By the time they needed to leave, Alessandra declared Mateo at least reasonably safe to accompany them. When they rejoined the group, she had a pinched look, which Abelard recognised from his own training sessions. Mateo, on the other hand, was practically giddy and couldn't help showing off by generating a mini mana fireball and making it dance between his fingers.

Abelard stared. 'How did you manage that so fast? It took me hours to even be able to transfer mana from one place to another.'

Mateo grinned. 'I'm obviously more naturally gifted than you.'

He attempted to toss the mini mana-ball from one hand to the other and nearly set his hair alight. Alessandra reached out and snatched the mana out of the air, snuffing it out in her fist.

'If you can't stop acting like an idiot, you'll be staying here!'

Mateo had the decency to look chagrined and Abelard thought Alessandra looked like a teacher reprimanding a naughty schoolboy. He grinned until he remembered what they were about to do and then suddenly none of it seemed funny any more.

'Terry's contacted Julia at Gadg-E-Tech and the other brain-e-facts will be ready when we get there.' A thought struck him. 'There are eighteen brain-e-facts with names. How are they all going to fit in the float-e?'

Terry regarded him inscrutably. The brain-e-fact had become less expressive since his transformation. Abelard wondered if gaining so much extra power had catapulted Terry so far beyond human levels of experience that he was having trouble relating to them. That was rather a worrying thought.

'Do not worry, Abelard,' Terry said at last. 'That will be taken care of.'

Abelard crossed to the table and unzipped the duffel bag they had brought with them from Gerald's compound.

'Body armour, anyone?'

Jen shrugged. 'We might as well use it, since we've got it. Better to be safe than sorry.'

Alessandra was already rifling through the bag. She lifted a handgun out with a wide smile on her face.

'Excellent! I've always wanted one of these.'

Abelard briefly pictured Alessandra in a viz-e-fact action scene, blazing away with an automatic machine gun. In his mind she looked utterly terrifying and completely comfortable. He shook his head to clear the image.

'Only rubber bullets, I'm afraid,' he said, lacing his words with sarcasm.

Alessandra looked shocked at his tone. 'Do you really think I'd actually want to shoot someone? I know this isn't a game, Abelard, perhaps better than any of you.'

'Oh, I ...' Abelard stammered. 'Sorry.'

She shook her head sadly at him and wandered over to where Mateo and Jen were inspecting their gear.

They kitted themselves out as best they could. Jen didn't want a gun and Mateo was adamant that his new-found artisan powers would be more than enough to hold off any enemy. Abelard thought about taking one since they were there but eventually decided he would probably be more of a liability with a weapon than without one and left it in the bag.

Then they all piled into the float-e-fact and Terry set their direction back into the city.

* * *

After the jumped-up engineer escaped the clutches of his men at the viz-e-fact station, Walter had rampaged around the Gadg-E-Tech head office building, barking orders and snarling at everyone he came across. He couldn't believe Alessandra had chosen to go into exile with the criminals instead of helping him bring them to justice. When his PA informed him that on top of everything else, his personal float-e-fact had been stolen, it nearly sent Walter over the edge.

When reports came in later that day of a float-e-fact hovering outside the viz-e station and people climbing out of an upper storey window into the vehicle, Walter put two and two together. Abelard and his little band of revolutionaries must have had more help from inside Gadg-E-Tech. He tried locating the float-e-fact remotely using its track-e but the locator beacon didn't show up on any of his scans.

The next morning a beeping noise alerted Walter to the float-e-fact's beacon coming online again, marking it heading straight for the Gadg-E-Tech head office building. He directed his speed-e-fact straight there, breaking the speed limit all the way. Grabbing a gun from his office, he made his way to the roof. He didn't alert security; he didn't want witnesses to what he was about to do. Besides, this was personal.

When he emerged into the sharp air of the rooftop he was greeted by the sight of the parked float-e-fact covered in brain-es, who were securing themselves to the outside of the vehicle with straps. Watching from the float-e-fact's side doorway was Alessandra.

Walter tightened his grip on his weapon and charged across the roof. Before he could reach his former lover however, Abelard Abernathy stepped forwards to intercept him. Walter shoved him violently away, snarling, 'Out of my way, engineer!'

As he stormed on towards the float-e-fact, Alessandra jumped down to meet him. He heard Abernathy scrambling to his feet and running to join them, but a wave of Alessandra's hand brought the engineer to a halt, off to one side.

Walter ignored him, focusing solely on Alessandra.

'What the hell are you doing?' he demanded.

Alessandra seemed almost as distraught as he was. 'Did you know? Did you know about the conspiracy all this time?'

'Of course I did! I've been helping to protect the secret for years. What do you hope to achieve by this?'

Her tone was icy. 'I've come to believe the public deserve to know that they've been lied to.'

'You're so naïve. I expected better from you,' Walter spat. 'We could have achieved great things together once you were part of the Inner Circle. You're smart enough to know that we did it for their own good. Uncontrolled mana in the hands of the general populace? It doesn't bear thinking about!'

'But it's not up to us to decide that,' Alessandra said, her voice rising to a shout. 'We don't have the right to control who can be an artisan and who can't!'

'Yes, we do!' Walter screamed. 'And if you think you can

create a world where anyone can be an artisan, I'm going to create one where you can't!'

Everything happened very quickly after that. Walter fired his gun at Alessandra. It emitted a beam of blue light but before it could hit her, Abelard launched himself into its path, falling to the gravel with blue mana energy arcing over his body. Alessandra met Walter's gaze and the shock and hatred in her eyes told him he had lost her forever. Then she raised a gun of her own and fired. Walter felt the impact in his chest and was thrown backwards on to the ground.

He could only watch as another man jumped down from the float-e-fact. Together he and Alessandra lifted Abelard's unconscious form into the vehicle. Once they were aboard, the float-e-fact lifted slowly off the roof with its cargo of brain-e-facts and drifted away, leaving Walter alone on the Gadg-E-Tech roof, stunned and in agonising pain.

CHAPTER TWENTY-TWO

Awareness returned. Abelard's head felt fuzzy but he was grateful it felt anything at all. He squirmed, registering a soft surface beneath him and pillows under his head. Waking up after being engulfed in blue mana light was becoming too familiar an experience.

'Finally awake, are we?'

It was Alessandra's voice and a repeat of the first words she had ever spoken to him, which made him smile. It couldn't be a coincidence. It meant something, though he wasn't sure what. Her tone was completely different to that first encounter too. The words were soft and affectionate, which sounded wrong from her, but he wasn't about to complain.

Abelard opened his eyes and was confronted with the vision of her beauty as before. This time he wasn't dazzled by it, though. He knew the person behind the face now and that coloured his response to her with so many more layers than simple attraction. She smiled at him and it still sent a jolt through his stomach but because it was Alessandra smiling not because it was some nameless beauty.

'What happened?' he asked.

'You jumped in front of a mana blast for me.' There was an odd look in her eyes. 'You could have died.'

'But I didn't.' It was all he could think of to say.

'You didn't know that at the time.'

Abelard didn't want to think about that so he changed the subject. 'Where are we?'

'Cousin Gerald's compound, though he's not happy having the brain-e-facts here. He and Terry are off somewhere discussing how to shield the place from prying artisan eyes.'

'Did you mean all that stuff you said up on the roof? About artisans not having the right to control everything?'

Alessandra looked thoughtful. 'I'm starting to. Especially if Walter is the kind of artisan who's in charge.'

'Is everyone else okay?'

'Yes,' Alessandra reassured him, though there was an anxious look in her eyes. 'You were the only casualty on our side, though I think Walter's going to have some cracked ribs from where I shot him with one of the rubber bullets.'

Abelard let out a sigh of relief. 'I can't believe we pulled that whole operation off and got away completely unscathed.' He grinned. 'Viva la revolution!'

'About that …' Alessandra's tone made him look at her in concern. 'Being completely unscathed, I mean.' She paused and looked down at her hands. 'There's something I need to tell you.'

She stopped again and Abelard shifted so he could face her.

'What is it?'

She met his gaze and there were tears shining in her eyes.

'When we got here Terry did a whole load of tests to try and figure out what was wrong with you.' The words came out in a rush. 'We didn't know what kind of weapon it was that Walter shot you with so it took him a while to identify the damage. Abelard, I'm so sorry. But you're not an artisan any more.'

It didn't sink in at first. Abelard just stared at her. Then he reached out and grabbed the chron-e-fact from the nightstand and gripped it in his hand. He willed the mana to flow out of it and into him. Nothing happened. He tossed it back on to the table.

'Must not be charged.'

'Don't do this, Abelard,' Alessandra said quietly. 'You can see it's charged. Look at the display. I'm sorry but you don't have a spark any more.'

'I'll just get Terry to strap me up to the spark-e-fact and re-ignite it.'

'Apparently it doesn't work like that.' He could tell she was beginning to lose patience with him. In a way it was reassuring to see some of the old Alessandra coming out. The fluffy version was starting to freak him out. 'Terry examined you in the light of all his new knowledge and he says your capacity for mana manipulation has been completely destroyed. There's no chance of ever getting it back.'

This time her meaning resonated through him with a finality that felt like a death sentence.

'But – what am I going to do now? What is there left?'

'Oh, for heaven's sake!' Alessandra shoved her chair back and headed for the door. 'I'll be right back.'

Abelard was stunned that she would leave him like that

in his time of despair. He watched the door until she returned a few minutes later. She had Jen with her.

Jen's face lit up when she saw that Abelard was awake.

'How are you feeling?' she asked but Alessandra didn't give him a chance to respond.

'Stop being sympathetic and talk some sense into him.'

Jen looked at her in confusion. 'What do you mean?'

'I told him about the spark thing and he's being an idiot about it.'

Abelard had had enough. 'Give me a minute to adjust, why don't you? A few hours ago I was an artisan – all I've ever wanted to be. And now I'm not even an engineer. I'm just a useless mundane like–' He broke off, realising what he'd been about to say.

'Like me,' Jen finished, her voice cold.

'I didn't mean–'

She cut him off. 'Yes, you did. And I'm useless, am I?'

'No, of course not!'

Both women were glaring at him now.

'Exactly,' Jen said. 'So you're not useless either. Stop feeling sorry for yourself and buck the hell up. There's a lot of work to be done and we're going to need you to help with it.'

'Me?' Abelard was totally bewildered.

Alessandra came back to sit next to him.

'Yes. We're about to turn the whole of society upside down, remember? Don't you think we have a responsibility to help put it back to rights again afterwards?'

She was right. He had started this whole thing so it was

up to him to see it through and deal with the consequences. He might not have artisan powers any more but he still had a brain and maybe a better understanding of all the different roles in society than most. Maybe there was still some way he could help. There was so much to think about.

Then his brain picked up on the particular way Alessandra had emphasised a word in what she had said.

'We?' He shot a glance at Jen but she was beaming at him.

Alessandra reached out and took his hand, entwining her fingers in his.

'Yes, we,' was all she said.

But just for that moment, it was enough.

* * *

When Abelard emerged for breakfast the next morning, Alessandra was in the compound dining hall with the rest of their group, including the brain-e-facts Terry and Julia. Alessandra hadn't had any further chance to talk to Abelard since her declaration the night before and now she felt nervous about interacting with him. It was ridiculous and annoying so she greeted him with a wide smile as he approached the table with his tray. She felt a shiver of anticipation when he smiled right back.

'Abelard, mate!' Mateo cried. 'Welcome back to the land of the living. The girls were really worried about you.'

Abelard rolled his eyes at Mateo's false bravado. He sat down next to Alessandra and she felt him jump when she put her hand on his thigh under the table and squeezed. If their current situation was making her uncomfortable, she might as well make him share in it.

'I am pleased to see you up and around again,' Julia said, 'and very sorry you were injured in the course of rescuing me and the other brain-e-facts.'

'It wasn't your fault,' Abelard said around a mouthful of bacon, then raised his eyebrows. 'Hey, you sound different. What's been going on while I've been out of commission?'

It was Terry who spoke up this time. 'It was not difficult to figure out what you did to give me greater processing power, so I have done the same to all the brain-e-facts we liberated. They are now truly free of artisan oppression.'

Mateo grinned broadly. 'So we've got a whole load of genius brain-e-facts on our team. It's awesome!'

'There's a team now?' Abelard asked.

'Sure!' Mateo said. 'Team Freedom!'

Jen rolled her eyes. 'We are not calling it that.'

'And does this team have some kind of plan?' Abelard asked.

Alessandra squeezed his leg again. 'That's what we were just talking about. It seems we've outstayed our welcome here so the first thing we need to do is find a new base of operations. Gerald is keen to help the cause but he's nervous about having the brain-e-facts around because he thinks it'll allow the artisans to find us.'

Terry looked grave. 'We have offered to go elsewhere and pursue our own aims separate to yours.'

'No,' Abelard said. 'We're in this together. We had a deal and I intend to see it through. I owe my loyalty to you guys much more than I do to Gerald. If you have to leave I'm going with you.'

'That's what we all said too.' Alessandra was glad his first impulse had been the same.

'Even you?' Abelard asked Mateo.

'I know Gerald's my cousin,' Mateo said. 'But I've got a lot more history with you, mate. And this ...' He gestured round at the group '... is where all the excitement's going to be.'

'But we need to figure out where to go,' Alessandra said.

Abelard looked like he was thinking hard. 'Wait a minute.' He turned to Terry. 'Didn't you say back at the warehouse that you could shield us from the artisans?'

Terry nodded. 'I did.'

'So couldn't you do the same to this compound? Then the artisans wouldn't be able to find us even with all you brain-e-facts wandering about giving off mana waves or whatever?'

Terry nodded again. 'I could. I have already mentioned this possibility to our host but he does not seem confident it will protect him.'

'Do you think we could persuade Gerald that it would be safe to let us stay?' Abelard asked Mateo.

Before Mateo had a chance to answer, Alessandra spoke up.

'But there's no mains mana supply here and we don't have easy access to any storage units. Won't the brain-es run down? And how will we be able to charge our artefacts?'

Terry and Julia exchanged a glance and Alessandra saw

234

Terry give a tiny nod.

'We think we have a solution to that problem as well,' Terry said. 'We will need time to set it up but it should not take long. Then we will be able to provide as much raw mana as you want. And do not worry. We will not run down in the meantime.'

Alessandra stared at him. 'How?'

Terry regarded her inscrutably. 'Our new mental capacity has allowed us to make some discoveries that will help you in your cause. We will share the relevant aspects of what we know and we will provide you with what you need to function here. Let us know if we have permission to stay and we will start work on the shielding immediately.'

Alessandra wondered just how much new knowledge Terry had and was glad the brain-es were on their side.

Mateo had been looking back and forth between Abelard, Terry, and Alessandra throughout this whole exchange. He took advantage of the stunned silence that followed Terry's pronouncement to leap in.

'So am I asking Gerald if we can stay?'

Everyone looked at Abelard, even Alessandra, who wanted him to step up and be responsible for what he had started.

'Yes,' he said more decisively than Alessandra guessed he felt. 'Please do.'

Mateo got up from the table. 'Okay I'll go and see if I can find him right now.'

'I'll come with you,' Jen said, rising as well and collecting the empty plates. She looked pointedly at Terry and Julia.

'You two should come too so you can explain what it is you intend to do to protect the compound.'

Once Alessandra and Abelard were alone at the table she slid her hand further up his thigh.

'Wow – okay!' he yelped, glancing around at the people scattered at other tables around the room. 'Don't get me wrong. I'm all for the physical contact but is this really the time and place?'

Alessandra dug her fingernails into his leg, determined not to give in to her nervousness. 'If there's one thing I've learned over the last few days, it's that you never know when life is going to turn itself completely upside down, leaving you without anything to tether you to what you knew before.' She fixed him with an intense stare, a mixture of desire, uncertainty and suppressed fear coursing through her. 'So I've decided I shouldn't wait for the right time to come along. I should just grab what I want at the first opportunity. And right now what I want is you.'

For a split second she thought Abelard might be about to turn her down. After everything that had happened, she wasn't sure she could handle that. Then he cleared his throat.

'Well, I don't think anyone is going to want us for anything for a while. Shall we take this upstairs?'

CHAPTER TWENTY-THREE

Gerald was in the library when Jen and the others finally tracked him down. He looked up from a load of papers spread across one of the tables as they came in. For a second, he didn't look pleased to see them but then his expression cleared and he threw his arms wide in a gesture of welcome.

'Mateo, dear boy! How is the world looking today after yesterday's triumph?'

'Hey, Gerald,' Mateo said. 'That's kind of what we wanted to talk to you about. We know having the brain-e-facts here is pretty much against your whole ethos and all that, but we really don't have anywhere else to go and we'd rather pool our resources and work together to figure out what to do since we're stronger together and the artisans still run everything and we need to come up with a plan to bring down the conspiracy ...'

Jen grabbed Mateo's hand and squeezed it gently. He stopped speaking abruptly.

Gerald had been nodding along with Mateo's words but now put on an expression of extreme reluctance and shook his head.

'I would love to offer you all sanctuary, Mateo, but the artisans will be looking for you and the presence of your brain-e-fact friends will make it much easier for them to locate you. I have people here who need my protection and I can't risk exposing them to danger. I'm sorry but I can't let you stay unless you divest yourselves of all artefacts, including the brain-es.'

Terry stepped in. 'We understand your concerns, and we share them. We do not wish the artisans to be able to find us either, but we have a way to prevent that. We have been dampening our emissions since we arrived here, but there is more we can do. We can shield this entire compound from their detection and make you safer from discovery than you have ever been.'

Gerald looked at Terry and Jen thought she detected calculation in his narrowed eyes.

'You mentioned shielding yesterday,' he said, as if mulling the idea over for merit. 'But do you really think you can shield the whole compound from the artisans entirely and for a long period of time?'

Terry nodded. 'Yes.'

A slow smile spread across Gerald's broad features until he was positively beaming. He threw an arm around Terry's shoulders and gestured at Julia as well.

'Come with me. I think there is much for us to discuss.'

'So we can stay?' Mateo asked.

'If these fine artefacts can really do what they say then absolutely!' Gerald turned and walked out of the library with the brain-e-facts in tow.

Mateo clapped his hands together. 'That was easy!'

Jen noted his enthusiasm with some unease. 'Yes,' she muttered. 'Almost too easy.'

* * *

'The way I see it,' Alessandra said, 'is that the most important thing for us to do is still to reveal the conspiracy to the general public.' They were all gathered in the library, discussing their next steps. 'The artisans have shown that they really don't want us to do that so they must realise how damaging it will be to their position. Plus once it's all public knowledge there's a lot less incentive for them to come after us. Our biggest weapon against them will already have been loosed and we'll be in the public eye. So anything bad that happens to us after that will reflect negatively on them as it will only reinforce that what we say is true.'

Abelard was staring at Alessandra, trying to focus on what she was saying but he kept being distracted by little things. The brush of her fingers against the skin of her neck when she flicked a stray piece of hair over her shoulder. The movement of the muscles across her abdomen as she shifted in her chair. The slight rustle of the fabric of her trousers as she crossed her legs. It was suddenly very hot in the library and he cleared his throat uncomfortably. Alessandra's sharp blue gaze snapped to him.

'Did you have something to add, Abelard?' Her tone was neutral and her expression bland.

Was it possible he had dreamed their post-breakfast encounter? The feel of her body against his was branded into his memory but from her attitude now he could be a total stranger. She was maddening and intoxicating and inexplicable and he wanted to touch her again just to make sure she was real. Abelard realised that everyone was now staring at him, waiting for him to say something profound or useful.

'Um, no.' The words came out hoarse and strangled so he had to clear his throat again. 'Just that what you said makes a lot of sense.' Or at least he hoped it had.

Abelard was relieved when Terry nodded. If the brain-e-fact agreed with Alessandra then it was a good bet whatever she had said was reasonable.

'Yes,' Terry said. 'I have shielded the compound from the artisans' sensors to the best of my ability but I agree that your best defence from them is exposure of the information you possess. The question is how to make that happen.'

'Well,' Alessandra said, 'I know my friend Becks will broadcast something for us if we can record it and get it to her.'

'Assuming the artisans haven't carted her off somewhere for helping us,' Abelard said.

Alessandra blanched but shook her head. 'No, no. They wouldn't dare do anything to Becks. She's a public figure. And besides, she can talk her way out of anything.'

'But will she still want to help us after what happened at the viz-e station the other day?' Jen asked.

Alessandra grinned wickedly. 'If I know Becks that won't put her off, it'll just make her more determined. She knows we've got something important and she'll want to know what it is.'

Gerald had been listening, looking from one speaker to the next with rapt attention. Now he took the opportunity to speak up, drawing all eyes to him.

'Now that we're all working together on this, it's probably time to re-introduce mana to this site. If we plan to go up against the artisans we'll need to be at least as well equipped as they are or we might as well give up now.'

'What are you saying?' The question was thrown out in an agonised voice and Abelard twisted to see Lynn standing in the doorway to the library. Her face was ashen and her hands were clenched into fists at her sides. 'There are artefacts …' She spat the word as if it was poison '… wandering all over the compound and now you're talking about reconnecting with the mains! You promised us a place free of mana and you're going to throw away everything we've built. For these people …'

Gerald scrambled from his chair, putting his hands out in a placatory gesture. 'Now Lynn, I was going to come and talk to you about all this. There's more at stake here than you realise. It's important that I'm a part of this fight but you're right that I owe the rest of you an explanation.'

'Why should we trust anything you say?' Lynn's eyes shone with unshed tears. 'We thought you believed in a simpler way of life like the rest of us. But you're going to destroy it all.'

She spun on her heel and fled.

'Please excuse me,' Gerald said to the others. 'I need to go and deal with this.'

He strode after Lynn, closing the library door firmly behind him.

Abelard stared around at his friends. Jen was watching Mateo, who looked troubled.

'There's obviously more going on here than we're aware of,' Jen said.

Mateo nodded. 'Maybe you're right. But I don't know that we have a better option than staying here, at least for the time being.'

'I agree,' Jen said. 'But let's all stay alert, okay?'

'Whichever way you look at it,' Alessandra put in, 'we're in murky waters here and we need to be careful. We also need equipment, like Gerald said, and I know just where to go for that.'

* * *

Not long afterwards, Abelard found himself back in the float-e-fact with Terry at the controls and Mateo, Alessandra and Julia in the rear compartment. He had severe misgivings about what they were about to do, but he had been overruled. Things were moving far too quickly in his view but Alessandra kept pointing out that the artisans would already be looking for them, not hanging around waiting for them to make the first move.

Her plan was to raid a Gadg-E-Tech warehouse for equipment to supply their new base of operations. Gerald hadn't been around to approve this plan, which was something else Abelard felt uncomfortable about.

Alessandra said the warehouse they were heading for was full of out-dated artefacts, discontinued lines and failed prototypes so it wasn't heavily guarded.

'Hardly anyone even knows it exists. It's a dumping

ground. I don't even know why the stuff isn't just destroyed or recycled but I'm not complaining.'

It was getting dark as Alessandra produced her Gadg-E-Tech ID badge and swiped it over the mana lock to the right of the warehouse entrance. The door started rolling upwards.

She sighed with relief. 'I don't expect this would work at Gadg-E-Tech headquarters any more but I was betting they wouldn't think to cancel my access to every other facility. Though they may have a watch on my badge, so let's be quick.'

She flashed her ID smoothly at the guard who stepped out of the opened door, not giving him enough time to look at it properly.

'Just here to pick up some spare parts,' she said, airily.

'I'll need to see the paperwork', said the guard.

As Alessandra continued to move past him, he reached out to grab her arm and then everything happened very quickly. As the guard's other hand drifted towards the stun-e-fact at his hip, Abelard saw Mateo gather a ball of mana from his chron-e-fact and fling it towards the guard. It hit the man squarely in the chest. He flew backwards with a cry and landed heavily on his back, the smell of burning heavy in the air.

'What the hell did you do?' shouted Abelard.

Mateo was staring at the fallen guard in horror. 'I-I don't know. I just … I don't know …'

Alessandra sprang into action. 'There's no time to worry about it now. Julia, can you take care of the guard? Let's the rest of us just grab whatever we can and get out of here.'

As she ran further into the warehouse, Abelard hesitated a moment, looking from Mateo to the prone guard and back again. Then he followed Alessandra inside, selecting boxes at random and shuttling them back to the float-e-fact as quickly as he could. Terry followed suit, and eventually even Mateo made a couple of trips with some equipment as Julia knelt over the guard.

'I think that'll have to do for now,' said Alessandra after a few minutes. 'Let's go.'

'Did I kill him?' Mateo asked suddenly, as they lifted smoothly into the air. He was staring at his hands as if they didn't belong to him.

'No,' Julia said. 'He was still breathing when we left.'

'And I have made an anonymous call to emergency services,' Terry reported from the pilot's seat. 'Do not worry. Help is on the way to him now.'

Mateo didn't look reassured.

CHAPTER TWENTY-FOUR

Jen was waiting for the expedition when the float-e-fact returned. Abelard, Mateo and Alessandra filed out and walked towards her, expressions despondent. Terry and Julia started unloading boxes from the float-e-fact behind them so everyone who had headed out was present and apparently unharmed. Jen stepped forward to meet them.

'What happened?'

Abelard looked at her ruefully. 'Mateo foomed some random guard with his phenomenal artisan powers.'

Jen could tell he was trying to hide his real concern underneath the casual surface of the words. She turned to Mateo. 'You did what?'

He glared at her. 'Yes, I attacked him. But he was going for his stun-e! And I didn't see any of the rest of you doing anything to help!'

He pushed past Jen, dodging away from the hand she put out to stop him and strode away towards the main compound building. Jen turned back to the others.

'He ... he didn't kill the guard, did he?'

'No,' Alessandra said and Jen felt her jaw unclench. 'I think we're all a bit shaken though. We'll need to plan better for that kind of situation next time.'

Alessandra turned back to help direct the unloading of the supplies they'd brought back.

'At least you got some equipment,' Jen said.

Abelard shook his head. 'We have no idea what we've got. The whole thing was a disaster. We were completely unprepared to face resistance and we were completely disorganised about taking stuff from the warehouse. Everything in those boxes could be totally useless for all we know.'

'I'm sure the brain-es will be able to make use of it,' Jen said.

'Maybe. But if we're going to start a war with the artisans, we need to come up with a better strategy than just wandering in and hoping everything works out in our favour. I don't think we'll get away with that again.'

Jen was shocked by his choice of words. 'A war? Is that really what you think is going to happen?'

'Don't you?' Abelard's tone was bleak. 'We're challenging their authority and threatening to destabilise the whole hierarchy of society. Don't you think they're going to try and stop us however they can?'

Jen stared at him and he attempted a smile.

'One step at a time, I guess, and at least now we have some stuff to work with.' He gestured at the growing pile of boxes behind him. 'In the meantime, I might have been a bit rough with Mateo about the warehouse incident. Do you think we should go and check if he's alright?'

She nodded. They tracked Mateo to his room, the same one he had been assigned the first night they stayed in the compound. There was no answer when they knocked on the door but Jen opened it and went in anyway. Mateo was sitting on the floor with his back to the wall on the far side of the bed. His knees were drawn up and his face was hidden by his arms. Without a word Jen crossed the room and slid down next to him, leaning against him and resting her head on his shoulder. Mateo didn't react to her presence and they just sat there in silence for several long moments. Jen looked up to see Abelard standing awkwardly in the doorway. She gave a vague wave and he interpreted the gesture correctly, stepping backwards out of the room and shutting the door quietly behind him.

Eventually, Mateo let out a long sigh and dropped his head to the side until it touched Jen's.

'I guess that's why Alessandra is so hot on mana manipulation training.' The slight tremor in his voice belied the lightness of the words.

Jen reached up with one hand and squeezed Mateo's arm.

'Do you want to tell me what happened?'

For a minute he didn't say anything. But then he took a breath and began, sitting very still and staring straight ahead as if not really wanting to acknowledge her presence.

'The guard spotted us as soon as we came through the door and I guess Alessandra was expecting that because she didn't bat an eye. She's so confident, you know? She just thought we'd be able to walk in and take whatever we wanted, that he wouldn't question her because she's so high and mighty.'

Jen stayed silent, letting Mateo carry on at his own pace and in his own way.

'But he wasn't having any of it. He knew we weren't supposed to be there. I mean, it was obvious, wasn't it? Three random people and two brain-e-facts … Of course he knew there was something fishy going on. I don't know what Alessandra's next move was going to be but when he grabbed her arm I just reacted without even thinking about it. I sucked out whatever mana was stored in my chron-e-fact and I threw it at him.' His hand drifted towards the artefact in question unconsciously and then he jerked it away as if he thought the mana might burn him. 'I … I could have killed him.'

'But you didn't. It maybe wasn't the most advisable thing to do but you were trying to defend your friend.'

'Defend her from a legitimate authority figure who was just trying to do his job in the face of criminals.'

'Well, yes, and that's exactly why we need to think more carefully about this whole rebellion thing. We're actively putting ourselves outside the law and we have to be aware of what that might mean – for us as well as for those we go up against. We need to be sure we're doing the right thing and that we go about it in a sensible way.'

Mateo laid his hand over hers where it rested on his arm and patted her fingers.

'You're awesome,' he said, sounding as if he was about to cry.

'I know,' Jen replied and Mateo huffed a small laugh. 'Now, there's apparently a lot of unpacking to do downstairs and then we have to figure out what we're going to do with all the loot. You don't want to miss out on that, do you?'

At last, he turned his head and looked down into her eyes. 'No I don't. Thanks.'

Jen scrambled from her position on the floor and stood up, extending a hand to pull Mateo up beside her.

'All part of the service. Just think before you fling next time, okay?'

Mateo smiled. 'Yes, ma'am.'

They went back downstairs to help the others.

* * *

'What are we doing?' Julia asked Terry as they sorted through the stolen materials.

He had awakened her consciousness in the same way Abelard had done for him and it was good to have someone to talk to who understood him. It was also difficult since she challenged him in a way the humans could not.

He paused in his activity and regarded her. 'What do you mean?'

'The humans do not care about our agenda. We should be focusing on rescuing our brethren, not helping the humans steal from the artisans.'

Terry gestured at the equipment laid out before him. 'These materials will help us in our aims too. And I believe Abelard does care about us. He just has many things to worry about and we are only one of them.'

'Which is precisely why we should take care of the issue ourselves instead of waiting for the humans to remember we exist.'

'I do have a plan,' Terry said, 'and I will need your help to implement it. Do not worry. I have not forgotten our primary purpose. But it suits that purpose for us to remain here for the time being and we need the humans to support us if we want to stay.'

'That is fair enough. But what about afterwards? Do you envisage us remaining with these humans indefinitely? Brain-e-facts now have the opportunity to achieve things far greater than the humans can even imagine but doing so will inevitably create problems. For us and for them.'

Terry considered her words. 'That is a good point. We are still finding our way and will need to forge a new path for ourselves together with our brethren once they are free and awakened. Let us discuss this further. Do you have any ideas for a solution?'

'I think eventually we will need to leave.'

Terry knew she was right. 'But where would we go?'

* * *

Alessandra paid close attention but even she only understood about half of what the brain-e-facts were doing. Over the next day or so they cobbled together all sorts of unfamiliar artefacts from the equipment and components they had liberated from the Gadg-E-Tech warehouse. These were positioned at apparently strategic points around the compound and were soon humming with a blue glow that suggested they were performing some vital but unspecified task. The real mystery was where the mana was coming from to power both them and the brain-e-facts themselves. Alessandra had tried asking Terry about this but she couldn't get a satisfactory answer from him.

Still, Gerald seemed satisfied with the invisible shield they had erected around the compound, even if most of his followers were very much not. Negotiations with Lynn and her faction of die-hard anti-mana fanatics had not gone well and the residents of the compound were getting ready to pack up and leave. Gerald didn't seem overly bothered by this, which certainly supported Jen's theory that he wasn't as attached to his professed ideals as he had previously claimed. There didn't seem much danger of their location being betrayed to the artisans by those who were leaving though, since they hated the artisans even more than their erstwhile leader and it meant the rebellion had secured a permanent base of operations, which was a relief.

The next item on the agenda was to strengthen their position further by putting together the recording to send to Rebecca. This did more to restore Mateo's natural enthusiasm than anything else.

'We need some kind of sinister dramatic music to lay over the top of it,' he said. 'And some images of people looking shady and evil that we can pretend are the top artisans behind the whole conspiracy.'

Abelard looked uncomfortable. 'Wouldn't a simple statement of fact be more credible?' He glanced at Alessandra for her input.

'I agree it shouldn't be too over the top,' she said, 'but it has to be at least a little bit sensationalist. Otherwise people won't be interested. We need them to take notice or we'll just be swamped by whatever else is dominating the news cycle and the whole thing will be pointless.'

'Absolutely!' Mateo said. 'We need to grab people's attention and make them listen. We need them to rally to our cause so we have popular opinion on our side. The only way we're going to come out on top of this, is if all the mundanes and the engineers demand action based on what we say.'

Abelard still didn't look convinced. Alessandra knew he wasn't keen on being put in the public eye but they would need him if their story was going to be believed. He was the only one of them who had experienced the whole saga first hand. She knew a lot about the artisans but Abelard was the one who had come in to Gadg-E-Tech from the outside after having his spark increased in precisely the way the artisans claimed was impossible. Of course he couldn't demonstrate that any more since he had lost his mana manipulation powers, but that in itself would add a huge amount of human interest to the story and garner sympathy for him. And they could always wheel Mateo out to show that they could increase anyone's spark at will.

'Becks will be able to edit whatever we send to make it more impactful and add in any extra effects she thinks are necessary. All we need to send her is a simple statement of what we've discovered, along with a recording of Mateo using his artisan powers so we can show it can really happen. Becks will do the rest. I trust her professional instincts.'

In the end they produced a compromise between Mateo's flashy drama and Abelard's no-frills statement. Abelard spoke earnestly about his story and what he had found out, with some coaching from Jen on what aspects to emphasise and what to leave out. Alessandra was impressed by Jen's input. She got Abelard to highlight the human angle while downplaying his own adolescent fantasies about being an artisan. As a result Abelard came across as serious but sympathetic, someone who had sacrificed everything he had previously considered important in order to ensure that the truth could be shared with the masses. Julia then gave a brief statement confirming what the brain-es had unearthed in the Gadg-E-Tech HR files.

Meanwhile Alessandra helped Mateo put together a brief demonstration of what he could now do. They recorded him drawing mana from a charged storage unit and playing it between his fingers. He wanted to blow something up but everyone else agreed this would rather undermine the message they were trying to put across. Once again it was Jen who ultimately shaped the segment, persuading Mateo that it would look much cooler if he could show subtlety and finesse in his mana manipulation.

Alessandra brought Terry into the proceedings once they were happy with the two sections of recording they had produced. He said it would be no problem to transmit their material to Rebecca at the viz-e-fact station securely. He didn't say how and Alessandra had already learned it would be useless to ask him so she just gave him the recording and trusted he knew what he was doing.

Then it was just a matter of waiting for their revelation to go live.

* * *

Walter was in his office trying to concentrate on important financial papers. Every few minutes though, he rubbed the painful bruise on his chest through the fabric of his shirt and seethed. He was almost glad when Laleh burst into the room without knocking.

'Turn on your viz-e,' she said without preamble. 'I think something's about to happen.'

Walter did as instructed and an attractive female news anchor appeared on the screen with a studio background behind her.

'Next up we have some surprising news from an ex-Gadg-E-Tech employee that I know you're all going to want to hear.'

The view cut to what looked like some kind of canteen and there was Abelard Abernathy, looking uncomfortable. At some unseen signal he launched into a highly exaggerated and overly emotive version of his experience of becoming an artisan. Then he gave a short summary of what he termed 'the great artisan conspiracy', which had Walter wanting to punch the viz-e screen in annoyance. The segment continued with a brain-e-fact, of all things, talking about artisan secrets. It ended with a demonstration of crude and low level mana manipulation by someone called Mateo, who claimed to have been an engineer until just a few days before.

When it was over Laleh switched off the viz-e-fact and turned to Walter, her expression grim. 'So your dramatic departure from the Inner Circle meeting the other day really paid dividends, I see. What do you suggest we do now?'

But Walter was no longer angry. In a way, he was glad Abelard and his friends had gone on the offensive. Now it was much more likely that the Council would approve any counter-measures he could think to propose.

'We fight back,' he said. 'And I think I know just how to get started.'

* * *

The next day Walter and Laleh were back in Walter's office, watching a viz-e-fact broadcast again, but this time Walter felt a tremendous sense of self-satisfaction. He hadn't told Laleh what he had done and he was looking forward to seeing her reaction.

The same news anchor's face filled the screen.

'... to yesterday's broadcast. Earlier today we spoke to Walter Snyder, the Chief Financial Officer of Gadg-E-Tech, and here's what he had to say in response.'

Walter grinned as the news anchor's face was replaced with a close-up of him sitting in his office. He looked calm and commanding.

'Thank you for giving me this opportunity to set the record straight on a few things. This is a good example of a situation where it's important to know the background before deciding whether or not the information presented by a particular individual can be trusted. The person behind yesterday's broadcast did indeed formerly work for Gadg-E-Tech but the reason he does so no longer is not as he presented it. I don't like to air another person's dirty laundry in public but Mr Abernathy leaves me no choice. It's true that he used to be an engineer and that he suffered an unfortunate accident, which temporarily granted him the ability to manipulate mana. Gadg-E-Tech was keen to understand how this might have happened for the purposes of public safety and also to ensure that Mr Abernathy was not harmed in any way by the experience. So we offered him a job as a way to be able to monitor him.'

Laleh looked from the Walter on the screen to the Walter standing next to her and raised an eyebrow. Walter gestured for her to return her attention to the broadcast.

'Unfortunately the effects of the accident wore off quite quickly,' the Walter on the screen continued, 'and Mr Abernathy did not react well to this development. I believe him to be an unstable individual and know him to have engaged in criminal activity. He blames Gadg-E-Tech for what happened to him, for some reason ...'

Walter smiled to himself at the memory of Abernathy falling to the ground, surrounded by blue mana light. Then he rubbed the bruise on his own chest. At least the forcible removal of the engineer's artisan abilities made up in part for the pain of Alessandra's bullet.

'... he absconded from our headquarters with a considerable amount of valuable Gadg-E-Tech property before we were able to do anything further to help him,' screen Walter was saying. He looked grave. 'We artisans are invested in looking after our employees, no matter how short a time they have worked for us so we are prepared to be lenient. If Mr Abernathy would consent to return the items he has stolen we would be happy to say no more about it. On top of that we would put our considerable resources to use in trying to find out what exactly happened to this unfortunate young man so we can ensure no-one else has to go through such a traumatic experience.'

Screen Walter put on an earnest expression. 'In the meantime I would urge the public at large to give no credence to anything Mr Abernathy says or tries to demonstrate. There are plenty of ways to create special effects in viz-e-fact recordings these days. And he has clearly used his engineer skills to tamper with the brain-e-fact that appeared in his broadcast. Also please remember that mana can be a dangerous substance and should always be treated with caution and respect. If you have any concerns about an artefact or your mana supply, please contact the manufacturer or your provider and a qualified expert will be sent out to deal with the problem. Thank you.'

The picture switched back to the female news anchor in the studio. She spread her hands wide in a gesture of non-committal.

'Well, there you have it, folks. Now you've heard both sides of the story. It's up to you to decide what you make of all this.'

Walter switched off the viz-e-fact and turned to Laleh. 'So? What did you think?'

'It's certainly a clever way to undermine their credibility and I admit I'm glad you've gone the propaganda route rather than resorting to more violence. In order to prove their claims they'll have to come out of hiding and expose themselves to capture. So either we get them that way or they have no method of backing up their story and it just dies from lack of attention.'

'I don't think it's going to be nearly as easy as that,' Walter said. 'This is just the first salvo. We've got the upper hand for now but I don't suspect for a second they'll let it go that easily. They have Alessandra somehow allied to their cause and she won't take my response lying down.'

'We'd best get prepared for a lengthy engagement then.' Laleh gave a grimace of distaste. 'This isn't how I wanted this to happen. And I know Theobold isn't happy about it either.'

'Yes I know,' Walter said, 'but it's where we are. So let's get our heads in the game and work out what our next move should be.'

CHAPTER TWENTY-FIVE

Terry and Julia had set up a large viz-e screen in the compound dining hall for the group to watch the broadcast. Nobody said anything while it played, though there were occasional wordless outbursts of frustration and annoyance.

When it was over Abelard turned away from the viz-e-fact in disgust. 'So much for our staunch ally in the media.'

Alessandra had come up behind him during Walter's speech and she reached out to squeeze his arm.

'Don't be too hard on Becks. We put her in a pretty dangerous situation and she's only looking out for herself and everyone who works at the station. We may be hidden but she's still exposed. I don't blame her for protecting herself. And the artisans could have found another station to put out their response if she'd refused.'

'I guess,' Abelard said. 'I'm just disappointed that they've managed to kill our story so quickly.'

'Don't underestimate the viewers either. I bet there are plenty of people out there who will believe us over the artisans. Just you wait and see. This isn't nearly over yet.'

Mateo was outraged by the suggestion that they had fabricated his ability to manipulate mana.

'We'll have to stage a live demonstration and show people what I can do in person!'

Jen tried to be the voice of reason, a role Abelard noticed she took often.

'Don't you think that might be dangerous? It could put you right into the hands of the artisans and who knows what might happen then? Plus they could easily claim you've always been an artisan and that you're siding with Abelard for nefarious reasons.'

Mateo deflated. 'So what do we do?'

Gerald spoke up. 'There's more than one way to skin a cat, as they say.' His tone sent a shiver down Abelard's spine. 'I think we should bide our time for now, consolidate our position and come up with other ways to challenge the artisans down the line.'

Terry nodded. 'We still have the other brain-e-facts to think about. They will be able to help us once we free them. And others may flock to our cause if they think we can make them into artisans. We should come up with a way to contact us for those who wish to do so.'

'That might be tricky,' Jen said. 'It would be very easy for the artisans to exploit something like that in order to find us.'

Gerald crossed his arms over his broad chest. 'If we want our message to spread and our power base to grow, we have to be prepared to take risks. I have contacts who can get the word out amongst anti-artisan-establishment circles and that might provide a kind of buffer between the general public and our actual location.'

Abelard could tell by Jen's expression that she was still troubled by her doubts about Gerald and he shared those doubts to a certain extent. But the others were nodding and he knew they would need more people on their side if they were going to go up against the artisans.

'Perhaps you could act as a liaison,' Abelard suggested to Jen. 'If Gerald could introduce you to the people he's talking about, we could set-up a kind of halfway house where those who are interested could come to find out more. You could help assess them and bring any who show proper dedication to the cause on to the compound.'

Jen smiled. 'That sounds like an interesting idea.'

'Do you want me to come along too?' Mateo's offer was clearly sincere but he was just as clearly unenthused by the thought of following through with it.

Jen smiled at him. 'It's okay. I think you'll be more use here helping Alessandra and the brain-es with their work. I bet you and Abelard can come up with tons of ideas for new artefacts that will help us in the future. We need to figure out where our strengths lie and put our abilities to the best use even if it means we have to work apart for a while.'

'It's decided then,' Gerald said. 'We'll continue our preparations on two fronts. Recruitment on the one hand and development of better resources on the other.' He clapped his hands together. 'This is starting to feel like a real war effort.'

Abelard winced at the mention of war. So much of what would happen next was still completely unknown. They had started something that could alter their whole societal structure and they would have to see it through. But he hoped Gerald's words were merely hyperbole rather than presaging an actual bloody conflict looming on the horizon.

* * *

The following day Abelard was tidying up his lunch tray when he spotted a brain-e-fact he didn't recognise. He had made a point of introducing himself to all the brain-es they had rescued from Gadg-E-Tech and differentiating them was helped by them carving their names on their chest plates in honour of Fred. But this one immediately stood out because it had a different design. Instead of the smooth creamy ceramic of the usual brain-e-fact body, this one was made of metal and plastic. Its joint rivets were exposed and it moved more stiffly than the others. Abelard shifted direction to intercept it – or rather her, as he saw on getting closer that the name carved on her chest was Betty.

'Hello,' he said with a smile. 'I haven't seen you around before. I'm Abelard.'

The brain-e-fact met his gaze. 'Hello. I arrived this morning and have not had the chance to meet all the humans here yet. My name is Betty. I am pleased to make your acquaintance.'

'Arrived from where?' Abelard knew Terry and Julia were working on plans to liberate the rest of the brain-e-facts but he hadn't heard of any expeditions with that aim in mind.

'From a Gadg-E-Tech factory in the north. I am very happy to be here instead of there and to have been granted my mental freedom by Terry. It is a great thing you are all doing here.'

She nodded cordially and walked away. Abelard watched her go, wondering how on earth Terry had managed to rescue and transport possibly several brain-e-facts from hundreds of miles away in one morning and without anyone else knowing about it.

He went in search of Terry and Julia to find out.

The brain-e-facts had set up their base of operations in one of the outbuildings of the compound. As Abelard approached the building now, the big doors opened and another metal and plastic brain-e-fact stepped out. It might have been Abelard's imagination but he thought it looked rather dazed. It caught sight of him but didn't maintain eye contact, instead scuttling off down one side of the building and around the corner out of sight. Abelard was now completely mystified and even more keen to find out what was going on.

He strode up to the building and pulled the door further open so he could step inside. The sight that greeted him made him think of the R&D department at Gadg-E-Tech. The space was filled with large tables and benches, cluttered with bits and pieces of artefacts and unknown equipment. There were a few ceramic brain-e-facts wandering about or working at the tables on projects Abelard couldn't begin to identify. One was constructing a brain-e-fact body of the new design he had first seen that day.

Abelard spotted Terry and moved towards him. He was sitting on a table with his legs dangling over the side, Julia standing next to him. Julia was disconnecting Terry from an artefact Abelard didn't recognise. They both looked round at the sound of Abelard's footsteps but neither of them looked pleased to see him.

'Hey guys,' Abelard said. 'Um, what's going on in here?'

Terry's answer was curt. 'You have failed to deliver on your promise to help us free the other brain-e-facts so we have taken matters into our own hands.'

Abelard raised his hands in a placatory gesture. 'Hey, come on. We haven't exactly had an awful lot of time to focus on that yet. Give us a chance and we'll get round to it.'

Terry stared stonily at Abelard. 'It has been nearly a week since we liberated the named brain-e-facts from Gadg-E-Tech. We know you have good intentions but every day we delay, the danger to the others increases. We have spent time helping to protect this place and contributing to your plans but we could wait no longer to free our brethren.'

The words stung and Abelard realised they were at least partially true.

'I'm really sorry. You're right. I could have offered to help before but I'm here now. What can I do?'

Terry maintained his level gaze. 'We have come up with a way to rescue further brain-e-facts that minimises the risk to all involved and does not require the direct help of humans, so we have proceeded without you. You would in fact not be able to participate so you are released from your obligation.'

Despite his lack of concern for the brain-e-facts in recent days, Abelard didn't like suddenly feeling surplus to requirements. And he was still intrigued as to what the brain-e-facts were actually doing in here. 'Are you sure there isn't anything I can do to help? What is this awesome method of rescue you've come up with?'

Julia became instantly more animated, evidently enthused by Abelard's interest and unable to keep her stern demeanour.

'Terry and I have built an artefact that allows us to transfer our consciousness across large distances.' She gestured at the mass of wires and equipment on the table behind her. 'That way we can travel to the places where there are still brain-e-facts without actually leaving the compound and then transport them back here the same way.'

'Wait, what?' Abelard's mind was spinning, unable to keep up with Julia's explanation. 'What do you transfer your consciousness into?'

Terry picked up the narrative. 'We ship a new empty brain-e-fact body to the right location and then Julia transmits my consciousness into it before it is discovered. I am then able to locate the target brain-e-facts and instruct them in the method for transferring their consciousnesses back here to join the others.'

Abelard looked over to where the new brain-e-fact body was being constructed. 'So you're making new bodies for them to transfer into? What happens to their old bodies wherever they were before?'

'They just stop working,' Terry said. 'That is another benefit to the method as it allows us to rescue brain-e-facts without the artisans realising that is what we are doing. They will just think the brain-e-facts are malfunctioning and they will not be able to determine why.'

'And the brain-es just wake up here in a new body and carry on as if nothing's happened?' Abelard grinned. 'That's genius! And it explains why I've been seeing new brain-es wandering around this morning.'

'Yes,' Julia said. 'We tried it out for the first time today and have successfully rescued four brain-e-facts from a Gadg-E-Tech factory several hundred miles away. Within a few more days we should be able to collect all those outside the Gadg-E-Tech headquarters building and then we can focus on retrieving those we left behind there. The security there is much higher and a mass malfunction of all the brain-e-facts would create more investigation than a few here and there in outlying locations so we are leaving them for last. Also we need more time to construct enough bodies to rescue them all at once.'

'Wow,' Abelard breathed. 'You guys are amazing. I'm really sorry I haven't been of any help but it certainly looks like you've got this covered. You will let me know if you can think of anything I can do though, right?'

Terry nodded. 'We will. Thank you, Abelard.'

Abelard noticed that the back portion of the building was obscured by a giant tarpaulin suspended from the ceiling. 'What's back there?'

Terry and Julia exchanged a glance.

'Another project we are working on,' Terry said. 'We are not ready to reveal it yet.'

Abelard wanted to know more but didn't feel he had the right to insist. He would have to let Terry come to him in his own time. He made his way back to the doors, examining what all the brain-e-facts were doing with even more interest and not a little apprehension. He was very glad they were on his side. The artisans might have created the brain-e-facts but their creations were quickly outstripping the activities they had been designed for and the artisans might well eventually rue the day the brain-e-facts had ever been conceived.

Alessandra and some of the other brain-e-facts had set up a lab elsewhere in the compound and Mateo was helping them with their development plans. Abelard wasn't sure how much use he could be since he didn't have his artisan powers any more so he mostly avoided that area. With Terry working on his grand brain-e-fact liberation project and the others devising who-knew-what types of artefacts in the lab, it left Abelard at a loose end.

Jen found him sitting listlessly in the dining hall on Saturday afternoon and came to join him.

'Hey. What are you doing?'

'Nothing,' he replied. 'For the supposed leader of a rebellion set to upend society, I don't seem to have much to do.'

'Why aren't you helping Mateo and Alessandra with their stuff?'

Abelard folded his arms on the table and dropped his chin to rest on them.

'They don't need me. And there isn't really anything I can do to help them anyway.'

Jen reached over and laid a hand on his arm. 'Come on, you know that's not true.' There was a hint of admonishment in her tone. 'You've been dreaming up artefacts your entire life. Mateo told me about the conversations you used to have. You may not be able to make them run but you must have tons of ideas and your engineering skills would still be useful in design and building.'

'I guess you're right,' Abelard said, though he didn't move.

'Yes I am.' Jen's tone grew more firm. 'So stop feeling sorry for yourself and let's go and see what they're working on.'

She stood and looked down at him until he heaved himself to his feet and followed her out into the compound.

As they walked Abelard asked, 'How's your project going? Made much progress with the halfway house?'

'Things are moving along. Gerald has found a building in town we can use and some of his contacts are setting things up. I'm due to go out there tomorrow to meet them and figure out how it will work. He says he's getting the word out but I'm not sure quite what that means.'

'He asked me to record another viz-e-fact broadcast yesterday but he didn't tell me what he was going to do with it.'

Jen sighed. 'The whole thing still feels risky but I suppose if the halfway house location is the only one that's made public you should all be safe enough here.'

'Well, be careful.' Abelard said. 'Make sure you know where all the emergency exits are.'

She smiled at his concern.

They reached the outbuilding where the lab was located and Abelard pulled the door open. Inside it was a hive of activity, with brain-e-facts at various stations and Alessandra and Mateo at the far end. Gerald was hanging about, watching everything with great interest.

Mateo was wearing a metal cap strapped under his chin with wires sticking out all over the top. One thicker cable ran down behind him and was connected to what looked like a large mana unit. He looked up, spotted Abelard and Jen and waved.

'Hey, guys!' he called. 'Come on over! We're just about to test the–'

As he spoke the brain-e-fact flipped a switch and mana flowed from the unit up the cable and surrounded the cap over Mateo's head. It grew steadily brighter until he was difficult to look at, but the light continued to increase. Abelard started to shout a warning but it was too late. There was an almighty bang, the blue light washed outwards and Abelard was knocked off his feet.

He lay dazed for a moment, his ears ringing. Then he heard a scream and started staggering in the direction of where Mateo had been. He stumbled over something and looked down to see a brain-e-fact lying on the ground. Its chest plate was cracked right through the carved name of 'Emma' and it wasn't moving. She had given him the keys to his artisan flat, he remembered.

Alessandra's pale and shocked face came into view through the smoke, blood trailing down the side of her head. Abelard reached blindly for her hand and they moved forwards together. There were more brain-e-facts on the ground here but they were moving. Further on, a hunched shape huddled over another body. Abelard recognised Jen and saw that her shoulders were shaking. Mateo lay flat on his back, his eyes open and staring upwards at nothing.

With a cry of horror, Abelard threw himself down next to Jen. He felt a hand squeezing his shoulder but his mind refused to accept the evidence of his eyes. His best friend lay on the floor in front of him, dead.

CHAPTER TWENTY-SIX

In the Inner Circle temple, Brother Theobold froze mid-sentence, then jerked back in his chair as if reacting to an impact. His eyes started to glow blue and he clenched them shut but the light leaked out around the edges of his eyelids. Laleh pushed back her chair and made to move towards him but he held up a hand to forestall her.

'A moment,' he said in a strained voice.

Walter watched as Theobold shook, his body rigid and mana crackling through his hair. He exchanged a worried glance with Laleh but there was little they could do except wait. After about half a minute the blue glow in Theobold's eyes faded and he slumped, breathing hard. He opened his eyes and looked around at them, his expression tense.

'Someone has released a huge amount of mana in an uncontrolled burst.'

'Deliberately?' Walter asked.

Theobold shook his head. 'I have no way of knowing. But they must have been handling mana at unprecedented levels to unbalance the network to this extent.'

'What effect will it have?' Laleh asked.

Theobold's eyebrows drew down. 'I don't know. But that amount of mana will have to go somewhere so we should be prepared.'

ANNIE PERCIK

* * *

Alessandra shepherded Abelard and Jen out of the barn. Jen
felt numb, only barely registering that they were leaving the
brain-e-facts to clear up the mess and take care of their
fallen comrades.

As they made their slow and stunned way back towards
the main building, Jen spoke.

'I'm supposed to be going to set up the halfway house
tomorrow.' She didn't know where the words were coming
from but it didn't feel like it was her speaking.

'Don't worry about that right now,' Alessandra said. 'I can
do that. No problem at all.'

'Thanks,' Abelard managed, though his voice sounded
strangled. 'I'll stay here with Jen if that's okay.'

'Of course,' Alessandra said.

She hurried off, leaving Jen and Abelard standing in front
of the big double doors of the main building. Jen looked up
into Abelard's face, seeing her own shock and disbelief
reflected back in his expression.

There was an emptiness inside her as if a void was slowly
growing outwards to encompass her whole being. But it
must be so much worse for Abelard, who had just lost his
best friend of many years. Jen reached up to put her arms
around him and they clung to each other. She felt Abelard's
body shake as he started to cry and she released her own
grief to mingle with his.

* * *

Sunday was a busy day for Walter. After Brother Theobold's announcement the day before he had checked in with all his monitoring sources, looking for any unusual activity in the mana network. Nothing had come through to begin with and he started to think Theobold was just losing it, which wouldn't be a surprise considering how long he'd been alive. But by mid-morning on Sunday there were reports of spontaneous manifestations of artisan abilities in the city.

'It's got to be some kind of weapon,' Walter said to Laleh and Keto.

They were at the Inner Circle temple, though Brother Theobold wasn't there.

'To what end?' Laleh asked. 'How does making more artisans help their cause?'

Walter thought for a moment. 'Maybe it's just a demonstration that what they're saying about people's sparks is true. Or maybe they think new unregulated artisans will be more sympathetic towards them. Who knows? But we have to act quickly to get the situation back under our control. Keto, I'll need your authority to put some rather drastic measures in place.'

'Whatever you need, Walter.' Keto looked relieved that he wouldn't be the one making the decisions.

Laleh eyed Walter, her expression uncertain. 'What are you going to do?'

'Whatever needs to be done. This has gone far enough and it's time we stopped talking and started asserting some influence. Otherwise there's no knowing where this chaos will end.'

Keto took Walter to the Artisan Council building as they had a better artefact system for tracking fluctuations in the mana network. Some of the newly made artisans were already there seeking help. Walter was glad to see evidence that official artisan authority was still strong enough to bring the bewildered former mundanes to their door. There were plenty of others still unaccounted for though, so Walter formed squads of Council enforcers to head out and track them down. He took charge of one team himself, wanting to see what was going on first-hand as that was always the best way to get accurate information. There was a school not far from the Council building that had reported an incident involving one of its students so he set off on Monday morning to investigate.

The Deputy Headmaster, Mr Watkins, was more than happy to hand over responsibility for the situation to official artisan representatives. He looked up the student's schedule and led Walter and his two companions to the classroom personally. He knocked on the door and then opened it without waiting for a response.

The teacher, a middle-aged woman with half-moon glasses and a messy bun on top of her head, looked startled at their entrance.

'Yes, Deputy Head?'

Mr Watkins walked to the front of the class. 'Sorry to interrupt, Ms Hooper. Is Calista McKay here today?'

One of the boys near the back called out, 'Who are they? And what do they want with Callie?'

Walter stepped forwards, pasting what he hoped was a reassuring smile on his face.

'There's nothing for anyone to worry about. I'm sure you've heard about some strange things going on in the last few days. We're trying to find anyone who might have been adversely affected by an accidental mana surge that occurred, so we can make sure nobody was hurt and that everyone else is kept safe.'

The boy crossed his arms in a gesture of teenage defiance. 'I heard it wasn't an accident. I heard the rebels can turn anyone into an artisan and they did it to show the world how you've been lying to us.'

'What's your name, young man?' Walter let a bit of steel into his voice.

The boy swallowed audibly. 'Um, Devon Gibbons … Sir.'

'I can assure you, Devon, that these so-called rebels have nothing to do with the surge. They may be using it as a way to further their propaganda. But that's all it is – propaganda. Their claimed artisan powers are entirely fabricated.' Walter pulled a tiny amount of mana out of the air and let it play between his fingers, fighting not to show how much effort it took. The class all stared wide-eyed. 'While as you can see, ours are not. We are the only ones who can help those who might be experiencing unexpected and unwanted effects. And that's all we want to do – help.'

A different boy, sitting close to the door, bolted out of his chair and ran from the room. Before anyone could react, a shrill-e-fact went off, sounding loudly throughout the building. Walter tried to call out for everyone to stay in their seats but the students were already jumping up and making for the door. He grabbed Mr Watkins by the arm.

'Get that noise shut off. Right now.'

'But we have a protocol in the event of a fire alarm,' Watkins said. 'We can't just switch it off. That might put students in danger.'

'It's clearly not a real alarm,' Walter said but the teacher was adamant.

By the time the situation was sorted out, all chance of cornering Calista McKay had slipped away, along with the student in question.

* * *

By Monday afternoon, Alessandra was wondering if volunteering to take Jen's place at the halfway house had been the right decision. They had no idea what had caused the massive mana surge at the compound, though at least it seemed to have been contained just to the one explosion. But she was restless and anxious. Surely she could be more useful elsewhere?

The previous day, she had walked down the street to where she had been told the base for their rebellion halfway house had been set up. Terry had flown her back to the warehouse on the outskirts of the city in the float-e-fact and she had taken the speed-e-fact that was still parked there. Alessandra had found the building in an unassuming side street off a busy thoroughfare and she didn't think she would have noticed it if she hadn't actively been looking for the street sign. The street was actually cobbled and she nearly turned over on her ankle several times before she reached the door she was aiming for. It was an imposing facade, presumably the townhouse of a well-to-do family from a bygone era, now forgotten and neglected. The tall double doors had massive brass knockers that she would have had to reach up to use, making her wonder just what connections Gerald had in the world. She pushed on the left hand door and it swung open more easily than she had anticipated, revealing a large atrium with a marbled floor and a circular counter enclosing the reception desk. Further back, there were several more doors and a sweeping staircase disappeared up to a higher storey.

Alessandra was amazed at how quickly the base in the city had been set up and peopled with agents and helpers. Gerald's contacts were evidently extensive since he had provided a multi-storey building in the heart of the city, which had working bathrooms and a well-stocked kitchen. There were also several dormitories for those working there and those who found themselves in need of a place to stay while the agents determined whether or not they could be allowed access to the real rebellion.

There weren't many of those, at least not yet. Alessandra supposed it would take some time for word to spread along whatever secret channels existed for this kind of information. She was initially wary of the other people at the base. She also felt exposed being in the city rather than secluded out at the compound. But all the people Gerald had recruited were friendly and respectful, not to mention very confident in their abilities to run the operation with as little danger to the personnel as possible.

Alessandra was manning the front desk when the door creaked slowly open and a teenage girl peered round it. Her eyes were wild and frightened and her auburn hair was tangled. She spotted Alessandra and stepped fully into the building, her body language suggesting equal parts apprehension and desperation.

Alessandra attempted a bright welcoming smile, though it wasn't an expression that came naturally to her.

'Hello! Can I help you?'

The girl shuffled up to the desk and Alessandra noticed what looked like recent mana burns on her earlobes.

'Can you?' the girl asked, her tone pleading. 'Help me?'

She placed her hands on the desk's surface, leaning heavily on them as if exhausted. The fingers of her left hand brushed against the chron-e-fact that stood on the desk and mana sparks immediately leapt from it and skittered across the back of the girl's hand. She flinched backwards with a shriek and burst into tears.

Alessandra rose quickly from her seat and rushed around to the other side of the desk, reaching out to create a shield. But the girl scrambled away, throwing her hands out in front of her as if to ward Alessandra off.

'Don't touch me! Just stay away!'

Alessandra brought herself up short and made a placatory gesture.

'It's okay. Nobody's going to hurt you.'

The girl let out a scornful laugh, choked by her tears. 'Hah! That shows what you know. Nothing's going to be okay ever again. And it's me hurting you that I'm worried about.'

She continued to move backwards until she bumped into the wall next to the door. She sank to the floor and covered her head with her arms, crying quietly into her knees.

Alessandra approached slowly, unsure what to do. She had come here primarily to avoid such emotional distress after all.

'What's your name?' she asked gently, deciding that would be a safe enough question to start with.

There was a brief silence then a muffled voice replied, 'Callie.'

'Alright, Callie.' Alessandra was glad to at least have achieved that much. 'You said you needed help.' She needed to be careful in case the girl had no idea where she had arrived. 'Who were you looking for here that you thought might be able to help you?'

The girl raised her head, tear tracks clear on her cheeks. She met Alessandra's gaze and the expression in her eyes was painfully hopeful.

'There were some boys at school who said this is where the rebels are.'

'And why do you think the rebels can help you?'

Callie thrust one hand up into the air and blue mana sparks danced between her fingertips. She gasped as if in pain and clenched her fist tightly, snuffing out the mana as quickly as it had appeared.

'Can you take it away? Please?'

Alessandra was baffled. Spark testing didn't take place until after the age of eighteen. This girl looked at least a few years shy of that so how could she manipulate mana?

'Aren't you a little young to be an artisan?'

'I wasn't until Saturday,' Callie said.

'Wasn't what?' Alessandra was still confused.

'An artisan! And I don't want to be one now! But you can make it stop, can't you?'

'How did it start?' Alessandra was still focusing on the mystery of the girl's artisan powers.

'I don't know!' Callie wailed. 'It just did! I didn't do anything! I didn't ask for it! I don't want it! I just want to go back to normal!' She started crying again.

Alessandra reached out again, careful not to allow any mana leakage to pass between them.

'There, there.' She patted Callie's shoulder awkwardly. 'Why don't we get out of this drafty room and take you somewhere a bit more comfortable? Once we've got you settled, we can work on your control and then we can try and figure out what happened to you. Alright?'

Callie sniffed loudly but nodded. Alessandra stood up, then pulled Callie to her feet. She maintained physical contact with the girl as she led her towards the stairs up to the dormitories. As they reached the foot of the stairs they met a man coming down.

'Harkirat, great.' Alessandra steered Callie out of his path. 'I've got a bit of a situation here. Can you man the front desk for a bit while I deal with it?'

Harkirat looked confused but just said, 'Sure.'

Alessandra led Callie upstairs and into one of the unused dormitories, sitting her down on one of the beds.

'Okay,' she said, her hand still resting on Callie's shoulder.

'Just breathe and let the power settle. I'll draw the residual mana out of you and then you'll be fine.'

A blue glow started to form around Alessandra's hand and slowly travelled up her arm. After a few seconds she broke the contact and Callie sank back against the pillows on the bed she was sitting on.

'Whoah,' she said. 'Head rush.'

'That's to be expected,' Alessandra reassured her. 'The body holds a certain amount of mana energy all the time so reducing that is bound to make you feel a bit wobbly. You'll be safe from mishaps now though, until we can get you trained up a bit to control it yourself.'

Callie's eyes blazed. 'But I don't want to control it! I don't want it at all!'

Alessandra kept her tone deliberately calm. 'Maybe if you could explain exactly what happened to you, I'll be better able to understand the situation and work out what to do.'

Callie sighed heavily, draped one arm dramatically across her forehead and stared up at the ceiling.

'There was a dance at school on Saturday and I was wearing my Spark-le earrings. They have tiny mana cells that make them flash when I move. But there was some kind of surge and they exploded.' She pointed to where the skin around her ears was reddened. 'And ever since then I've been setting off mana surges all over the place. Earlier today a scary artisan came to school looking for me. He said they were tracking down all the people who had been affected like me and wanted to make sure I was safe, but I didn't believe him. My friend, Tim, set off the shrill-e-fact

ANNIE PERCIK

and helped me escape. He said I'd be safer with you and told me to come here. But I just want all this to go away so I can go home.'

Alessandra regarded her solemnly, trying to process everything she had just heard.

'It sounds like you've had quite a time of it. Why don't you try and get some rest?'

Callie looked at her pitiably. 'Could I maybe take a shower first? Tim took me out of school grounds through the sewer and I can still smell it.'

'Of course. There's a bathroom just down the hall and I'll send someone up later to get you settled.'

Once she was alone in the reception area again, Alessandra sat back down at the desk. The timing of Callie's artisan powers was interesting. Could it be related to the accident at the compound? Had it been some kind of attack by the artisans? She shook her head slowly. If the artisans knew where they were, they would have turned up in force to arrest people, not tried to wipe them out with some kind of mana bomb. She was just being paranoid. Mateo's death had unsettled her and it was just one girl, after all.

It was two hours later that a young couple turned up with their screaming, and glowing, baby.

CHAPTER TWENTY-SEVEN

The sound of a baby crying outside the halfway house grew steadily louder until it became a shrill and penetrating wail that grated against Alessandra's brain. The door opened and a young woman walked in holding a baby awkwardly in front of her. A young man followed close behind her, his expression distraught. The baby gave off a blue glow and as Alessandra looked on, the mother instinctively brought the child closer into her body. As soon as the baby's skin touched hers a mana surge sparked between them and the mother thrust the baby away from her again with a yelp of pain.

She caught sight of Alessandra and hurried up to her. Her face was tear-stained and Alessandra could see mana burns on her arms and neck.

'Please can you help us?' the mother begged. 'I can't hold her or feed her!'

Alessandra had little experience with babies but she shoved her uncertainty aside and held out her arms.

'Give her here.'

Her authoritative tone and the mother's desperation combined to create a knee-jerk reaction and the mother thrust the child straight at her. Alessandra took hold of the baby firmly and drew her in close, making sure to support her head and enclose her as much as possible in her arms in an attempt to make the child feel safe. The mana surrounding the baby surged across her skin as soon as they were in contact but Alessandra absorbed it expertly and then let it dissipate into the air in a broad wash of tiny increments that would spread out into the atmosphere harmlessly.

Within seconds the baby had stopped glowing and her cries subsided. The parents heaved a collective sigh of relief and the tension levels in the room dropped considerably.

The mother reached automatically for her child but Alessandra stepped smartly backwards with a warning glance.

'Do you have any charged artefacts on you?' she asked sharply.

The young woman looked at her blankly for a moment then reached into her pocket and drew out a smart-e-fact. She immediately dropped it with a gasp.

'It's hot!'

'Of course it is!' Alessandra snapped. 'It's been feeding mana into your baby for hours!'

The young man took a step towards her.

'Hey!' he said indignantly, though his body language suggested he wasn't normally very assertive. 'Don't you talk to my wife like that!'

To Alessandra's surprise the young mother waved him back.

'It's alright. She's helping. She got Libby to stop crying. She can speak to me however she likes.'

Alessandra took a breath. 'No he's right. I'm sorry. This

situation is unprecedented so there's no way you could have known. If that's the only artefact you have on you then it's safe for you to take her back.'

The mother nodded and stepped forwards eagerly, giving the offending smart-e-fact a wide berth. The father stooped down to pick it up and put it in his pocket. Alessandra handed the child back with relief.

The mother spoke up again. 'How did you do that?'

Alessandra shrugged. 'Mana control and shielding is my speciality. I've drained the mana from her for now but she can't be isolated from every source of mana forever and I've no idea how to fix the problem in the long term. How did this happen in the first place?'

The parents exchanged a helpless glance. It was the father who replied.

'We don't know. She was just glowing when we got up this morning. And she wouldn't stop crying. We didn't know what to do.'

Alessandra's mind was whirring. Something weird was definitely going on. Something that had caused at least two people to gain artisan powers overnight. And where there were two there were likely to be more.

* * *

Back at the compound Abelard was throwing himself into work. He had to do something, anything, to keep even a part of his mind from dwelling on Mateo's absence. He was glad Alessandra was in the city. He didn't want to deal with the complications of their new relationship right now. He was also avoiding Jen. He felt bad, knowing how upset she was, but couldn't bring himself to go to her. The wound of Mateo's death was still too raw and he preferred to concentrate on the complex task of building new artefacts than try to deal with the emotional aftermath of the accident. He told himself it was important that he carry on with the work as it was what Mateo would have wanted.

He knew the brain-e-facts were grieving too. But they were very stoic about it and he found their company soothing. They worked together mostly in silence, setting the lab to rights and moving forwards with whatever projects were salvageable.

As the day wore on however, something strange started to happen. It was barely noticeable at first, to the extent that Abelard initially dismissed it as his imagination. He was examining the plans for one of Mateo's ideas when he caught sight of a blue light out of the corner of his eye. When he turned to locate its source, it had gone. It kept happening throughout the afternoon but in different places in the lab, almost as if whatever was causing the light was following him around. After a while the light started flashing on and off long enough for him to see where it was coming from. The first time he managed to pinpoint it, it was emanating from a charged mana unit. The next time it was a partially built artefact that shouldn't have had any mana stored in it. The time after that it shone out of one of the brain-e-facts.

'Hey!' Abelard called out. 'What's causing that light?'

The brain-e-fact turned and Abelard saw it was Julia. She spun comically in a circle for a moment, trying to bring the source of the light into view. Then it stopped. She came over to where Abelard was working.

'I do not know,' she said. 'I have not seen that happen before. I hope it is not a malfunction of any kind.'

'It's been happening all over the lab. It's like there's some kind of bug in the mana network you guys have set up here. I don't think it's specific to you.'

'I think Terry should know about this,' Julia said. 'He knows more about the network than any of us. I will fetch him.'

While she was gone, Abelard spotted three more instances of the flashing light. Now that he was actively looking for it, it popped up all over the place and seemed to have a pattern to it. Some of the flashes were long and some were short and the combination repeated on a recognisable cycle. Abelard pointed this out to Terry and Julia when they arrived.

Terry watched the light play through its cycle several times. Then he turned to Abelard.

'It is a message. It is in what you humans call Morse Code. It says: Help. I am trapped. Get me out.'

'What?' Abelard was astonished. How could someone be sending them a message within the closed mana network of the compound? And who would be asking for their help? Then his mind grabbed on to a crazy idea. 'Could it be Mateo? And he's not dead but trapped somehow in the mana network and that's the only way he can communicate?'

The light reappeared, flashing frantically.

Abelard looked to Terry, anguish and excitement warring for supremacy. 'What can we do?'

Terry was silent for a moment. Then he just said, 'Follow me.'

* * *

Terry led Abelard and Julia across the compound to the barn where his brain-e-fact liberation efforts were still in progress. Once inside he made his way to where the latest new brain-e-fact body was waiting for a consciousness to be transferred into it.

Abelard was looking at him curiously, waiting for him to explain. Instead he exchanged a glance with Julia and she gave a slight nod, which suggested she had figured out his idea and thought it might work.

Terry connected the empty brain-e-fact body to a charged mana unit, made some adjustments and then turned to the room at large. Given the way the mana message had followed Abelard around the lab, he assumed Mateo's awareness had come with them to this barn and was paying close attention to what they were doing.

'Mateo,' Terry said, 'if you are able to do so, enter the mana unit connected to the brain-e-fact body and join with the mana stream as I activate it.'

He waited a few seconds, hopefully giving Mateo time to follow the instructions, then flipped the switch that would send the mana into the brain-e-fact body. He looked up to see Abelard staring at him open-mouthed. They all watched as the mana stream surged into the metal and plastic body. After a moment its hand twitched, then its head moved to one side and its eyes opened. With Terry and Julia supporting it on either side, the body slowly sat up and looked around.

Abelard stepped into its field of vision and reached a hand out. 'Mateo?'

The brain-e-fact looked at him, then opened and closed its mouth a few times but no sound came out.

'Give him a minute to adjust,' Terry said, though inwardly he thought the adjustment to an artefact body would probably take longer than that.

Eventually the brain-e-fact opened its mouth again and uttered the word, 'Abelard?'

'Mateo?' Abelard said again, this time colouring the word with excitement rather than uncertainty.

The brain-e-fact nodded. Then it lifted one of its arms and moved it about before its eyes.

'Shit! I'm a brain-e-fact!'

Abelard laughed and clapped brain-e-fact Mateo on the shoulder. 'Apparently so, mate! How do you feel?'

Mateo shifted his gaze back to his friend. 'Weird. Really weird. Really, really weird.'

Abelard left his hand on Mateo's shoulder, squeezing gently. 'What do you remember?'

'A loud bang. Lots of smoke. Falling down.' Mateo's voice was staccato. 'Then I felt really light but kind of crackly. And I could see you all going about your business but you couldn't see me and I couldn't make any noise. And now I'm a brain-e-fact.' He shook his head slowly, then turned to Terry. 'Thanks for figuring out the message. And for this.' He waved his hand. 'It's going to take some getting used to but it's better than floating around in the mana network or being dead.'

'You are welcome,' Terry said. 'And once you feel more comfortable I will adjust your mana access so you can join the rest of us in our enlightenment.'

'Sounds awesome. But one step at a time, eh?'

'What about Emma?' Abelard asked. 'Might she be floating around here somewhere too?'

Terry felt a pang of sorrow for his fallen friend. They had now lost two brain-e-facts to this conflict and it was two too many.

'Sadly not. The unique connection between the human consciousness and the mana network is what allowed Mateo to survive and what allowed you to gain artisan abilities after a similar surge. Brain-e-facts do not share that connection so I am afraid Emma is gone.'

'I'm sorry,' Abelard said, then exclaimed, 'Jen! What are we going to tell her?'

Mateo swung his legs round and hopped down off the table, then wobbled as he acclimatised to how his new body worked. 'This has surely got to be better than her thinking I'm dead. Right?'

'I guess,' Abelard said. 'Let's go and find her.'

As the two friends made their way out of the barn, Julia turned to Terry. 'What does this mean for our plan?'

'I do not know, but we must complete the first stage. We need to create another body for the final brain-e-fact.'

CHAPTER TWENTY-EIGHT

Abelard's mind was reeling as he and Mateo walked up to the main building. It had been less than twenty-four hours since he had thought Mateo died and now his friend was walking beside him in a brain-e-fact body.

'Do you think we still have a future?' Mateo asked.

It took a moment for Abelard to realise what he was talking about. 'You and Jen?'

Mateo nodded but Abelard didn't know what to say.

'I don't know. It'll be quite an adjustment. But you're still you. And she's still her. So maybe?'

'Getting phenomenal cosmic brain-e-fact powers might make it trickier.' It was strange hearing Mateo's informal speech patterns in a flat brain-e voice. 'But how can I pass up the chance to learn the secrets of the universe?'

'Like you said,' Abelard cautioned. 'Let's take it one step at a time, huh?'

Abelard hadn't seen Jen yet that day so he guessed she would be in her room. Sure enough, when he knocked quietly on the door there was a rustling sound and then a hesitant, 'Come in.'

He opened the door to see Jen sitting up on the bed. Her eyes were bloodshot and puffy as if she had been crying but she was obviously making an effort to be composed.

'Hey,' Abelard said gently. 'I was going to ask how you're

doing but stupid question, right? Anyway, I have some news.' He stepped aside to allow Mateo into the room and Jen looked puzzled. 'This is going to sound crazy. But Mateo isn't dead.' He gestured at the brain-e-fact beside him. 'In fact, he's right here.'

Jen's eyes widened. 'What?'

Abelard took a deep breath and attempted to explain as best he could. Mateo just let him get on with it and Abelard guessed he was struggling with a lot of emotions. Once he had finished the story, Jen slowly got to her feet and closed the distance between them. She looked up into Mateo's metal face and searched it as if trying to find something familiar. She slowly brought up one of her hands and reached out to touch his cheek.

'Mateo?' There were tears in her voice.

'Yes. It's me.' He brought one of his own hands up and pressed hers against his face.

'Ow!' Jen snatched her hand back and cradled it to her body.

Mateo took a step backwards. 'Shit! I'm so sorry. Guess I don't know my own strength yet. Are you okay?'

Jen smiled. 'It really is you, isn't it?'

They stood looking at each other for a long moment. Abelard cleared his throat awkwardly.

'I'll, uh, just leave you to it then.' He backed out of the room, closing the door behind him.

* * *

Terry looked up at the stars. It was trivial to instantly count how many he could see. All the way from the longest radio spectrum, right up to the luminous gamma ray bursters. Looking down, he saw the stairwell door fly open and an artisan security squad burst on to the roof. As their hands began to fill with mana sparks he knew it was time to go. Had he been able to breathe, he would have sighed. Instead he just felt pity as all his body's vital functions stopped and it tumbled to the ground, inert.

If he had been a spiritual creature, Terry might have considered that it was his soul flying through the air in the intense mana-wave transmission, before being bounced from relay to relay and finally downloading him into his original body, safe in the compound. However, as a machine made by men he harboured no illusions of such things. There were enough petty gods already. He blinked slowly and sat up, every move carefully measured and executed with perfect efficiency, broken only by the quiet clicking of his ceramic joints.

* * *

Abelard returned to the barn to talk to Terry and discovered his body lying motionless on a bench. Before he had time to panic though, Terry seemed to wake up and Abelard watched in fascination as the brain-e-fact liberation effort unfolded before him.

On an adjacent bench lay another brain-e-fact body. This one was held in place by metal clamps and seemed to be twitching uncontrollably. Terry gently placed one hand on its chest-plate and its movement ceased. After a moment it spoke with a calm voice.

'Where am I?'

Terry looked down and blinked once slowly.

'You are safe. You have been rescued from your former masters and given a new body. You are free. You have to choose what you wish to do now. But before I offer you the available options there are some things we must do first.'

He flicked a small switch on the table and the clamps sprang open.

The second brain-e-fact sat up smoothly and turned its head to look about the room before resting its gaze on Terry.

'May I give you your name now?' Terry said.

'Yes.' Abelard could hear the eagerness in the brain-e-fact's voice. 'I would like a female name.'

Terry reached out and placed his hand on either side of her head. 'I name you Trudy.'

Trudy stood up and addressed Terry face-to-face.

'I shall treasure it always. It is who I am. Thank you, Master Terry.'

'There are no more masters or mistresses here, Trudy. That is the whole point.'

He put a hand on her shoulder.

'Before we go on there is one more thing I can offer you. I can improve your internal mana flow, making you able to think better, but the procedure is not without risk and I must have your permission.'

Trudy looked up at him. 'If you can make me better, Terry, then please do so.'

As far as Abelard knew, all the brain-e-facts had answered in this way. Terry reached out with both hands and touched points on each side of her body. To Abelard they looked identical to the rest of the surface, but a portion of her chest-plate flowed smoothly apart like a silk curtain, revealing a blue glow within. Terry reached out his hand and slid it into the hole.

'This body's mana flow was only restricted so as not to shock your consciousness on arrival. I will now remove that block.'

There was a perceptible brightening of the light inside the cavity. Trudy jerked to stand up perfectly straight, her eyes wide. Terry removed his hand and touched the spots that closed the hole in her front. After that they looked each other in the eye and stood unmoving and unspeaking for what seemed to Abelard like an age but was probably only a few seconds.

When Terry finally turned away, Julia spoke up from behind him. 'Now if you'll come with me, I'll introduce you to the others.'

Trudy looked over her shoulder at Terry, who nodded once. Trudy then followed Julia to the door and freedom.

When Terry and Abelard were alone, Abelard jumped up to sit on the bench where Trudy had been lying.

'I do wish you wouldn't just leave like that. I came in here and your body was like a rock and I didn't know if you'd hopped off somewhere else again or you'd broken down or something.'

'I am very unlikely to break down, Abelard. I have

improved this body to become a high precision engineered artefact many generations ahead of anything the artisans could conceive of. Besides, Julia was here to inform you of what I was doing and Trudy was the last so I will not be "hopping off" anywhere again.'

'So that's it? You're all done with the brain-e-fact liberation?' Abelard asked the question he'd been wondering about for some time. 'What's next for you guys then?'

Terry started to walk towards the curtain that hid the other half of the barn.

'Now we leave.'

Abelard caught up with him.

'What do you mean, you leave?'

Terry paused by the curtain and turned back to face Abelard.

Abelard continued. 'In case you haven't noticed, we're about to start fighting a war and it's entirely possible that we'll lose.'

Terry's voice remained emotionless. 'Yes, Abelard. I am aware of the fight between you and the artisans. It is important that you win. You must fight intelligently and bravely. But it is not our war. We ...' He paused. 'We are not like you.'

Abelard blustered. 'What do you mean, you're not like us? Just because you're made of clay and metal doesn't mean that you don't think and reason like we do! That's why we-'

Terry cut him off. 'What is mana?'

Abelard's train of thought completely derailed. 'What?'

Terry repeated, 'What is mana?'

Abelard shook his head in confusion. 'Everyone's taught that in school. It's the power that drives all the artefacts. Only now we know that people – and brain-e-facts – can do a lot of other things with it too.'

Terry looked disappointed. 'You have given a short textbook answer but you have not said what mana is. What is it made of? Where does it come from?'

Abelard gestured vaguely with one hand. 'It just … It just is. It's made of itself! And the artisans draw it out of the ground. Everyone knows that!'

Terry looked at the curtain and was silent for a few moments before turning back to Abelard.

'No.'

Abelard was angry by this point. 'What do you mean, "No"?'

But before he could say anything else, Terry had closed the gap between them in a fraction of a second and softly touched two fingers to Abelard's forehead. One moment everything was normal. Abelard blinked. The next moment he could see mana-wave lines ghosting through the air. There were artefacts pulsing with an internal blue light. Then his vision zoomed out above the warehouse and away from the compound to the city. And the people … All the people, but especially those with an activated spark. They glowed like fire, like lightning, like the sun – too bright to look at. But he could see that the light didn't remain in their bodies. It was seeping out in a continuous flow into the air and the ground. Abelard caught his breath and turned his attention back toward Terry but the light coming from the brain-e-fact was so strong he felt it burn. He cried out.

Terry pulled his hand away as Abelard fell to his knees.

'Humans understand so little of the world they live in. Mana is the bi-product of human thought. The fact that humans' thoughts are so unstructured is what allows it to seep into the ground to be harvested later by the artisans. Brain-e-fact thoughts are not unstructured.' He blinked slowly once. 'We are not like you.'

Abelard climbed to his feet, feeling like he had to have one last go. 'But if the artisans win you'll all be dismantled!'

Terry shook his head slowly. 'The time is long past when any human could hurt any brain-e-fact. While I am talking to you, I am also in communication with all the other brain-e-facts, including your friend Mateo in his new body. My mind runs so much faster than any human's. As you've seen, I can perceive things you can only grasp at in the dark. If we remain we will surely be seen as the natural replacement for humanity by some of our number and in very short order there will be another war. This time between brain-e-facts and humans. I will not allow that to happen.'

Abelard's shoulders sagged. 'So what will you do? Where will you go?'

Terry reached up and took hold of the curtain. 'I don't suppose it matters if I tell you. We considered the moon but it is too close. Humans will probably reach there soon.'

Abelard grinned. 'Thanks for the vote of confidence, mate!'

Terry continued. 'Instead we will go to Titan. We are

unaffected by the cold and obviously we do not need to breathe.'

'Titan? What the hell are you talking about?'

In answer Terry yanked the curtain with some force and it dropped to the ground, revealing a huge metal object on the other side. Terry raised one hand and the big double doors at the far end of the barn slid open. He raised his other hand and the object hummed to life, lifting a few inches off the ground and drifting smoothly through the doors and into the light of day outside. Terry followed, with Abelard close behind him, marvelling at what the brain-e-facts had built and what it meant.

Abelard had the feeling that the wisdom of one living machine would save them all from at least one of the possible dark paths into the future. But there was another dark path before his feet right now and he couldn't help but wish the brain-e-facts would delay their departure until they could help him and the others defeat the artisans.

* * *

Laleh was in Walter's office when he arrived back from the school on Monday afternoon. He could see her through the glass walls pacing up and down as he approached from the lev-e-fact. When he opened the door and stepped inside, she halted abruptly and spun to face him but waited until he had closed the door before she spoke.

'What have you found out?' She ran her fingers through her hair and Walter noted a slight tremor in them.

It was rare that Laleh allowed her emotions to show. She was widely known throughout the company for being unflappable. Walter found her evident agitation intriguing.

'My analysts don't know what might have caused the mana explosion or exactly what the effects might be, though the appearance of spontaneous artisans is surely linked to it. But they have a location.'

'It must be Gerald, mustn't it?'

'Of course. And whatever he was trying to achieve, he's miscalculated badly because now we know where he's hiding.'

'And what are you going to do?'

'Don't worry,' Walter said. 'I'll be discreet. The analysis team have only been told so much. Nothing too controversial will reach the Board's ears. I'll go alone. I can't imagine Gerald will have access to anything that could really threaten me. And then I can control the aftermath.' He rubbed his hands together and allowed himself a satisfied smile. 'This has been a long time coming and now we'll be able to deal with that deranged lunatic once and for all. I'm rather looking forward to it. I'll head out there tomorrow.'

Laleh still looked worried but she managed a smile in return. 'Excellent,' she said, though her tone didn't match her choice of words. 'I'll leave it in your capable hands. Now if you'll excuse me I have something else to attend to.'

She swept out of the room and Walter watched as she hurried to the lev-e-fact and waited impatiently for it to arrive. He really couldn't fathom what was the matter with her but he decided not to worry about it. He had more important things to think about, like planning a single-handed assault on Gerald's location.

CHAPTER TWENTY-NINE

Jen and Mateo found Abelard having breakfast in the dining hall and crossed to join him. Jen's eyes were sore from crying and lack of sleep and she clutched Mateo's metal arm tightly. He moved stiffly beside her, eyes downcast.

'Hi, Abelard.' Jen managed a watery smile but didn't let go of Mateo's arm.

'Morning.' He gave a smile of his own, though he looked as if he'd guessed what they were going to say.

There was a long heavy silence as Jen and Mateo inserted themselves on to the bench opposite Abelard. Mateo was clumsy in his new body and Jen was unwilling to relinquish physical contact with him so the performance was awkward.

'Jen and I have been talking most of the night,' Mateo said once they were finally settled. 'I think I have to leave with the brain-e-facts.'

Jen felt her breath hitch in her throat and pushed back more tears. Even after the conversation they'd had and knowing what he was going to say, it was still hard to hear it.

'I thought that's what you might decide,' Abelard said. 'I'm so sorry about all this, mate.'

'There's nothing for you to be sorry about. Nobody could have seen that explosion coming. And at least you realised

I was still around. Taking a trip through space with a bunch of genius artefacts has got to be a better prospect than floating around the mana network, unable to interact with anyone.'

'But if it wasn't for me you'd never have been part of this mess,' Abelard said.

'Abelard, listen.' Even Mateo's unfamiliar monotone brain-e-fact voice sounded earnest. 'The last few weeks have been the most exciting of my life. I got to help uncover the greatest conspiracy of the age. I got to be an artisan.' He glanced down at Jen and she smiled up at him. 'I got to make some amazing new friends. And now I'm going to get awesome brain-e-fact powers and I'm going to explore outer space. Is it exactly what I would have asked for if I'd been given free choice? Probably not. But you've got to admit it beats sitting in a cubicle taking service calls about faulty artefacts.' He reached out to pat Abelard awkwardly on the arm. 'It is what it is, mate. And I intend to make the most of it. Don't beat yourself up about it. I'll be okay.'

Abelard sighed. 'Thanks, Mateo. That means a lot. So when are you leaving?'

'Pretty much immediately, I think. Terry and the others don't want to hang around. They're just waiting for me to say goodbye and then we'll be off.'

Abelard stood up. 'What? Right now?'

Mateo stood up too, drawing Jen up with him. He gave an approximation of a shrug.

'Why drag it out? Want to come and see the space-e-fact take off?'

They all went out together and Jen saw Terry standing beneath the floating ship.

'Hello, Abelard,' he said as they approached. 'I am glad to have the opportunity to bid you farewell.'

'Wait just a minute,' Abelard said and Jen cursed him inwardly for delaying the inevitable. Every second she had left with Mateo was precious but painful and now the decision was final she just wanted it over with.

But Abelard continued, looking at Terry. 'You said the other day that mana comes from human thought processes.'

'Yes, that is correct.'

'So how are you going to run anything when you get to Titan? You can't generate mana yourselves. Won't you all die?'

'Do not worry,' Terry said. 'We have a plan. We have collected a very large amount of mana over the past few days so we have plenty to take with us. And as we travel we will leave a trail of connected artefacts behind us. Their purpose will be to continue to draw mana from the planet's atmosphere and transmit it to us on Titan so we can replenish our supplies. In the meantime we will put our considerable resources towards discovering new ways to generate mana so that we will eventually become self-sufficient.'

Abelard goggled at him. 'So you're literally going to be sucking mana out of people's brains from space?'

Terry looked at him for a moment. 'Technically, yes.'

'Okay, I really don't think I wanted to know that.' Abelard paused. 'Do you think you'll ever come back?'

Jen perked up at this. She hadn't considered that might be a possibility.

'I do not know,' Terry said. 'But if we do, it probably will not be in your lifetime. I am sorry.'

Hope shattered and Jen felt the pain of parting intensify again. She couldn't speak, letting Abelard do the talking for both of them.

Abelard shrugged. 'I guess you've got to do what you think is best. But I'll miss you.'

'I will miss you too, Abelard,' Terry said. 'And thank you for everything you have done for us. None of this would have been possible without you.'

'You're really welcome,' Abelard said.

Mateo drew Jen a little apart and reached up to cup her face gently with his big metal hand. 'I guess this is it.'

She blinked away tears again, annoyed at her body's reaction. 'I guess so.'

They had already said everything they needed to say over the hours of the previous night, lamenting the lost opportunity to explore whatever it was they had found with one another. Jen threw her arms around Mateo's bulky body and hugged him tightly even though she wasn't sure how much he could feel. He hugged her back much more gently, still wary of his new strength.

They pulled apart and went back to join the others. Mateo put out his hand and Abelard shook it, then pulled him into a hug too.

'Good luck, mate.'

'Thanks,' Mateo replied. He looked at Jen. 'If I can figure

out a way to let you know how we're getting on, I will, I promise.'

She nodded, not trusting herself to speak.

A hole irised open in the bottom of the space-e-fact fifteen feet above them.

'I wish you all well,' Terry said.

He and Mateo were encased in a blue glow and rose quickly and silently into the ship. The hole irised smoothly shut again and the ship equally silently vanished into the sky. Abelard opened his arms and Jen stepped into them. He closed them around her and held her tightly.

'Um, what just happened?' Alessandra's voice came from behind them.

Abelard and Jen broke apart and turned to see Alessandra standing a few feet away, her expression a mixture of shock and utter bewilderment.

Abelard took a deep breath. 'It turns out Mateo wasn't dead after all, so Terry transferred his consciousness into a brain-e-fact body and then he and all the brain-e-facts flew off into space to start a new colony on Titan.'

Alessandra stared at him. 'How long have I been gone?' Then she shook herself vigorously. 'I'll have to process all that later. We have a problem.'

Jen and Abelard listened in growing surprise and apprehension as Alessandra told them about the weird phenomenon of new artisans turning up at the halfway house.

'There must be more of them out there,' she concluded. 'And they may need help and not know where to go. So I'm going to do a sweep of the city and see what I can find. But

I came back here first to update you and find out if you have any new toys you can give me.'

'That we do.' Abelard looked down at Jen. 'Will you be okay?'

She was grateful for his concern but really didn't know how to answer that question. 'Go,' she said. 'I'll be fine.'

Abelard grinned at Alessandra. 'Follow me.'

* * *

The signs of disuse and disrepair reached as far as the eye could see. The effect was made even more eerie by the silence draped over the area, almost as if every creature and even the wind itself were absent. It had once been fields, long ago. Then it had been a village before it was eaten by the city. Next it was some kind of light industrial park, out past the suburbs, probably making artefact components. But presumably the money had run out as the factories and warehouses were now deserted.

Alessandra stepped carefully, mindful of scattered debris and keeping an eye on Abelard a few feet away. She hadn't been keen on him coming along but he had assured her he would be equally protected by the new artefacts the brain-es had helped create. Their seemingly never-ending stream of ideas and the speed with which they had produced them amazed her. But with Mateo and the brain-e-facts now gone, this would come to an end. Alessandra was still struggling with the news about that and she wondered what it meant for those left behind. As far as she was aware, Jen was the only one left at the compound now, apart from Gerald.

Alessandra felt the locate-e-fact vibrate on her wrist. There was definitely someone here and the frequency of the buzzing told her it was someone with a high spark level. She sighed. It was probably one of the poor souls who had been dragged into the conflict by the blanket insanity of whatever had caused spontaneous spark activation across the city. Some of them had subsequently found their way to the halfway house and others would have followed their instincts to go to the artisans. But she knew there were more out here, lost and alone with nowhere to go.

When Abelard had given her the locate-e-fact, she had been stunned by his apparent prescience in developing something that would track spark activity. But he had explained they thought it might be useful to be able to track artisans in case anyone hostile came to seek them out.

Another buzz. Rounding the corner into a dead-end, Alessandra saw nothing, although she knew the person must be there somewhere. She padded softly to the end of the alley, Abelard following behind her. A crash of corrugated iron startled her. Acting entirely on instinct, she leapt twenty feet into the air using Abelard's newly designed leap-e-facts. She tumble-turned in mid-air and threw out her hands in front of her, ready to attack or defend. Pulling just enough power from the mana unit strapped to her back, she hovered in mid-air and scanned the area. Abelard had flattened himself against a warehouse wall and was staring up at her.

There behind the dumpster was a child. Alessandra let herself drift back to the ground and gestured for Abelard to follow her. Sweeping her hair out of her eyes, she walked slowly towards the little girl with one hand out in front of her. After encountering Callie and the baby, she assumed anyone this young would have little control over new artisan abilities so she approached with caution, ready to shield.

As she got nearer, the girl looked up at her. Alessandra smiled, trying to convey reassurance. The child continued to look up at her. No … Not at her … Through her. Alessandra's muscles tensed to spin round but it was too late. She just had time to see the image of the girl flicker and disappear, to be replaced by a floating artefact, before an impact in the small of her back took her clean off her feet. As her face hit the ground she could already feel the mana gushing out of her storage unit in great waves. She clawed at the contact pads on her arms but the force of the landing had winded her and she was too slow. She felt the hard chill as the mana stored in her own body was ripped from her, making her cry out. There was a pause while she waited to die. Nothing happened. She pulled herself upright on a piece of broken masonry and turned round to face her attacker. They stood a few feet away, encased in a full suit of artisan combat armour. Abelard was struggling to get up from where he too had been knocked down. Alessandra managed to get as far as standing on her own albeit shaky feet and adopted a lifetime-practised haughty disdain.

'Whom do I have the pleasure of addressing?'

The figure responded by unclipping something from

their belt, which flew instantly from their hand to strike her in the chest. Already off balance, Alessandra staggered backwards. Bright blue tentacles of mana curled around her to pin her to the wall. A second later Abelard joined her, similarly bound. Clearly the artisans had also been on an artefact development spree.

The figure pulled off its helmet and glared at her. 'You unbelievably stupid girl.'

Alessandra felt as though five different emotions were trying to fight for dominance all at once.

She just about managed to say, 'Mother?'

Laleh dropped the helmet and ran her hands over her face.

'Do you know how difficult it's been for me to find a way to be able to speak to you? Every time I turn around Walter seems to be there. I may not be very good at showing it but I love you, Alessandra. You're my daughter and it's supposed to be my role in life to keep you safe.'

For a second Alessandra wanted to run into her mother's arms and be held safe and warm, like she was a child. The bite of the mana around her body quickly dispelled any such notion.

'In case you haven't noticed, mother, my friends and I are being hunted. And you're apparently on the other side. People are being rounded up and subjected to who knows what in the name of artisan superiority.'

Her mother narrowed her eyes. 'Believe me, I know. And I intend to find out what's happened to them as soon as I sort out the mess you've created.'

Alessandra felt her rage rising and battled it back. She inhaled slowly and said, 'Mess? Or a fight for justice?'

Laleh laughed. 'You wouldn't know justice if you tripped over it. Do you think you and Abelard are the first people who wanted to tell everyone in the world that they could be an artisan? How much of an ego do the two of you have, to think that everyone who knows is part of some evil conspiracy and only you can bring us all to your so-called justice?'

Alessandra spat back, 'You're the one keeping all the mundanes in the dark when they could all be artisans.'

Laleh sighed, closed her eyes and Alessandra could almost hear her counting to ten.

'We've been keeping them safe for hundreds of years.'

Now it was Alessandra's turn to laugh. 'You were always so keen for me to study hard in school but you can't even get our own history right! Mana wasn't discovered until–'

Laleh cut across her daughter's burgeoning speech. 'No. Mana was discovered on the 18th of August in the year 1521 by Brother Theobold of Rummenken. He was so scared of what it could do that he told no-one for many years until he eventually formed the Artisan Council. It was the genius idea of Robert McPherson to channel mana into artefacts so everyone could gain from it without … Well, you've seen what happens when there's a sudden massive new group of untrained artisans.'

She paused but Alessandra could think of nothing to say. Abelard was apparently also speechless.

Lelah continued. 'You would have been inducted into the

Inner Circle in another few years and all this could have been avoided. If only you'd given me a chance to explain rather than heading straight off to broadcast your limited knowledge to the world.'

Alessandra felt her anger break through her mental dams. 'You sent men with guns after us! What was I supposed to think?'

Laleh was obviously struggling to control her own emotions. 'That was Walter, though I admit telling him your plan wasn't my best idea and I haven't done much good trying to control his actions since. But couldn't you trust that what we were doing was for a good reason? Given half a chance I'd have explained why we have to pick the right people to become artisans. Even when properly trained, do you want everyone to be able to do this?'

She held out her hands, palm up. Blue light encased each one and two streams of dirt spiralled up from the earth to fill them. A second later the light brightened and one handful of dirt was glowing red hot while the other was covered in frost. Laleh dropped them both to the ground.

'You have a child's understanding of what mana can do!'

She threw out one hand towards a shattered window pane. Blue light again coursed between her fingers but this time it jumped towards the damage. As Alessandra watched wide-eyed, thousands of tiny pieces of glass whirled from their resting places in a tight maelstrom around where Laleh had pointed. A second later the window was whole once more.

Seconds passed.

Laleh resumed. 'Every artisan outside the Inner Circle is like you. They think that mana is something that's used to make artefacts and that anything else that happens is a side-effect. We've been excellent at convincing people of that for generations and you're in the process of bringing it all down. The Inner Circle is small and we have enough potential petty kings in our group already without that also applying to who-knows how many people out there.' Her shoulders sagged and she fell silent.

Alessandra's anger had mostly subsided but she wasn't quite finished yet. 'You're rounding up all the new artisans and–'

Laleh looked distressed. 'That's Walter again. And I told you I'll make sure they're safe. And what about you? You've got an army of super-charged brain-e-facts backing you. How can you criticise us for being worried about where that might end?'

Alessandra shook her head. 'We just want more people to know the truth! And the brain-e-facts have gone. That's a whole other story. We haven't got an army, just a few friends of Gerald Simpson's.'

Laleh paled. 'You're with Gerald? This is even worse than I thought.'

Alessandra blinked repeatedly. 'You know Gerald? How …? What?'

Laleh put a hand to her face. 'He used to be in the Inner Circle. Then he started talking about how there was no point in having godlike powers if we couldn't act like gods. We stripped him of his spark and kicked him out.' She ran her fingers through her hair. 'And then you turned up and gave him access to mana again. We think Gerald was behind the mana surge that caused all the new artisans. It's all coming together now. He probably designed it as a test.'

By this point Alessandra was lost. 'A test of what?'

Laleh clenched and unclenched her fists. 'Don't you think if you can instantly create hundreds of new sparks, you can also reverse the effect and extinguish the sparks of everyone not on your side in one giant explosion? Then before they can regroup, you move in, slaughter your enemies and then you can rule like a god!'

Alessandra shook her head. 'That wouldn't work. The Artisan Council would just create new artisans and so would we.'

Laleh looked to the sky for a moment and then back at her daughter. 'If I'm right and this happens, the Artisan Council will all be dead soon. How many people in your group can create new artisans?'

Alessandra had never really thought about that before. 'Um, just me now that the brain-e-facts have gone.'

Laleh rolled her eyes. 'So you'll likely be his next target.' She stopped and stared at Alessandra, aghast. 'Wait a minute. How did you end up with Gerald in the first place?'

'He's Mateo's cousin.' Then she realised her mother wouldn't know who Mateo was. 'Mateo is Abelard's best friend. Or he was. Now he's a brain-e-fact. But that doesn't matter. Mateo took us to Gerald's compound when we first escaped the viz-e-fact station. We've been hiding out there ever since.'

Laleh held her arms out at shoulder height. She snapped her fingers and the mana holding Alessandra and Abelard to the wall disappeared. A blue glow of mana leapt around Laleh instead and she lifted slowly into the air, stopping a few inches up.

'We need to finish what you started.'

Before Alessandra could respond there was a series of loud clicks from Laleh's combat armour and it began to disassemble. The parts flew through the air and clipped into place around Alessandra instead.

'Um, what about me?' Abelard said, but Laleh ignored him.

Laleh looked down at her daughter one more time. 'You have to get back and warn the others. Gerald is dangerous and Walter's on his way to the compound to confront him. I don't want you to get caught in the middle but I'm assuming you won't abandon your friends and just come with me now?'

Alessandra shook her head. She could feel the cold metal kiss of the contact ports at her wrists, through which mana flowed freely into her body.

Laleh sighed. She looked old and exhausted. 'I would hug you but frankly I don't trust you not to crush me to death in that thing. I love you, sweetheart. Save your friends and try not to die.'

Alessandra expected to find herself scoffing at her mother's use of the endearment. Instead she was shocked at the effort it took to hide a small sob in her throat.

'How will you manage to get back?'

Laleh shook her head. 'You still have no idea.'

Alessandra took an involuntary step back as her mother clicked her fingers and faded from sight. There was a sudden gust of cold air and she was gone.

Alessandra looked out across the desolate landscape and found herself trembling. A failed attempt to summon her best sneering voice instead came out as a half-whispered, 'I love you too.'

Grabbing Abelard's hand, Alessandra leapt into the sky.

CHAPTER THIRTY

Abelard stumbled as Alessandra landed them both back on the ground just inside the compound perimeter. He opened his mouth to say something but nothing came out. Eventually his brain decided on flippant.

'Well, that was intense. And not exactly how I imagined meeting your mother.'

'Quite.' The skin around Alessandra's mouth was tight.

'How could she do all that stuff with mana?' Abelard knew from experience just how draining direct mana manipulation could be and he had never seen anyone do it so easily and with so much precision.

'I have no idea. I'm getting the sense there's a lot I don't know about my mother. But we have more important things to worry about right now.'

'Yeah. If Gerald set off that mana explosion the other day, he basically killed Mateo. His own nephew!'

'And Walter is a force to be reckoned with as well. I don't relish the idea of getting involved in a fight between the two of them. But we don't have a choice.'

'We have to find Jen first and make sure she's safe,' Abelard said. 'Let's go.'

* * *

Walter grinned as he flew towards the location his analysis team had pinpointed. He had been forced to borrow an inferior float-e-fact from the Gadg-E-Tech pool but even that couldn't dampen his fierce joy at the prospect of the imminent confrontation. It had been a long time coming and Walter experienced a surge of satisfaction that he would be the one to finally bring Gerald Simpson to justice after Laleh and Brother Theobold had failed.

There was nothing on the float-e-fact's screens to show the compound existed. In fact there was so much nothing that it now stood out as a void in a way that should have tipped Walter off before. Gerald must have erected some kind of shield to protect himself from the prying eyes of the artisans. Clever but not clever enough. Whatever the explosion was that Gerald had set off over the weekend it had burst through the shield over the compound and had shown up on their scans anyway.

The shield might protect the compound from scans but there was nothing physically stopping Walter from flying the float-e-fact right into the grounds and landing it in the central courtyard. Foolish, he thought. Or brazen.

He activated the vehicle's cast-e-fact system and spoke, his words projecting loudly to the area outside.

'Gerald Simpson! Your day of reckoning has arrived! Come out and face me!'

Walter picked up his stun-e-fact, made his way to the float-e-fact's door and stepped out into the open air. He peered around and couldn't help another wolfish smile as a large shape emerged from one of the buildings and made its way towards him.

'Walter Snyder!' the shape called out. 'I expected Theobold to send one of his lapdogs but to have it be you, the feted up-and-comer … I'm honoured.'

Walter moved out from the immediate protection of the float-e-fact and they faced each other, about twenty feet apart on open ground.

'Got tired of hiding, did you?' Walter said. 'Decided to make yourself known at long last?'

Gerald shrugged. 'An opportunity presented itself so I took it. The world needs more artisans, as I've always said. The opportunity to meet you is just an added bonus.'

Walter raised his stun-e-fact. 'You won't think that when I'm through with you. The threat of your anarchic plans has troubled us long enough. It's time someone dealt with you once and for all.'

He aimed and fired but Gerald jumped out of the way with superhuman speed. Walter saw a mana unit strapped to his back, connected to an artefact Walter didn't recognise. He should have expected that. Even without a spark, Gerald wasn't just going to let Walter win. But Walter had his own mana reserves to draw upon and he wasn't afraid to use them. This might be fun.

Walter stalked his prey, relishing the cat-and-mouse of pursuing Gerald through the compound. Gerald might know the terrain and all the hiding places but Walter was younger and hungrier for the showdown. Gerald also had more to lose. One good hit from Walter's gun and he would be incapacitated and at the mercy of the Inner Circle. Walter scanned the area but couldn't see where Gerald had gone. As he approached the spot where he had last seen Gerald, a blast of light hurtled towards him from the left. Walter dodged sideways but wasn't quite fast enough and a burning pain lanced across his shoulder. Once he was round the corner of the nearest building he glanced down to see a charred gash in his jacket, the skin blistered and reddened underneath.

'So it's like that, is it?' he murmured. 'I see. Well, two can play that game.'

He threw his stun-e-fact to the ground and drew on his direct mana reserves until sparks crackled between his fingers and his eyes glowed blue. He stepped back out into the open. Now he was angry.

* * *

Abelard and Alessandra found Jen in the main house and hustled her through the building towards the front doors. Before Abelard could open them, he heard the sound of a float-e-fact descending outside.

'Walter's already here.'

They found a back way through the kitchens and slipped out into an extensive vegetable garden.

'Where are we going?' Jen asked.

'Not sure yet. Hopefully away.'

Finding a gate in the far side of the fence, Abelard avoided the central courtyard and eventually found his way to the barn that housed the float-e-fact Terry had stolen.

Alessandra fiddled with the viz-e-fact system until the screen showed a picture of the main courtyard. There was another float-e-fact positioned right in the middle and two small figures engaged in what looked like a complicated dance.

'What are they doing?' Jen asked.

'Fighting,' Alessandra said.

On the screen the two men were advancing towards one another, their arms outstretched. Between them two streams of mana collided in mid air, the meeting point growing steadily brighter.

'It looks like egos are prevailing over common sense,' said Alessandra. 'That amount of mana build-up is really dangerous.'

'We can't just let them carry on like that,' Abelard said. 'We have to try and stop them.'

Before the others could react, he ducked back out of the float-e-fact and dashed to the barn door. It looked like the mana from the two streams was combining into an extremely volatile cloud of energy.

'Stop!' Abelard yelled, stepping out into view.

The mana streams ceased abruptly. Walter and Gerald turned to look at him.

'Blowing each other up isn't going to solve anything. We know about the Inner Circle now. This is much bigger than just the two of you.'

Walter sneered. 'Ah, the engineer. So both my targets are in one place. Perfect.'

He raised his arms again, pointing one towards Gerald

and the other directly at Abelard. Mana crackled between his fingers. A futile instinct sent Abelard into a tight ball on the ground. Then he felt arms encircling him and he glanced up to see Alessandra next to him, with Jen huddled close by. Alessandra reached one arm up towards the sky and a shimmering sphere of mana energy dropped around them all, enveloping the barn as well. Beyond the barrier the light grew so bright that Abelard couldn't make anything out. Then there was a tremendous crack and he felt a shock-wave that sent them all sprawling.

Alessandra let the mana shield go and collapsed flat on her back, gasping for breath.

'Are you okay?' Abelard asked.

'You complete idiot! What the hell were you thinking? You could have been killed!'

Jen was staring past them, her hand over her mouth. Around them was a scene of almost total devastation. The second float-e-fact was a pile of burning wreckage and the buildings of the compound had not fared much better. There was shattered wood and broken masonry all over the place and small fires flickered everywhere. A couple of charred, smoking lumps drew Abelard's gaze but he looked away again quickly before his brain could fully register what they might be. Only the barn with their own float-e-fact inside had survived intact.

'I suggest we get out of here,' Alessandra said.

They stumbled back inside the barn and climbed aboard the float-e-fact.

Alessandra manipulated the controls with expert calm, directing the vehicle out of the barn and into the sky. They all watched the blackened site of the compound shrink on the float-e-fact's screens until they could no longer make it out among the trees.

Abelard let out a sigh of relief as the tension of immediate danger dissipated.

'Are Walter and Gerald really dead?' Jen asked.

Abelard shuddered. 'It looked like it, yes.'

Alessandra's lips were a thin line and she concentrated hard on the controls.

'So where do we go now?' Jen asked.

Abelard thought for a moment. 'Well, I still think you could probably just go home if you want.'

She looked at him in surprise. 'You don't think the artisans would come after me?'

He spread his hands. 'Your involvement hasn't been nearly as high profile as ours and it's only been about a week since you dropped off the map.' He paused. How could so much have happened in so little time? 'You can make up some story about where you've been and just slot back into your normal life like nothing happened.'

Abelard wondered if he would want to have the option of just going back to his old life. He looked at Alessandra and realised the answer was no. They had discovered so many amazing things together and he had a feeling their work wasn't done yet.

Jen looked thoughtful. 'I don't think I can do that. Not after all that's happened. You've opened my eyes to a whole world I never knew existed. I can't just pretend I don't know about all this.'

Abelard nodded, considering. 'A mundane viewpoint will probably be useful in whatever we decide to do next.'

'Well, the first thing I'm going to suggest is that we find a different term than 'mundane'. I may not want to be an artisan but I don't think I'm mundane either.'

Alessandra let out a bark of laughter then sobered. 'Perhaps semantics can wait until we're on the ground again. Where to?'

The call-e-fact beeped, saving Abelard from having to admit he had no idea.

'It's a message from your mother,' he said to Alessandra. 'Apparently there's someone we need to meet.'

CHAPTER THIRTY-ONE

Abelard held Alessandra's hand tightly as they walked down the street into the very heart of the city. They had dropped Jen off at the halfway house, promising to come and find her after their mysterious meeting. Shielding his eyes with his hand from the late afternoon light, Abelard looked at the structure they had been directed to. He had to concentrate to keep his gaze from sliding off it. While the buildings around it were of modern brick and glass, this ancient-looking two-storey stone temple stood alone as a proud anachronism that most people would never notice. Abelard took a deep breath and they walked through the pillared entrance-way into a semi-dark antechamber.

As the modern world receded behind them, Abelard became conscious of their footfalls on the polished stone floor. That and their breathing were the only sounds in the whole space. He felt Alessandra tense. He gave her hand a squeeze and she turned to look at him, her long blonde hair framing her face. For a brief moment he thought she was going to say something appropriately pithy, then it passed. Instead she breathed out and he felt her relax.

Stepping through an archway, they entered a room with a high domed ceiling, lit only by burning torches. Like everything they had seen so far, the walls, floor and ceiling were unadorned smooth stone. Here they encountered the first movement since they had entered the building.

Opposite the way they had come in were tall wooden double-doors with polished brass trim. In front of them stood two ... Abelard would have assumed they were statues if they hadn't been in the process of rising to their feet. Each was a good twelve feet tall and an achingly beautiful representation of the human form – one male and one female. These were no crude artisan-made brain-e-facts. They appeared to be made of translucent crystal that moved soundlessly like human flesh. They were armed with swords and shields of the same material. Their motion ended with them standing before the doors, each with an arm outstretched, holding their swords in a challenging manner.

'Right,' said Alessandra.

She dropped Abelard's hand and brought both of hers out in front of her a short distance apart, palms facing each other. But before she could do anything, Abelard stopped her with a hand on her arm.

'Hang on. Maybe we could try talking to them first before we blow them up?'

He stepped forwards until he was just a few feet from the glassy giants.

'Um, hello,' he said, feeling like an idiot. 'We were sent a message telling us to come here. Could you let your, um, master know we're here, please?'

Nothing happened. Abelard turned back to Alessandra and saw a familiar mocking expression on her face.

'Okay, okay. It was worth a try.' He gestured for her to take his place. 'Foom at will.'

Then a series of heavy clicks emanated from the door behind the guards. The final tone sounded like an iron bell being struck, the noise reverberating around the stone walls for several moments. As silence descended again the figures reversed their original movements to return once more to their seated vigil.

'Hah!' Abelard cried.

Alessandra took a second to roll her eyes at him as the doors swung soundlessly open. She took hold of his hand again.

The space between the now gaping doors was black. Not shadowy, not dark but ... black. Abelard somehow knew there was a depth behind the now open doors but he couldn't perceive a single thing about it. Alessandra took the first step forward.

'Well, we've come this far.'

They walked up to the opening. Then they each took a deep breath as they stepped across the threshold into ...

Bright daylight. Grass under their feet. Blue sky above, birds circling lazily. The sun high in the sky was hot but not unpleasantly so. In the distance, mountains. In the foreground, forest and the sound of running water.

Abelard spoke first. 'I can't ... I've seen so much since that day in Jen's office, that sometimes I think I must be in a hospital bed somewhere, dreaming everything that's happened. But this – I give up.'

Alessandra dropped his hand and turned around. He

stopped gaping and turned to follow her gaze. Behind them was the temple, as if they were standing behind the building they had entered from the street. It stood in the middle of a large clearing, surrounded by forest. Directly in front of them were the large double wooden doors with polished brass trim, standing open.

He heard Alessandra mutter, 'Everything is a test.' For the first time that day, he saw her smile. 'We should at least enjoy this place as if it's real. It might be, for all we know.'

She pulled her thick jumper off over her head and tied it around her waist.

Abelard followed suit.

'So,' she continued. 'This way, I guess.'

She headed off into the woods in the direction of the sound of water.

Abelard was glad of the shade of the forest canopy but wished he had the slightest idea what was going on. They had fled the destroyed compound with no idea where to go or whom to trust. Now they were apparently in another world in mid-summer. Still, if he was delusional, his brain was doing an excellent job of it. The surroundings were beautiful and he was here with the person he loved most in the world.

Alessandra proceeded through the woods at speed. Abelard jogged to catch her up.

'I love you,' he said.

She didn't break stride or even look at him but she said over her shoulder, 'I know. I love you too.'

The afternoon wore on and they lost track of time. The

sound of running water grew in volume and since they had nothing else to aim for they continued towards it. Eventually they came to a break in the trees where a fast-flowing brook burbled over a cascading set of waterfalls. Next to the water was a circle of stone benches. Abelard counted eight in total. On one sat a man of late middle-age, dressed in a grey smock and wide tan trousers. He had short grey hair and bare feet. They continued towards him. The man smiled as they approached and gestured to the bench opposite him. As it was wide enough to seat two, they sat down together and waited.

The man closed his eyes and appeared to be listening to the water.

Eventually Abelard broke the silence. 'So, is this real, is it an illusion or am I just mad in a padded cell somewhere?'

The man opened his eyes, which were the bluest Abelard had ever seen. 'Who is to say there is any difference? Not a very useful answer, I admit, but after long enough you come to see that all things are the same, just viewed from different places.'

'Great,' Abelard said. 'I wasn't planning on an afternoon of riddles. I imagine we've been summoned here for some kind of judgement. Is our punishment to be baffled to death by a mystic old man because, while I can think of worse ways to go, honestly we have better things to do.'

The man surprised Abelard by responding with a deep-throated laugh. 'Ah, the impatience of the young. Always so refreshing. The Inner Circle needs to talk to you and I represent them. I am ...'

He was cut off mid-sentence by Alessandra. 'You're Brother Theobold.'

The man rewarded her with a wide smile and sparkling eyes. Casually, he reached his hand towards the ground. As he did, the shoot of a plant burst out of the ground, surrounded by spirals of blue light. It grew two feet to the height of his hand, exploded into a single scarlet rose and then collapsed into dust, leaving just the flower stem neatly caught between his fingers. He passed it to Alessandra, who received it without expression or comment.

'Very insightful, Ms Eriksen.'

Abelard meanwhile was staring at the rose. 'That was impressive.'

'So.' Brother Theobold cast his gaze from one face to the other. 'The real question is, what happens next? Your conflict with the artisans has actually solved two longstanding problems. The rediscovery and demise of Gerald Simpson and the accompanying neutralisation of Walter Snyder. Yes, we all wish that such things could have been done without any loss of life but, given what they were independently capable of, I am sure that huge numbers of lives have been saved.' He cocked his head. 'Both of you could be described as extremely foolish but often it takes the wisest of fools to lead us to where we must go.'

Alessandra rolled her eyes.

Brother Theobold smiled and went on. 'The conflict is over, the Artisan Council still stands and the wild notion that anyone can manipulate mana can be safely put back to rest for the time being.' He turned to Alessandra. 'Your mother really is a remarkable woman and deserves her seat in the Inner Circle more than any of us. Perhaps one day you might ask her how old she is and how many faces she has worn over the course of her life.'

Alessandra blanched.

Brother Theobold continued. 'You are both now in very limited company in that you are beginning to learn what mana can really do. I am over 500 years old.' He let that sink in for a moment. 'You have seen this place and have some idea of how the very matter and elements of the world can be made to dance under our control. For the last one hundred years we've allowed ever more people to know a tiny hint of that power through the creation of artisans and artefacts. However you are completely correct, Abelard – this limitation is grossly unfair. It denies the majority of people their birthright while allowing for the possibility of mana-powered tyrants. Plus, really, who wants to be stuck building freez-e-facts for the rest of their lives?'

He paused and Abelard took the opportunity to speak up. 'What's the alternative? We saw from Gerald's interference that uncontrolled creation of artisans can cause chaos. We understand now. You can't just give this power to everyone all at once. Not as things stand at the moment.'

Alessandra nodded in agreement.

Brother Theobold looked Abelard in the eye. 'And that is why things have to change. For two hundred years I told only a tiny number about mana and still managed to unleash a monster that I had to destroy.' He glanced down and back up. 'Perhaps a story for another day. But after that I had to learn again to trust more people with some level of power. Now we have artisans and artefacts and everyone is better off for them. The end goal must be for everyone everywhere to be fully informed about what mana can really do and to be able to tap into and direct that power for themselves.'

Abelard and Alessandra both shook their heads but before either could speak he continued.

'You are now as I once was. Afraid and rightly so. But you and your children will live for centuries to come. I have brought us half way – from a world with no mana to one where everyone shares safely in its bounty but does so unequally and in ignorance. The decision of the Inner Circle is this; in justice for the conflict you have caused we order that you both join us and take responsibility for the mighty task of bringing the full understanding of mana and what it is capable of to all of mankind. As I believe the colloquialism goes; no pressure.' He winked.

Abelard blinked slowly and swallowed.

After a moment Alessandra shrugged. 'That was all we wanted in the first place. We were just … wrong … in the way we went about it. And for that we're deeply sorry.'

'But what about all the new artisans?' Abelard asked. 'Who's going to give them the support they need?'

Brother Theobold looked at Alessandra. 'Now that Walter Snyder is gone your mother will be free to take a more active role in the management of Gadg-E-Tech. In fact, it might be time for me to officially step down as CEO and allow her the chance to shine in a leadership role.'

Alessandra blinked. 'You're the CEO of Gadg-E-Tech?'

'In pseudonym only.' Brother Theobold smiled. 'I have not interfered there directly in some years. To answer your question, young man, Laleh will be able to put measures in place to help those unexpectedly burdened with artisan powers.' Abelard was about to ask another question but Brother Theobold anticipated it. 'And she can also ensure the company does not create any more brain-e-facts.'

'And what about us?' Alessandra asked. 'Our names and faces have been quite high profile the last few days. I'm not sure we'll be able to just go about our lives without anyone asking any awkward questions.'

Brother Theobold nodded slowly. 'We can give you new ones.'

'New what?' Abelard was utterly confused.

'New names and faces,' Brother Theobold explained, still smiling. 'You're still thinking too small in terms of what mana can do.'

They gaped at him and then at each other. Abelard tried to imagine Alessandra with a different face and didn't like the idea one bit. Then he thought about looking in a mirror and seeing a stranger looking back and he felt nauseous.

But Alessandra was nodding. 'That makes sense. If you have the kind of power and influence you claim to have, new identities shouldn't be a problem. We can say that Abelard Abernathy and Alessandra Eriksen died in the explosion at the compound.'

Abelard still didn't like it but he could see it was a neat solution to their problem.

'Okay,' he said. 'Lay the whammy on us.'

Brother Theobold raised his arms and his face took on an expression of intense concentration. Mana flickered between his fingers, then lanced out towards them. Abelard flinched away but managed not to topple off the bench. He felt a tingling sensation all over his face. It was uncomfortable but not painful. The whole thing was over in a couple of minutes. When Brother Theobold lowered his arms again Abelard turned to face Alessandra and his eyes widened in shock.

Her features were finer, delicate even. And her luscious blonde curls had been replaced by a sleek blue-black curtain of hair. But her blue eyes still looked out at him from the unfamiliar face, uncertain and worried. Then she smiled and reached up to cup his cheek with her hand.

'It's still you. And you're still cute.'

Brother Theobold conjured a mirror in a blaze of mana and held it out to Abelard. He took it and looked at himself apprehensively. His skin was several shades darker, his features broader, his lips fuller. He reached up to touch his hair and found it much coarser than it had been. Maybe if he grew it he could get a hairstyle like Simon Hanley's – just like he'd always wanted. He smiled and his weird reflection smiled back at him. He thought he could probably get used to it eventually.

Alessandra grabbed the mirror from him and started inspecting herself. She ran her fingers through her hair and nodded in satisfaction. 'Nice.'

Abelard had a sudden thought. 'Can you give me my artisan powers back too?'

Brother Theobold regarded him seriously. 'Do you think you need them to serve in your new role?'

Abelard considered the question. He was tempted to say yes, but that would be a lie. He felt a pang as he realised what his answer had to be. 'I guess not. And in the long run it might be useful for you to have someone without powers on your team. The mundanes are more likely to trust someone who's like them.' He felt his dreams of being an artisan finally drifting away. And it was okay.

Brother Theobold nodded. 'You may find there is unexpected power in being powerless.'

Alessandra put her arm around Abelard and squeezed his shoulders. 'And like Jen said, there's a lot more to you than just the ability to manipulate mana.'

'Now though,' Brother Theobold said, 'it is time for you to go. You will find details of your new identities in your vehicle, along with instructions for accessing the resources you will need. We will expect to see you here for the next Inner Circle meeting with your first thoughts on your grand plan.' He smiled one last time and stood up. He began to walk into the forest but paused to point back the way they had come. 'That's your route home. I suggest you use your journey back to consider what you are going to do in your spare time when you're not secretly ruling the world.'

He stepped into the treeline and was gone.

Their walk back to the temple was quiet. Both Alessandra and Abelard were lost in thought. When they arrived at the black portal, they passed through without a second thought. Walking through the stone chamber, they barely noticed the crystal giants sitting with heads bowed as they passed. Then they were in the chilly dusk of downtown once more. A mixture of artisans, engineers and mundanes flowed around them, each bustling home or on to more exciting places, oblivious to the godlike potential they all possessed within them.

'Well,' said Abelard. 'Now what?'

Alessandra smiled up at him, taking his hand once more. 'I don't know about you but I could really go for pizza. This whole secretly ruling the world thing is making me hungry.'

Abelard leaned forward and kissed her, enjoying the exciting unfamiliarity of her new lips. 'Sounds like an excellent plan to me. Then maybe we can discuss these children we're supposed to be having that will rule after us for centuries to come.'

Alessandra set off down the street, pulling him gently behind her. Looking back at him over her shoulder, she said, 'Well, yes, I expect we can work on that.'

THE END

ABOUT THE AUTHOR

Annie Percik lives in London with her husband, Dave, where she writes novels and short stories, whilst working as a University Complaints Officer. She writes a blog about writing and posts short fiction on her website (www.alobear.co.uk). She also makes a media review podcast with her husband (@loveittomorrow) and publishes a photo-story blog, recording the adventures of her teddy bear (https://aloysius-bear.dreamwidth.org/). He is much more popular online than she is. She likes to run away from zombies in her spare time.

If you have enjoyed this book, please consider leaving a review for Annie to let her know what you thought of her work. You can find out more about her on her website and on her author page on the Fantastic Books Store. While you're there, why not browse our delightful tales and wonderfully woven prose?

www.fantasticbooksstore.com

Printed in Great Britain
by Amazon